**Edmund reached out
a large hand toward her.
"Come here, Mistress Hall."**

Gwyneth hesitated only a moment, went up a step, then gave him her hand, dwarfed by the size and heat of his. She knew that her face flamed red as she suddenly imagined that hand touching her in ways her mother had described. He drew her the rest of the way up the stairs until she stood at the top, staring into his massive chest. His fingers firmly took her chin and lifted her face until she had no choice but to stare into his pale eyes. There were flecks of darker blue there, and she studied them in wonder.

"You have but a moment, mistress," he said. "Decide now if you will marry me."

Other **AVON ROMANCES**

Coming Soon

And Don't Miss These
ROMANTIC TREASURES
from Avon Books

GAYLE CALLEN

HIS BRIDE

AVON BOOKS
An Imprint of HarperCollinsPublishers

AVON BOOKS
An Imprint of HarperCollins*Publishers*
10 East 53rd Street
New York, New York 10022-5299

Copyright © 2002 by Gayle Callen
ISBN: 0-380-82110-9
www.avonromance.com

First Avon Books paperback printing: November 2002

Avon Trademark Reg. U.S. Pat. Off. and in Other Countries, Marca Registrada, Hecho en U.S.A.
HarperCollins® is a registered trademark of HarperCollins Publishers Inc.

Printed in the U.S.A.

10 9 8 7 6 5 4 3 2 1

To my wonderful critique group, the Packeteers: Ginny Aubertine, Laurie Bishop, Lisa Hilleren, Theresa Kovian, Jenna Mindel, Amber Schalk, and Chris Wenger. Over the years, we've given each other writing advice and support, but best of all—friendship and laughter. The memories sustain me.

And to Chris Wenger, for valiantly answering my last-minute, desperate, "Can you quickly read my manuscript and tell me what you think?" pleas. You'll never know how much I appreciate your help and encouragement.

Prologue

England
1591

"My wife is dead." Sir Edmund Blackwell folded his arms across his chest and stared into the faces of his wife's parents. "I am sorry for your grief, my lord, but I do not understand why you felt the need to see me. After all, you know how she died."

He'd been summoned from Yorkshire to Earl Langston's estate in Lincolnshire to face the two people who'd conspired to make the last few years of his life a nightmare. He knew they blamed him for their daughter's poor choices. When he arrived, he'd been offered no refreshments, only led through the great hall with its racks of spears and suits of armor, as if the threat of their military power was supposed to daunt him. The gallery where he now faced them ran the length of the mansion and let in the sun through stained-glass windows, which cast muted color everywhere. He was seated on a heavily carved chair. Dour ancestral portraits glared down at him; the earl and his countess did the same from a cushioned bench. A polished table stood as a barrier between them. Buffets and cupboards were scattered down the length of the room, decorated with china or covered with Turkish carpets.

Lord Langston, a thin, cold man, made no effort to conceal his contempt. "As part of Elizabeth's dowry, we gave you Castle Wintering and its lands, which is an ancient part of our family estates. We merely wish to buy it back from you now that our daughter lies at peace."

Edmund resisted the urge to voice his disgust. Their daughter hadn't let herself have peace in life, so why would she be blessed with it in death? He had hoped that with time, he and Elizabeth would have grown to suit each other, but she and her parents had made sure that had never happened.

But give up Castle Wintering? Give up what he'd worked so hard for, the only source of income he had left? *Never.*

Edmund returned the cold stare with one of his own. "I have invested much time and labor in the estate, and I wish to continue." He started to rise.

"If this was all you had to discuss, we could have done it through letters."

"Please sit down, Sir Edmund," said Letitia Langston, his wife's mother. Where her husband pretended civility, she let malice glitter behind her eyes. "We could force you to sell us the land. After all, there are already those who believe you were the cause of my daughter's death."

He remained standing above them, knowing that his size usually frightened people. He narrowed his gaze at Lady Langston as her threat seemed to coil around him. What more proof did he need that they had planted this lie even as far away as Castle Wintering, all in an attempt to manipulate him? Would it ever end? "And we both know that that is a lie. I have already agreed not to publicize the details of her death. Do you wish me to change my mind?"

Edmund knew his own threat was a gamble, for they were a very powerful family. Yet their weakness was the merest thought of a scandal connected to their family name.

The countess's fingers were white where she gripped her skirt at the knees.

Before she could speak, her husband interrupted. "Blackwell, we have another suggestion for the dilemma presented to us."

"There is no longer a dilemma between us," Edmund said tightly.

"Then there is *your* dilemma."

He stiffened but remained silent.

"You have land, Blackwell, but you no longer have the money to make it succeed."

Not a difficult thing for their spies to discover.

"Thanks to you—and your daughter."

Lady Langston slammed her hands onto the table between them, but her husband touched her arm.

"I am resourceful," Edmund continued, "and will get what I need for Castle Wintering."

Lord Langston said, "I have a solution to your problems—all of them. We regret that there are those who blame you for our daughter's death. We would like to offer you a new bride."

Edmund tried not to let his astonishment show. He had known Elizabeth's parents had something planned, but he never would have guessed *this* attempt at manipulating him. "I am not interested in marrying so soon, my lord."

Lord Langston continued as if Edmund hadn't spoken, and his eyes glittered with challenge. "The girl is of good bloodlines, as she's a cousin of mine through her mother, and her father was knighted by the queen. By offering another relative in marriage to you, we prove to the world that we do not believe the rumors about our daughter's death."

Edmund controlled his bitter laugh. Another Langston wife? They had said nothing that would induce him to marry someone from their family again.

"There is a substantial dowry involved, of course," the earl said slowly, as if dangling bait.

And it was the perfect bait. Money was the one thing he desperately needed, now that his wounds prevented him from earning his living as a mercenary.

The Langstons were offering him a way out—but at what price and for what twisted reason? He could only imagine the kind of woman they wanted to saddle him with. But what choice did he have?

"Sit down, Sir Edmund," said Lord Langston.

He sat. "Why are you doing this? Are you trying to rid yourself of this girl?"

The earl leaned back in his chair, not bothering to hide his triumphant smile. "She is a good girl whose family is not wealthy. We've taken her under our wing. She is used to hard work and will be an asset to you."

That Edmund doubted. Why should a cousin of Elizabeth's know anything more than beautiful clothes and what court functions to attend? If he actually went through with this farce, he would handle marriage much differently.

"Show me the bridal contract."

Lord Langston reached into a cupboard behind him and brought forth a sheaf of papers, which he pushed across the table.

Both of Elizabeth's parents were watching Edmund closely now.

As he bent over the contract, the thought of another Langston bride made his stomach churn. His instinctive reaction was to refuse, but he had to be smarter now, to weigh the advantages. Castle Wintering's potential was enormous, with the land so perfect for raising sheep, and the wool trade prosperous. And he had yet to have the land explored for mining opportunities. But all of this required money. He desperately needed this estate, even if it meant matching wits with the Langstons.

The contract was brief and the language precise. There was only one clause that Edmund had to read twice, a provision that should he die without a male heir, the land would return to Langston hands. He glanced at them, and the earl's lip curled as if he knew exactly the clause Edmund was reading.

They really wanted their property back, did they not, even if their heirs had to await Edmund's death?

He sat back in his chair and studied Elizabeth's parents with narrowed eyes.

"You are still suspicious," the earl said.

"Every dealing I have had with you has made me that way."

"Then let us be open about the hostility between us. You seduced our daughter and forced that marriage, and now she is dead."

Edmund gritted his teeth, knowing all the critical things Langston had left out of his summary.

But he would let some of that go for now. "And while I was away, you threatened my steward to make sure two years' worth of profits from Castle Wintering went for Elizabeth's lavish accessories rather than grain and cattle. Why should I trust you now?"

"There will never be a time for trust between us, Blackwell. If you choose not to accept this . . . arrangement, you shall lose the land for taxes, and who do you think the queen will agree to sell it to?"

"Then why are you interfering?"

The earl leaned forward, and his lips curled back over his teeth. "Because this is personal between us, Blackwell. Consider this a challenge, a duel of wits between you and me. If you accept, you shall have the money to begin the restoration of Castle Wintering and a woman to give you an heir. But always you will have to wonder what I'm planning, how I've manipulated this situation to win. The money and land aren't as important to me as knowing you'll be humbled in the end. Dare you take that chance?"

For several moments, Edmund could only stare at the old man, feeling hatred suffuse the gallery. And by God, he returned their feelings. "And what do I win if I solve your plots?"

"Your freedom from me. You will already have the money and a gently bred bride to begin a new life."

"And if I lose?"

"But you're already close to losing everything, are you not, Blackwell?"

How Edmund longed to defeat Langston in battle, the honorable way. But it could not be. He desperately needed that money—and he needed to defeat Earl Langston once and for all. Already he had a plan simmering in his mind.

He took a quill pen, dipped it in ink, and signed his name at the bottom of the contract.

"Your challenge is met, Langston."

Chapter 1

London
One week later . . .

"**G**wyneth, we have news of the most excellent kind," said Earl Langston. "We have found you a husband."

Feeling suddenly light-headed, Gwyneth Hall tried to keep herself from gaping at him. "A husband, my lord?" He had never shown interest in helping her family—his cousins—before. Why now?

Stunned, she sat back in the cushioned chair and tried not to feel overwhelmed by the opulent withdrawing room in her cousin's London mansion. Painted angels hovered above her on the ceiling. Somber portraits of people she'd never met decorated the darkly paneled walls. While a timid maid served her spiced cider, the earl and his wife smiled like they were baring their teeth.

They'd only invited her to their home once, a few months ago, when they'd needed a companion for their daughter, Elizabeth, while her husband was out of the country. Gwyneth had accepted, glad to experience more of London than her poor corner of it. Instead of a companion, she had been an unpaid servant, seeing to her cousin's wardrobe. But Elizabeth was dead now, and Gwyneth had promised to keep the circumstances a secret. Was this offer of a husband a payment for her silence?

"How old are you now?" Lord Langston asked.

"I have three and twenty years."

"And I believe your father does not have dowries for his four daughters."

She saw the earl glance distastefully at her garments, knew her green woolen gown with its simple linen ruff at the neck might as well be rags to him. But besides her gloves, she wore a hat with a narrow brim that her mother had given her tilted at a smart angle. She felt proud of her appearance.

Her back stiffened as she lifted her chin. "My father works hard, Lord Langston, but he has grown sickly over the last several years."

"I understand, my dear. That is why I have taken it upon myself to provide you with a dowry."

She narrowed her gaze. "And why would you do this?"

She heard Lady Langston inhale with a hiss, and the earl's smile thinned.

"Because, girl," said Lady Langston, "we cannot give you in marriage to Edmund Blackwell without it."

Edmund Blackwell? The name echoed about in her head like a stone thrown down a rocky cliff.

"Elizabeth's husband?" she finally managed to say in a faint voice, though her tongue felt swollen. The husband her cousin had cried over?

The earl nodded. "He has an estate to run, and we feel that a wife will ease his burdens and provide companionship."

Gwyneth well remembered trying to start awkward conversations with Elizabeth. Once she had asked if hers was a love match, because she'd always thought the Langstons wanted to marry her to a nobleman. Elizabeth had only burst into angry tears and refused to discuss it.

"Elizabeth died but six weeks ago," she said in bewilderment. "He needs a wife this quickly?"

Lady Langston shook her head. "Do not think he agreed to it easily, girl. It is a difficult thing to lose such a woman as my daughter was. But he understands the reality of needing the dowry for his lands and a woman to run his household."

But of course he needed the money most of all; she could see that immediately. Such was the way of things in marriage. She had hoped it would be different for her, that she'd have a man to love and a family to care for.

And there was no saying she couldn't have that yet. She had spent her life learning how to be a good wife and had despaired of ever getting the chance—until recently, that is, when a prosperous merchant had begun to court her. He was twice her age and had lecherous intentions, but he offered a gift of money that would bring her family back from the edge of poverty, and he had wanted no dowry, which in itself made him attractive to her family. She would be one less daughter to worry about feeding.

But Edmund Blackwell would offer no money. How would this help her family—help her sisters with dowries?

Suddenly her hope soared as she glanced from the earl to his wife excitedly. "Forgive my curiosity, but does this mean you will be so kind as to offer my sisters dowries as well?"

Lady Langston gave her a frosty, knowing look, as if Gwyneth was begging for ownership of all of their estates. "Your mother is family. We are offering to ease her burdens by seeing one of her daughters settled. Is your greed so great that you demand more?"

Gwyneth felt the blood drain from her face. "My lady, you misunderstand me. I am grateful for this opportunity, and only wish to make my decision with all the facts available. I only ask that I might meet Sir Edmund before I decide."

"He has already returned north to Yorkshire because the grain harvest is well under way." The earl already seemed distracted, as if her concerns were unimportant.

"There is no choice, girl," said Lady Langston coldly. "He needs a wife, and we have already offered you to him. The marriage contract has been legally signed."

Gwyneth stared at her clenched fists, trying to quell her rising panic. The decision had been made without her. Did Sir Edmund leave so quickly because he did not want her to see him? She tried not to think about the cold, bitter tone of Elizabeth's voice whenever she spoke of him.

Yet she had been wishing desperately for another man to choose as her husband, because she soon would have been forced by her conscience to marry the merchant. Was an ugly stranger better than an old man whose odor often lingered after he had left the room?

Although her cousin Elizabeth had complained about her husband leaving her alone when he went to France, she had never said that he mistreated her—and he *had* put up with her selfishness. Of course, Gwyneth had heard the rumor that he killed Elizabeth, but Gwyneth herself had been there at the end of her cousin's life, while Sir Edmund had been with the army in France. Malicious gossip was only for people with little else to occupy them, and she gave no credence to it.

Surely if she was a good, hard-working wife to

him, she could persuade him to offer small dowries to her sisters. After all, wasn't she bringing a large dowry to him herself, thanks to the Langstons?

"What are you thinking about, my dear?" Lord Langston asked.

"I am thinking how kind you are to offer a dowry for me, my lord," Gwyneth said firmly, looking up in time to see them exchange relieved glances. "When will Sir Edmund come to London for the ceremony?"

"He cannot spare the time," said Lady Langston. "He is sending an escort to bring you north to Castle Wintering."

The name of the castle sent a strange chill through her. She inwardly berated herself for foolishness, even as she imagined how lonely her new life would be. She wouldn't be getting married amidst a family celebration—not her family anyway. None of her three sisters could be spared from the family bakery to travel with her. She would be alone with her new husband. She had to force aside thoughts of a wedding night with a man she'd never met.

Earl Langston stared out the window at the receding figure of his cousin Gwyneth and allowed his satisfaction to show.

His wife came to his side. "Everything worked out as we planned."

"Aye, my lady wife. Blackwell signed the contract, and Gwyneth agreed to it. Not that she had much choice. The pressure I would have put on her father might have been . . . distressing to his health. And she'll be away from London, where she cannot cause trouble with what she knows about our daughter."

"If only Blackwell had been willing to sell us the property instead. The gall of that baseborn churl to obstruct us! We could have begun mining immediately. You said if we started rumors that he killed Elizabeth, he would have no choice but to do as we wished. She was so unhappy that it was apparent to all that he was at fault."

"Patience, Letitia. The steward at Castle Wintering has made certain that all the servants understand that Blackwell killed Elizabeth but that we cannot prove who Blackwell hired to do it. And Blackwell has done as we wished—he's taking another Langston bride. We shall send the bailiff from our Durham properties to witness the wedding. Then he can examine the ore site to see if Blackwell has discovered it. If it is undisturbed, the lead ore will wait."

She flung up her hands and strode away from him. "But you have made certain we must wait *years*. It will take many female brats before that barbarian realizes that Alyce Hall's branch of the family never has boys. Since the marriage contract states that the property returns to us if he has no sons, this could last beyond our death!"

"And you do not wish to provide for your sons' future?"

At least she still retained the ability to blush, the earl thought with his usual exasperation.

"But I wish to provide for ours as well, you fool," she said.

When she returned to his side, he gripped her arm tightly to hold her still. He watched her blanch and enjoyed her wince. "Do you not yet trust my abilities, my lady wife? After all, Black-well believes that we've raised Gwyneth as al-most our ward."

She bit her lip. "I trusted you with our children, and our daughter ended up married to an igno-rant monster. And now she's—"

He quickly spoke before the inevitable self-pitying tears began. "Elizabeth chose poorly, Leti-tia, but we have begun to remedy the insult to our family. I have not fully informed you of the extent of my plan."

Her stare was skeptical. "And I am supposed to trust this? You challenged him, when we could just have waited for him to lose the estate to taxes."

He softened his grip, and her shoulders re-laxed. "I was correct about the rumors of murder forcing Blackwell to accept our offer, wasn't I? Then trust me in this. I would not risk the chance that he would grovel to a wealthy friend for the money. Edmund Blackwell will fail as a land-holder long before we have to care what brats he sires. I've already made certain of it. And then the land will be ours again, and he will be ruined."

Gwyneth had never imagined how difficult it would be to leave her family. Her father's frailty weighed on her, and she prayed that she would see him again someday. Would her new husband ever bring her to London to visit her parents?

They had once lived on a farm north of the city, when her father had been whole and could support his family by working the land. They'd been so happy there. His illness had necessitated their move to London, where her father could guard merchants, a less demanding occupation. Even that had eventually proved too much for him.

Now her three sisters would have to assist their mother without her. They supplied several of the London bakeries with their baked goods, and Gwyneth had always been the one to deal with their customers.

But her mother reassured her and displayed genuine enthusiasm and gratitude because Gwyneth would finally have a home of her own. She even calmed Gwyneth's fears about her wedding night with an explanation of what would happen. Although Gwyneth was grateful for the truth, she worried about doing such things with a stranger. And what if he wasn't as gentle as her mother said husbands should be?

The trip to Yorkshire took ten long days. Sir Edmund's soldiers were pleasant, especially the ser-

geant in charge, Sir Geoffrey Drake, who had a
good-natured smile and seemed too irreverent to
be a military man. Even his garments were too
rich for a soldier, but a soldier was what he professed himself to be. She was grateful for the
friendship he offered her, and interested to realize
that he seemed to be Sir Edmund's friend as well.

Thank goodness for Lucy Tyler, who'd insisted
she accompany Gwyneth. She was a tall, thin girl,
with startling black hair and ambitious eyes,
who'd often had to walk the streets selling the fish
her father caught. They had met the first day
Gwyneth's family moved to London. They had
been two little girls dealing with the danger of city
life and had become good friends in the process.

The day before Gwyneth was to leave, Lucy
had volunteered her services as companion and
maid, hoping to send money home to her own
struggling family. It was a great relief to Gwyneth
not to face the wild north all alone.

On the last part of their journey, they rode
through the broad, fertile plains of the York valley,
and Geoffrey pointed off to the northwest, where
the Pennines rose flat-topped to the sky. He explained that Castle Wintering was in Swaledale,
the valley of the River Swale, which flowed from
the Pennines. But for the wedding, Sir Edmund
would meet them the next day in Richmond.
Gwyneth's dulled nerves roared back to life as she
realized she would be married on the morrow.
What would her groom look like? She'd spent the

entire journey trying to remember everything Elizabeth had ever said about him, but her cousin's usual conversation had been only about herself.

In the morning, she and Lucy were escorted into Richmond, a village of stone houses in the shadow of Richmond Castle, which had been built on a cliff above the River Swale. While Gwyneth's stomach tightened with nervous spasms, she consoled herself with the thought of a warm bath at an inn before she would meet her husband.

Geoffrey dashed those hopes as he rode alongside their coach. He informed her that she and Sir Edmund were returning to Castle Wintering today after the wedding ceremony.

"Sir Geoffrey!" Lucy protested, leaning over Gwyneth's lap to look out the window. "Mistress Gwyneth is a bride. Surely she can prepare. She never even met the man."

He shrugged, his expression reluctant. "I understand, ladies, but Edmund . . . he has much to do. The letter I just received—"

"I am sorry, Geoffrey," Gwyneth said, "but I shan't marry until I can change into my best gown. Please find a suitable place."

"There's no one who will see you but Edmund and myself. We'll be late—"

Her heart did a little flip of disappointment on hearing that not one of Sir Edmund's friends and villagers would be coming. "Regardless, I am changing. Do what you must." She had never felt so certain of anything. Her life was out of her control—but how she met her fate was not. She would not be wed wearing dusty travel garments, with her face full of perspiration and dirt.

Soon they turned into a quiet church courtyard with benches and a garden on one side and a graveyard on the other. While Geoffrey went inside the church, Gwyneth and Lucy stepped out of the coach and stared up at the largest black stallion they had ever seen. Its back was well above Gwyneth's head, and it seemed to roll its eyes as if possessed by the devil. It tossed its shiny mane and snorted at them, and the silly childhood fear of horses that Gwyneth thought she'd conquered came flooding back.

It had to be Sir Edmund Blackwell's horse, and she stayed well away, wondering about the size of the man who could ride such an animal. Geoffrey returned with the black-robed vicar, who smiled and bowed as he escorted her to a small chamber at the rear of the church. Lucy followed with the gown, and they were left alone.

Gwyneth felt unreal as she washed her body with tepid water from a basin. She had wanted to bathe and perfume herself, but it was not to be. She could only put on the blue cloth gown over her smock and petticoats and allow Lucy to button it up the front. Before she left London, her mother had cheerfully told her that she'd lowered the square neckline to display the assets Gwyneth was bringing to the wedding, but she had not realized how exposed she would feel. She tried to tuck a piece of lace in her bodice, but with a frown, Lucy removed it and tied a long scarf about her waist.

When they went back to the courtyard, Geoffrey rose from the bench with a smile and motioned for them to sit.

Minutes passed, and Gwyneth's nerves were stretched taut. Lucy got up to wander through the garden, sniffing roses and daisies. Gwyneth couldn't move her legs to do the same. Why did Sir Edmund make them wait, if he was in such a hurry?

Wearing a smile, Lucy eventually came back, holding up a circlet of blossoms. "I've made ye a garland for your hair, mistress."

Gwyneth felt foolish tears sting her eyes as she bowed her head and let the girl place the flowers in her hair. "Lucy, please, I've been your friend forever. Call me by my name."

"Soon ye'll be Lady Blackwell, mistress," she said soothingly. "Won't that be fine?"

When she heard a door open at the top of the stairs, Gwyneth shuddered and slowly looked up.

Chapter 2

S ir Edmund Blackwell—for who else could it be?—stood before the doors of the church, clothed in a loose leather tunic, belted at the waist, over plain cloth breeches. A cloak was thrown back on his shoulders. He was taller than any man Gwyneth had ever seen. His shoulders filled the door frame, and surely he'd had to duck to step outside. She didn't think she could have put her arms around his barrel chest. His devil-black hair was cropped in layers close to his head. His clean-shaven face had the hard, spare lines of a granite cliff, not handsome, but impressively male and darkened by the sun. This was a man who'd seen more of battlefields and death than home and family. There was no welcoming smile or even nervousness. Beneath his frowning brow, pale blue eyes the color of a dawn sky shone out at her, assessing, and maybe finding her lacking.

Gwyneth remembered her manners and slowly rose from the bench. His piercing, uncomfortable gaze slid down her body and back up. She thought of introducing herself, but he never even looked away, as if he just . . . knew her, knew everything about her.

"You are Mistress Gwyneth Hall."

It was a statement of fact, said in a deep voice that rumbled through her chest.

"Sir Edmund." Sweeping into a curtsy, she wanted to breathe a sigh of relief at how normal she sounded.

Still standing at her side, Geoffrey smiled. "My sincerest apologies for not thinking to introduce the two of you," he said in a voice that sounded strangely cheerful in the tense silence.

But she couldn't look at Geoffrey for staring at her betrothed.

Edmund reached out a large hand toward her. "Come here, Mistress Hall."

Gwyneth hesitated only a moment, went up a step, then gave him her hand, dwarfed by the size and heat of his. She knew that her face flamed red as she suddenly imagined that hand touching her in ways her mother had described. He drew her the rest of the way up the stairs until she stood at the top, staring into his massive chest. His fingers firmly took her chin and lifted her face until she had no choice but to stare into his pale eyes. There were flecks of darker blue there, and she studied them in wonder.

"You have but a moment, mistress," he said. "Decide now if you will marry me."

Could he see into her soul? The whole scene felt unreal, with the midday sun beating down on the garden and courtyard. His soldiers had come from behind the building and now stood watching. But here, in the doorway of the church, where she was cast in shadow, the day seemed cold and this man radiated the only heat to be found.

He . . . tantalized her, awed her, even frightened her, but only because of the way he made her emotions shiver in her chest and weaken her knees. She had never felt this confused before, certainly not on meeting any other man. But he wasn't just a man. He was an enigma, a challenge. Her life was about to change, and she was ready for it.

"I shall marry you, Sir Edmund." Her voice rang clearly through the courtyard.

She could hear a sigh of relief spread through the soldiers, and she watched her groom's eyes look upon her speculatively.

"Have you made *your* decision then?" she suddenly asked, and almost wished she could bite back her bold words.

Geoffrey chuckled into the silence, but Sir Edmund only continued to stare at her, his hand on her face, each fingertip a hot coal that burned her.

Had her words been reckless? Would he even now send her home disgraced and penniless?

Each breath Edmund inhaled seemed to him a struggle of enormous proportions—all because of one small, fragile-looking woman who stood proudly before him.

Gwyneth Hall, his bride.

He had first glimpsed her sitting beside the garden in a shaft of sunlight while he had stood in the cold shadows of the church. Now he kept his fingers on her face because the touch of her warm skin brought to life long-buried emotions, and he needed that reminder of what to guard against.

He'd made his own plans guaranteed to best Earl Langston. He would use the dowry to rebuild his lands, and when he'd earned enough money, he would repay the dowry and annul the marriage, breaking his ties with the Langstons. Seeking an annulment meant he could never bed his bride. He had thought that would be easy if she was anything like her cousin Elizabeth. He had convinced himself that the Langstons would give him a woman past her prime, an ugly cousin whom they'd been unable to marry off.

But instead, Gwyneth was a delicate maiden, her hair hanging freely in golden curls about her shoulders. No strand looked the same shade of yellow, and the differences seemed a riotous blend of color shining about her face. Her skin had seen a touch of the sun, which had mellowed an Englishwoman's usual pasty complexion into a feast of pale peach. Her eyes, so unafraid and bold, were warm brown with the palest hint of gold like her hair.

And when he had looked down her body, his vow of celibacy hit a low blow to his groin. Gwyneth wore a maiden's gown, cut low to show a groom the wonders that awaited him on the wedding night. The slopes of her breasts were the same mellow peach color, and between them lurked a valley of shadows and promise. She did not have Elizabeth's ethereal beauty, but Gwyneth Hall was lush in her own delicate way, with an earthy sensuality that made him think of home instead of just a place to live.

He dropped his hand from her face.

God above, he would not do this again, he thought. It was a good thing that he would forgo this wedding night. He had allowed his lust for Elizabeth to overcome his good sense—with disastrous results. She'd proven that a woman was not the sum of her appearance.

Though Gwyneth's eyes might be windows deeper into herself, he would not trust what he might see there. She was a pawn in Langston's game, and it was up to him to find out how deeply she was under the earl's control.

Edmund scrutinized her until he saw apprehension awaken in her eyes. "Aye, girl, my decision is made. Mr. Collins?" He turned to the

clergyman, who stiffened abruptly at the sum-
mons. "Bring your prayer book. We will wed."

The marriage ceremony there on the church
steps bound Gwyneth's life to that of a stranger.
Sir Edmund watched the vicar as if it was nothing
to him to marry someone he'd never met, while
she stared at her groom's profile, with its strong
nose and square jaw. At the right time, he put a
gold ring on her finger, and the ring felt heavy
with new obligations. At the end, she raised her
face for his kiss, but his lips only touched her
cheek. Her unease sounded the first of many
warnings.

Geoffrey broke bride cakes and handed them
about to the wedded couple, the soldiers, the
vicar, and Lucy. Gwyneth drank from the same
cup of wine as her new husband, celebrating that
the marriage was properly done.

And then it was all over, and she was bound
forever in wedlock to Sir Edmund Blackwell. She
was a man's wife, and it still felt so very strange.

Watching her new husband walk down the
stairs, she realized what he had concealed by remaining at the church door: he was lame. One
knee did not bend like the other, and he had to
take each of the stairs one at a time. Once on flat
ground, he walked with an awkward gait, bringing his permanently straight right leg forward.

Suddenly Sir Edmund turned and caught her

staring at him. He arched his brow, but she only
smiled, for such a deformity mattered not a whit
to her. When he turned abruptly away, her smile
died.

"Geoff," he called, "saddle the horses. I cannot
be gone long from the castle."

"But Edmund," Geoffrey said, glancing almost
guiltily at Gwyneth, who still remained on the
church stairs, "I have already sent one of the men
to procure a meal at a nearby inn."

Geoffrey lowered his voice, but she still heard
him.

"It *is* her wedding day, Edmund."

She slowly walked down the stairs and was
surprised when Lucy clutched her hand, staring
at Gwyneth's new husband in fear.

Sir Edmund looked up at the sun and then
sighed. "We will spare the time, then. My lady?"

He turned back to Gwyneth, who released
Lucy and hurried to his side, then hesitated when
she caught sight of his warhorse.

"Aye, my lord?"

"There is no need to take the coach through
these narrow streets. You shall ride with me."

Before she understood what he was about, he
caught her hand and pulled her closer, then
swung her up in his massive arms as if she were a
puff of wool. With eyes that felt wide and too dry,
she stared at his horse.

"My lord, please stop!" she cried, stiffening and
trying not to struggle.

His face went dark, and in a low voice he said, "If you do not wish me to touch you, at least have the decency not to show my men."

Gwyneth had no idea what he meant, but she shook her head anyway. "'Tis not that, but your horse. I—I—" She felt like such a fool, and her voice dropped to a pained whisper. "I am afraid of horses, my lord." She prided herself on her strong mind and calm will, and it brought her near tears to have to confess such a foolish weakness to her new husband.

She lay curled in his strong embrace and pleaded with her eyes, wrapping her arms about his neck. He stared at her for a long time, and then she felt his palm slide down her thigh. She gasped at such a familiarity, even as she tried to remember that he was her husband now.

"You feel strong enough to walk," Sir Edmund said.

She heard the soldiers laughing at his words and felt his tension ease. Somehow she had embarrassed him, and her foolish confession had made it go away. She was grateful at least for that. He set her down, then turned for the reins of his horse and limped at her side.

Geoffrey led the party down a few streets, past the market cross in the center of Richmond, and to a prosperous three-story inn. Every building here seemed to be made of the same gray stone and roof slates, but what made it pretty were the flowers planted along the roads that wound up the hillside. Gwyneth found herself wishing that they could live in a town like this.

As she followed her husband into the cool interior of the inn, she tried to remember the few things she knew of him. Geoffrey was loyal to Sir Edmund and had said little of him. All Gwyneth knew was that he'd been knighted on the field of battle.

He was supposed to be a common man, little schooled in the way of the nobility. For this she was grateful. Although noble blood ran in her veins, she had not been raised at court and was glad her husband would not think less of her for that. Her mother had taught her a smattering of French and Greek, her numbers, and something of the countries of the world. Like any lady, she'd learned to sing and embroider, but it was truly in a kitchen that she excelled—not a ladylike accomplishment, but one she was proud of.

They entered the warm, gloomy public room of the inn, and she watched as people at the benches and tables went silent as the armed party passed. She saw looks of fear that she well understood. Geoffrey led them into a private dining chamber with its own lead-paned windows to let in the sunlight, then bade her sit at her husband's side. The soldiers seemed at ease with their lord and sprawled wherever they wanted. Geoffrey sat down in their midst and soon had all the men laughing. Lucy struck up a tentative conversation with the vicar, which left Gwyneth with no one to talk to—but her husband.

She quickly realized he was not a talkative man, but she could not blame him. She wasn't certain what to say either. Instead, she watched him eat.

And was pleasantly amazed. Her *mother* could not have faulted his manners. He ate with a politeness and cleanliness that intrigued her. Did he learn such things among soldiers? If not, where? But how to ask one's husband why he didn't have the table manners of a boar? She experienced the sensation of his sleeve brushing hers, of his head and shoulders above hers. He was such a big man.

The silence was pressing on her with a heavy weight. She found herself filling the void with images of the two of them alone in a bedchamber. As her husband, he had the right to do anything he wanted to her, and she could not refuse him. She would be wearing the night rail her mother had given her, and her husband would be wearing . . . what? Did men wear nightclothes to bed? She didn't even want to think about that.

"Sir Edmund?" she said.

He glanced sideways at her, said, "Aye?" then took another bite of lamb.

"What is Castle Wintering like?"

Again he gave her that inscrutable glance. "Like?" he echoed almost distastefully. "'Tis a place to live, a place to work."

"Have you always lived there?"

This time he turned his body to face her. On the bench, his knee brushed hers, sending interesting shivers through her. She lowered her lashes and swallowed a spoonful of pigeon pie that she'd barely chewed. It seemed to stick in her throat.

"You are Elizabeth's cousin, are you not?" he asked.

Bewildered, she nodded.

"Did she not talk of our marriage?"

"Nay, my lord," she said, unwilling to reveal the few angry things Elizabeth had said.

One of his eyebrows rose, and it was apparent he didn't believe her. "I was given Castle Wintering as part of my wife's dowry only two years ago."

"Oh," she breathed, realizing he was almost as new to the area as she was. "Then where was your first home?"

He tore a piece of bread from the round loaf. "Too many places to mention."

Gwyneth didn't know what to say to that. She sensed he didn't want her probing deeply, and though she waited, he had no questions of his own.

Amidst conversations and laughter, she sat in pained silence next to the man who wanted to know nothing about her but would expect to share her bed and know her body intimately.

But she certainly wouldn't feel sorry for herself. At least his scent was pleasant, not unbearable, as the merchant's had been, and his features were attractive, though hard. He couldn't be more than ten years older than she. She had known an arranged marriage would be difficult, but she would willingly brave anything, even an indifferent husband, if it meant helping her family.

Edmund looked out across the room and chewed another piece of bread, though it might have tasted like dirt for all he knew. Anything to keep the woman from asking questions. Why couldn't she make this easy and be afraid of him—though for a moment, he remembered how startled and sick he'd felt when he'd lifted her up and thought she was frightened of his touch. When it had turned out to be his horse—his horse!—he had been almost too relieved.

What was wrong with him? He shouldn't be having this much trouble remembering who she was.

She acted differently from Elizabeth and her parents, but that was probably part of the plan. When he looked into her seemingly honest face, he was supposed to forget her family and fall under her spell. He glanced sideways at her as she toyed with her stewed fish. Surely that gown was part of the plan, too.

He swigged a mouthful of ale to wash down the dry bread and continued to stare at her now that she wasn't watching. His height enabled him to look down her bodice, and if she moved the right way, he would see everything. She hadn't done that yet, but it didn't keep him from hoping. If he couldn't touch, at least he could look.

He heard someone clear his throat and glanced up to see Geoff watching him, a grin stretching his face. Edmund narrowed his eyes at him, but Geoff only raised his goblet in a toast toward Gwyneth, who didn't seem to know that anything unusual was going on around her.

Geoff mouthed the word "chamber," and pointed above him. Edmund understood the reference immediately and gave a quick shake of his head. No, he would not take her to bed here. He wanted to be back in his own lair, where he had plenty of places to escape her plots.

"My lord?"

He turned his head and found Gwyneth staring up at him, those golden-brown eyes seeing into him, mesmerizing him. This was not a good sign. "What is it?"

"I must . . . leave the room for a moment."

Her dark-fringed lashes were lowered, and a becoming blush swept over her cheeks.

"Take your maid with you. I do not want you alone here."

She nodded, motioned to the dark-haired girl, and they both left.

The mood in the chamber became considerably more boisterous, and he caught his men winking and elbowing one another while raising their tankards to him. He knew what they were thinking: she was an agreeable wench to take to bed. He downed the rest of his ale and thought of the night ahead, when he would send Gwyneth away from him.

Geoff slid onto the bench at his side. "Before the wedding, you asked me to keep my eyes open for anything suspicious."

"And?"

"People walking by the courtyard walls of the church often lingered to stare but never for long. Except for one man."

Edmund stiffened. He was not about to explain his strange marriage to Geoff, but he had asked pointed questions about Gwyneth's journey north, which had been enough to make his friend curious. "What did this man look like?"

"Not poor by any means. His garments were subdued but expensive in cut and fabric. I did not recognize his face, but I couldn't help noticing him because he wore a strange fur hat on a hot summer day."

"What did he do?"

"Nothing but watch the entire ceremony, which was peculiar in and of itself. After you'd said your final vows, I turned, and he was gone."

Edmund urged Geoff to rejoin the merriment, then sat and wondered how closely Earl Langston was watching him.

When Gwyneth descended from the second floor of the inn, she steeled herself to return to the dining chamber and her husband's silence. This time she would make merry conversation and have him laughing in a trice. She was usually good at talking with people.

But Sir Edmund and his soldiers had already gathered in the taproom, obviously impatient to be on their way home.

Home. She so wanted that word to mean something to her marriage. Right now all it made her think about was the small cottage in London that had been the center of her world. She started to imagine what her parents and sisters were doing at this moment, but she had to force the thought aside as it made tears well up in her eyes. She would not cry on her wedding day and make her husband think she was not grateful to him.

Outside, village boys were holding the reins of the troop's horses. Sir Edmund and Geoffrey tossed coins to them, and the boys merrily ran away. Gwyneth remained staring up at her husband's horse, so much larger and wilder than the rest. It seemed to watch her as it pawed the ground, ready to kick.

The men were paying little attention to them, and all mounted their horses as the two women waited. Gwyneth was impressed by how easily Sir Edmund swung his lame leg over the horse's back. Once he was mounted, the injury didn't seem to bother him, though the leg was held stiff and straight. The horse seemed totally under his command, like one of Lucifer's minions.

"Milady," Lucy said into her ear, "Methinks they forgot us already."

Gwyneth frowned and waited, but the men were talking and gesturing like the rough soldiers they were, and Geoffrey and Sir Edmund were conversing, their view blocked by the soldiers. She was not about to walk into the midst of those horses to get their attention. Her husband would remember her soon enough.

But the horses began to move off. The women exchanged glances, linked arms, and started to walk behind them, carefully stepping over the horses' leavings.

Suddenly Sir Edmund's horse separated itself from the others, and he wheeled the animal about and came toward them. Gwyneth froze, barely stopping herself from shrinking back. He guided the animal sideways as he looked down upon her.

"Lady Blackwell, were you going to walk all the way to Wintering?"

For one moment, she thought her husband's straight lips might have twitched with amusement at his own folly. Or was she just longing for the gentle humor she so enjoyed with her family?

And then she realized he'd called her by her new name, and she felt like a different person, a stranger.

"Sir Edmund, I assumed you would eventually remember me. But just in case, we had planned to return to the coach."

He frowned and leaned forward on the pommel, staring down at her. "The coach will have a difficult time these last few miles up the dale. It is very rocky and uneven. 'Twould be best if you rode with me."

"No, my lord. I have traveled in that coach for more than a week now, and I assure you that my . . . posterior is quite accustomed to bouncing."

Sir Edmund's eyes widened, and now she was certain she saw laughter there.

"Have I said something humorous, my lord?"

Lucy gripped her elbow harder and hissed in her ear, "Gwyn, I think yer words could be taken for . . . bed talk."

"Bed talk?" she repeated a little too loudly.

To her mortification, her husband seemed to choke as he whirled his horse about.

"To the coach, then!" he called to his men.

He did not offer her a ride this time, and it was just as well. Her face was as red as her mother's roses.

Chapter 3

~~~⌒○⌒~~~

Gwyneth and Lucy clung to each other as the coach threatened to tip over because of the steep grade of the road. Sir Edmund was right, but she just couldn't give him the satisfaction of admitting the truth. He would only want her to get up on his fiendishly tall horse. The thought of sitting on such a wild animal terrified her. But the coach was slowing everyone down, and she could see her husband glancing at the setting sun with obvious impatience.

Impatience for what? she wondered, feeling a little shiver of nervous excitement. Could it be that he was anxious to come to their wedding bed, that he thought her too beautiful to resist?

Gwyneth knew she was getting carried away by her fancies. He didn't have to resist her; he had earned the right through marriage to do whatever

39

he wanted to her. She chewed on her lip and imagined the kind of lover he would be. Would he hurry, or would he take his time to make her feel comfortable? Her mother had told her that the latter was important in a man, that it was a husband's duty to make his bride feel cherished. She could not imagine Sir Edmund Blackwell whispering poetic words in her ear.

As the road leveled off, Lucy tugged on her arm and pointed out the window. "Milady, look!"

"Surely 'tis not more sheep," she teased.

Lucy just rolled her eyes and leaned farther out. Gwyneth peered past her shoulder. The road was following a small river. Rocks broke up the smooth flow of the water and also littered the grassy slopes of the steep hills. Far in the distance, where the valley narrowed, a small castle cut into the hillside. Its single turret pointed to the sky. With the sun setting, only the opposite side of the valley was still light; the castle blended in with the shadows.

" 'Tis lovely," Lucy breathed.

Gwyneth could only agree. She'd only been a little girl when they'd lived on a farm, so she had almost forgotten what such open spaces felt like. It was freedom, wild and pure as the wind that blew her hair about. It was peace, without the London sounds of hawkers shouting their wares and the jingle of many horses crowding the streets. Could it become her home? Or would her husband always make her feel like the second wife, the intruder?

Gwyneth leaned out the other window and saw Sir Edmund in the lead, practically standing in his stirrups as he leaned forward. No matter how impassive he'd seemed back at the inn when they'd discussed his estate, she could tell by his proud expression that he thought of Castle Wintering as his home. Though he'd lived there only two years, it was apparent he put his heart and soul into it.

Geoffrey caught up to him, and a challenging glance between them sent them galloping down the dirt road like mischievous boys. The soldiers streamed behind them, shouting and taking bets amongst themselves. Cheering on her husband, Gwyneth waved her own hand in exultation. When she couldn't see them well any more, she sat back in the coach, wearing a smile that wouldn't leave her face.

Lucy was watching her with bewilderment.

Feeling embarrassed, Gwyneth asked, "Is something wrong?"

"For a woman who never met her husband before their weddin' day, ye seem awful happy."

Her smiled faded as she contemplated Lucy's words. "All along I have had no choice in this matter. Why should I make it worse on myself and everyone else by being miserable?"

Lucy lowered her voice and couldn't quite meet her eyes. "Are ye not . . . afraid?"

"A little," she conceded.

"He's a big man—a stranger."

"Aye." Gwyneth's anxiety rattled back to life. She glanced out the window again. The sun was totally behind the hills now, and the closer they got to Castle Wintering, the more something seemed wrong. Clearly there had once been a high wall encircling it, for now she could see rubble where it had collapsed in sections. There were no people on the road except them, although along each side of the valley, she could see herds of grazing sheep and cattle and the occasional shepherd. Farther up the valley stretched acres of orchards and gardens and farmland. But the closer they got to the castle, the more decayed and overgrown it looked, hunched against the hillside, a dark, silent presence marring the valley.

Finally they passed between the broken gates and into a large courtyard carpeted with weeds growing in random tufts. She could see outbuildings along the walls and the last soldier leading his horse into what had to be a stable. But except for Ranalf, their coachman, she and Lucy were alone. Somewhere a door slammed, and then there was silence but for hens clucking in the dirt.

"They forgot us again," Lucy said morosely.

"They're taking care of the horses after such a long trip." Gwyneth put her cloak over her arm as Ranalf opened the door. She stepped down stiffly onto a wooden box he pushed into place for her, then to the ground. When he doffed his cap, she touched his arm.

"Ranalf, thank you for the care you've shown us," she said.

"Sorry for that last bit," he said, pulling his head lower into his shoulders. "A mite rough."

"The roads are not your fault, now, are they?"

He grinned and shook his head.

Gwyneth looked about, watching as the gloom cast shadows everywhere. "Ranalf, do you know where the servants are?"

"No servants stay the night, Lady Blackwell. Not since—" He broke off and blushed.

"Not since . . ." Gwyneth repeated.

"Not since the last mistress died, milady."

"Why is that?" She gave Lucy a puzzled glance and saw that the girl's eyes were huge. "I see that the soldiers stay."

"Oh, yes, milady, in the barracks. We all know there's no truth to the rumors, although it be difficult to convince the villagers."

"What rumors?" Lucy asked before Gwyneth could stop her.

Ranalf's face was now a fiery red. "I be speakin' when I shouldn't. Forgive me, milady. I'll go take care of the horses."

He hopped up to his coachman's box, grabbed the reins, and guided the horses toward the stables. The women were left standing alone, because even the cart with their trunks had already gone lumbering by. A chill seemed to be rising from the ground and swirling about them, even though summer was not entirely over.

Gwyneth took a deep breath. "Well, shall we enter the castle?"

"Are ye certain 'tis safe?" Lucy asked, sliding her hand under Gwyneth's elbow.

Gwyneth patted her hand. " 'Tis perfectly safe, and our home now—well, my home at least. You don't have to stay, Lucy."

"Oh, nay, milady, I can be as brave as you."

The two of them marched arm in arm to a large set of double doors that looked whole and sound. After they walked up three stone steps, Gwyneth knocked, but it sounded like only a tap against the hard wood. The second time she made a fist and pounded. Though she heard a satisfying echo inside, no one came to greet them.

She was becoming annoyed now, so she grasped the latch, lifted it, and swung the door wide. Inside was a massive old medieval hall, with sooted rafters high above her and a hearth taller than she at each end of the room. There was even a set of rusty armor on either side of a dark doorway, as if standing guard. Two walls had tapestries covering them, but they were too dark and stained to make out.

"Oh, my," Lucy finally breathed with dismay.

Gwyneth was glad it wasn't she who had expressed such an opinion first. But she shared it.

Though there were fresh rushes on the floor and a large, clean table before one of the hearths, the hall looked unlived in. For one aching moment, she remembered the warm fire and happy laughter of her own home.

There was a sudden rustle of rushes from a dark corner, and to her horror several shapes rose up. With a shrill squeak, Lucy grabbed hold of her arm again. They heard the first low growls, and she realized with relief that it was a pack of dogs. But the growling continued, and the animals began to slink around both sides of the table, coming toward them. There seemed to be so many of them.

"Should we run, Gwyn?" Lucy cried.

In a calm voice, she said, "I think 'twould be the worst thing to do. Remain still. They probably just want to see who we are. They are Sir Edmund's dogs, after all." That sounded so foolish, but she could think of nothing else to say, not when her own fright was rising in proportion to Lucy's.

They were still standing there, frozen, when one of the many doors opened and Sir Edmund limped into the hall. There were joyous barks all around, and the dogs dashed for him, circling him and nosing his hand and bumping his legs. While Gwyneth and Lucy sagged against each other, he rubbed the animals, saying "Good dog" over and over.

He stopped abruptly when he noticed the

women, and Gwyneth couldn't help wondering if he'd forgotten again that he was married.

"There you are, my lady," Sir Edmund said, frowning. "I was wondering where you had wandered off to."

She wanted to say they'd been abandoned and could have been attacked by wild animals for all the thought anyone gave them, but she restrained herself and instead gave him a tired smile. "When we saw no one in the courtyard, we decided to come inside, Sir Edmund. I hope you do not mind."

He frowned. "Not at all. I assume the dogs did not startle you."

She wanted to roll her eyes. Did all men think that a pack of smelly dogs was a welcome touch in a woman's household? And there were ten dogs!

"I saw Mrs. Haskell before she returned to the village," Sir Edmund continued, "and she said she'd left supper for us in the kitchen."

"Mrs. Haskell?"

"The housekeeper." He looked down at papers he held in his hand, even as he still absently petted the dogs. He gestured over his shoulder. "Follow this corridor to the end, and you'll reach the kitchen."

Gwyneth walked toward him, feeling Lucy cling to her elbow, as if the dogs had been the final insult to the girl's idea of a proper welcome. Several of the large animals approached them and began to sniff at their skirts.

"Will you not eat with us, my lord?" Gwyneth asked, putting out a hand and sighing with relief when one of the dogs only licked it.

Her husband didn't even lift his head. "I have business to attend to."

She stiffened at his dismissal of her. She understood that she was not an important part of his life yet. That might come with time, and she could be patient. But there was still the wedding night, which he probably wouldn't ignore.

She and Lucy walked around Sir Edmund as if he were a statue in their way and entered what seemed like a dark hole in the wall. She almost wished one or two of the dogs would accompany them. But the oppressive stone corridor was short, and there were torches in wall brackets to light their way. The kitchen itself was almost cheery, with a hearth and oven built into one wall and a heavy wooden table with benches. A full kettle steamed over the fire, and as both women inhaled the wonderful scent, they smiled at each other.

Edmund waited until he was certain Gwyneth was gone before he flung the papers onto the table and sank into a cushioned chair before the hearth. It was the end of summer, so no fire had been lit, but he could have used the cheerfulness. Samuel, his favorite hound, dropped his big head on his knee, and Edmund fondled his furry ears.

He almost wanted to follow the women into the kitchen and listen to them talk. Since Elizabeth had died and the rumors had begun to spread that he'd killed her, the last of the servants had found places in the village to live. They needed his employment but were too afraid to spend the night, as if he only murdered people in their beds.

He wiped a hand down his face, then through his short hair. He couldn't blame them. They had at first thought of him as their savior, the man who released them from service to the Langstons. The earl had always taken much of Castle Wintering's profits without reinvesting it in the estate. But after Edmund had become the owner of the castle, Elizabeth had used her parents and the steward to get at the profits for herself. He'd been forced to go back to mercenary work. He'd spent months away from this place—his first real home. He loved it here, even the harsh winters, but he had to support it somehow. So Elizabeth had remained in London at court, and he'd traveled with the army one last time.

But Castle Wintering was home, even though it had suffered much ruin wrought by war. Its curtain walls had been shot down by cannon fire, and it had almost been given over to the rats under the earl's rule, but Edmund could see a future here. It would simply take time—and money.

But there was a bride along with the dowry, and already the hall smelled different, and he could imagine feminine laughter drifting from the kitchen. One of the dogs sitting near the corridor sniffed and whined. Edmund knew how he felt.

He closed his eyes and leaned his head back against the carved wood of the chair. He almost wished he could tell Gwyneth she wasn't a real wife to him. How else could he explain that he wouldn't be coming to her bed?

But then she'd go running home, and the dowry would be withdrawn, and he'd be back where he'd started, without money to pay the taxes or buy the grain for the winter sowing. And he wouldn't have bested Earl Langston.

He had no choice but to let Gwyneth think he was merely thoughtless and cruel while he bided his time before sending her away. When the estate had earned enough money and he annulled the marriage, he would give Gwyneth a dowry to lure a new husband, to set her free of the Langstons, if she wished it. Then he'd find his own bride, a common girl without noble relatives, who would give birth to a son to inherit the castle and all his hard work.

When enough time had passed for Gwyneth and her maid to be finished eating, Edmund stood up and motioned the dogs back to their corner, though they whined their dismay. He went down the corridor toward the kitchen, keeping silent as he approached the doorway. He hesitated, for he could see his new wife perfectly, with firelight flickering across her pretty face, her eyes bright with laughter, and her smile—

He took a deep breath and fought the desire that he'd kept simmering low out of sheer willpower. Lust was an annoyance, but he'd live with it.

When he stepped into the kitchen, their faces lifted to his. The maid's laughter died immediately, while Gwyneth quickly hid what could only be nervousness behind a shy smile. 'Twas a shame he couldn't tell her there was no reason to be nervous about the wedding night.

He turned to the maid first, and she seemed to shrink from him, which he was used to. "What is your name again, girl?"

"Lucy Tyler, milord," she said in a small voice.

"As you can see, Lucy, you have your choice of chambers here. The servants' quarters are—"

But he caught her panicked look at Gwyneth.

"Sir Edmund," Gwyneth interrupted, "might Lucy have a bedchamber closer to mine? She has never been away from home before."

He heard the unspoken implication that Gwyneth had never left home either. He couldn't imagine anyone calling Langston House a home, but that only proved why he must be wary of her.

"I have no problem with this. Come, I'll show you to your chambers."

He lit candles at the kitchen fire, handed the holders to Gwyneth and Lucy, and then led them back to the hall. Joyfully the dogs gathered round them. He watched Lucy stiffen with terror, but Gwyneth smiled and reached to pat the nearest furry neck. As a pack, they all trooped to a corridor across the hall. He could smell the damp, unused odor of the place. If he had really wanted to make Gwyneth despise him, he should have made sure the tower room wasn't prepared, but he'd found he couldn't do that to a woman. Mrs. Haskell wouldn't have approved of such rudeness anyway.

At the last chamber before they reached the tower, Edmund opened the door and walked in, motioning for the dogs to wait outside. Gwyneth and Lucy followed him inside. Though the room hadn't been used in years, it was decently furnished, and had a fresh pile of wood in the hearth. The maid glanced around with her big, dark eyes, then back at him with barely concealed horror.

He forced himself to be gruff instead of sympathetic. "The servants' quarters were readied for you, Lucy, but you chose not to use them. I shall send the servants to help you clean it on the morrow as well as bring your things up."

"Aye, milord," she murmured.

When Lucy knelt before the hearth, Edmund could see her hands shaking as she fumbled with the wood. Brushing her aside, he knelt down on one knee to start the fire for her. He felt a little foolish with his injured leg straight out to the side, but the women would get used to it. Soon the fire began to glow, chasing the room's shadows away. He saw Lucy assess the large bed and the carpet before the hearth, and thought she relaxed a bit.

But she still followed them back into the corridor. Lucy could spend the night with Gwyneth and it wouldn't matter, because he had no intention of joining his wife.

When they came to the tower, the dogs suddenly stopped. They paced about one another, growling and whining. Elizabeth had never liked the dogs, and it was obvious they had long memories.

" 'Tis all right," Edmund said, "get up if you're going."

Then they were barking cheerfully and chasing each other. Following the dogs, Edmund, Gwyneth, and Lucy wound their way up the stairs that hugged the circular walls. He pushed past the dogs and opened the door into a chamber that was spacious and well furnished, with glass windows that looked out on the valley in four directions. The dogs followed him in first.

It was Elizabeth's chamber, her sanctuary, where she'd spent the majority of her time and money when she wasn't in London. No luxury was too expensive for her. He could only look upon this room with distaste, for it reminded him too much of her. He had seldom set foot here, especially not after the first year of their marriage. The thought of lying in the same bed with Elizabeth had grown repulsive.

He turned to see Gwyneth's reaction, but she was on the tower landing, fighting to get past the dogs and still keep a hold on a cowering Lucy. Edmund suppressed a laugh, though she glanced at him sharply as if she recognized his amusement and disapproved. He barked a command at the pack, which promptly swept back down the stairs. The two women pressed themselves against the stone wall as every dog in the pack of ten brushed their skirts. He knew from experience the amount of hair they left behind.

When she was finally in the room, Gwyneth turned about, looking everywhere, even as Edmund lit tallow candles one by one at the small fire in the hearth. When he stood up, he saw her looking at the massive four-poster bed. The touch of trepidation in her eyes turned to embarrassment when she saw him watching her. Then she straightened her shoulders and turned about as she absorbed the room.

"Sir Edmund, 'tis quite lovely here," she said.

"You'll enjoy the view from the windows when the sun is up."

Her delighted smile beamed at him like a far-off light in a storm, beckoning and entrancing. When he didn't stop staring, she turned shy and cast down her lashes. The need to send Lucy away and bar the door against all intruders was such a powerful force that he came up on the balls of his feet as if to heed it. Every part of him yearned for what her smile promised, and that was what finally stopped him.

It wasn't true, that smile, for they were strangers to each other.

Chapter 4

Gwyneth felt her smile die as Sir Edmund's eyes suddenly went from the blue heat of flames to a pale glacial color. The chamber that had seemed welcoming in its luxury now seemed dwarfed by his size and his cool detachment. She wanted to ask if she had done something wrong but felt hindered by their very strangeness to each other. They were in their bridal chamber, and all he had to do was send Lucy away and they'd be alone. Certainly Gwyneth was frightened, but she was ready to consummate her marriage, to begin the duty she owed her family.

But instead he looked down at her coldly, a broad, tall stranger, and the shivery heat that she had hoped to feel again was gone.

Lucy backed toward the door. "I'll leave ye be, milady—milord."

Edmund shot Lucy a quick glance. "Nay, your mistress needs your help."

Without another word, he limped past Lucy and began his halting descent of the stairs. Biting her trembling lip, Gwyneth went to close the door but instead remained to watch him. He never looked up, and as the staircase curved down, he dropped out of sight.

When even his bobbing shadow was gone, she slowly closed the door and leaned back against it. Lucy was staring at her, wide-eyed.

Gwyneth gave her a perfunctory smile and went to open her trunk, which must have been brought up while they ate.

"Lady Blackwell," Lucy began in an uncertain voice, "what do ye make of him?"

Gwyneth held up a hand. "Do not speak of him. We shall unpack and settle in. 'Tis a beautiful chamber, is it not?"

"Aye, milady." She bowed her head and opened the trunk, beginning to set out a small pile of garments.

For once, Gwyneth could not bring herself to help. She gave in to a need to explore her new chamber. The walls were hung with expensive tapestries, not painted canvas, and there were even framed paintings of gardens and cottages. A large cupboard held a basin and ewer and was scattered with more lotions and washes than she could imagine having a use for. Her nose tested each fragrance, and she planned which lotions she would use first. There were balls of delicate, fragrant soap next to the softest towels she'd ever touched. Part of her relaxed and rejoiced, because Sir Edmund had prepared a special place for her, as if he meant to give their marriage a real chance for happiness instead of treating it like a duty.

But she should have known it would not be so easy.

"Lady Blackwell!" Lucy suddenly called in a strange voice.

She turned and found the girl bent over a coffer, one that had already been in the chamber. Slowly Lucy lifted up a pile of red velvet, and as she shook it out into the shape of a gown, emeralds and pearls sewn to the bodice glittered in the candlelight. Both women gasped.

"Gwyn!" Lucy whispered, as she carefully placed the gown across the bed and lifted out another. "Aren't they heavenly?"

Gwyneth felt a shock run through her at the expense and beauty of the garments. Had Sir Edmund had these made for her? For a moment, the fantasy she'd dreamed of each night almost became real. He wanted to cherish her; he wanted to be a true husband to her. He just didn't know how to go about showing it when they were together. But then she recognized the next gown, black and white satin scattered with tiny diamonds.

These were Elizabeth's gowns.

She shook her head in disbelief at how wild and

foolish her thoughts had almost become. Of course they were Elizabeth's. Sir Edmund had agreed to marry Gwyneth only a few weeks ago, certainly not enough time to have a whole wardrobe created for a woman he'd never met. She knew with certainty that Sir Edmund had meant nothing cruel by giving her a dead woman's garments. Such richness and expense shouldn't go to waste, and most women would have welcomed the gift.

But she didn't want to share Sir Edmund with the ghost of her cousin. Then realization struck, and she looked about her in sorrow. This was Elizabeth's chamber, the best in the castle. She'd spared no expense on the fine tapestries that kept out the drafts, while the rest of the household suffered.

Was there supposed to be a dark message in Sir Edmund's giving her this chamber? Did he want her to understand that she'd never measure up to his first wife? But she'd known the shallow, self-centered woman Elizabeth had been. If only she knew more about what kind of marriage they'd truly had.

Perhaps Sir Edmund was only grateful to be given another chance and wanted his second wife to have the best comforts the castle had.

Or maybe he didn't care one way or the other.

Gwyneth hugged herself and watched Lucy exclaim over each new garment and accessory. Finally the girl looked excitedly over her shoulder, but her smile died when she saw Gwyneth's face.

"Milady?"

"Pack them away, Lucy. I cannot accept them."

"But why? Surely I never knew such lovely things existed."

"They were his first wife's garments."

Lucy gave an apologetic shrug. "Such things are done, milady."

"I know. But she was my cousin too. Would you mind putting them away? Then we'll just close the coffer and have someone remove it on the morrow."

Lucy nodded, her shoulders drooping, and finished the task while Gwyneth hung her own small selection of gowns on pegs in the wall.

When she was done, Lucy straightened and said, "I guess 'tis time to send for hot water for a bath, milady. I see a tub over there in the corner."

For a moment, Gwyneth sighed at the thought of finally being clean after such a long journey, until she remembered the state of her new household. "I can't. There are no servants to carry up the water."

"*I'll* do it," Lucy said indignantly. "'Tis your wedding night. He should have seen to it."

"None of that." Her voice was stern, but she finished with a small smile. "And I'll not have you hurting yourself carrying buckets all over this castle—and probably getting lost too."

Lucy reluctantly grinned. "I was beginnin' to wonder how I would find me mornin' meal."

"Then that's settled." She walked to the fire, took a small kettle of water from the floor near the hearth, and hung it on a hook above the flames. "There's already water here, and I can wash as I usually do. From now on, when I want a bath, I'll have to see to it in the middle of the day."

"Gwyn!" Lucy said, scandalized.

She laughed. "Help me unbutton my gown, and then you can go to your bed."

When Gwyneth was wearing only a smock, she smiled and handed a candleholder to Lucy. "Off with you, now. Sleep well."

The girl hesitated at the door. "Are ye sure ye don't want me to stay?"

"He'll probably be here soon." Her breath caught a little. "I'd best be alone."

Lucy nodded, opened her mouth as if to say "good luck," but seemed to think better of it and just smiled before she held the candle out above the stairs. "I'll likely break me bloody neck."

Gwyneth heard the whisper and smiled as she closed the door. It was suddenly very quiet in her new bedchamber. But it wouldn't be for long. Her husband would be here soon, and she didn't want to start her marriage with his disappointment.

Quickly she stripped off her smock, then stood on a towel before the hearth to wash herself. Though it was summer, there was an ancient coldness in the castle that made her shiver as the water ran down her skin. Or maybe it was only her nerves making her teeth chatter.

She toweled herself dry and dressed quickly in the new night rail her mother had given her. It was plain, gathered at her neck and wrists, but of a delicate, sheer fabric that quite made Gwyneth blush at how much it revealed. But her mother had promised that a man would like it.

Next she had to decide where to wait for her husband. For only the second time, she let her gaze slide to the large bed, with its four high posts, heavy bed curtains, and a canopy over the top. It was so big, there was a set of little stairs to climb up to it.

It was big enough to fit a man like her husband, and she shivered as she imagined lying in it with him. Or would he go to his own chamber to sleep, as some men did? Her parents shared a room, and she so wanted to enjoy the kind of love they had.

She almost giggled nervously as she went back to the question of where to await her husband. In bed? No, it would seem too obvious. Yet to sit in a chair before the fire felt ridiculous, since she wore so little clothing.

She settled on a perch at the edge of the bed, with her feet resting on the steps. Once she stopped moving, she could hear the absolute quiet of the castle. She was at the highest point, and below her it was almost empty. She had never felt much stillness in her life, because her parents' cozy cottage was always full of running feet and laughter. But that life was gone, and it was time to make her own.

Several minutes passed, and she shifted into a more comfortable position. Surely Sir Edmund knew Lucy had retired to her own chamber. Or was Gwyneth supposed to send for him?

But no—he would have asked. He must want her to wait. When he was finished with his work, he would come to her.

But an hour passed, and she found herself pacing the wooden floor. Soon she was looking through another coffer for needlework, anything to pass the time as her nervousness melted into a sick dread. She'd foolishly left her own embroidery in the coach. But there was nothing useful to occupy her hands, no books to occupy her mind.

Where was he?

Finally, when Gwyneth had watched the moon rise into the night sky and it was well past midnight, she blew out the candles and crawled up into the bed she'd avoided. Lucy had thoughtfully turned down the covers, and she now slid beneath the icy sheets and pulled the blankets and coverlet up beneath her chin. She huddled there, her back against the headboard, her face pillowed on her knees, and tried not to cry.

Her husband wasn't coming.

When she finally admitted it to herself, a single tear fell from her welling eyes, and she angrily brushed it away. She would not cry. Surely there

was a reason why Sir Edmund did not come—
maybe he'd drunk too much, celebrating with the
soldiers, as men were wont to do. Or maybe he'd
fallen asleep going over the castle accounts; he
seemed so diligent in his work.

Or else, once again, he'd just forgotten her.

It was so difficult to imagine such a thing, yet
he'd spent the day forgetting he had a wife. But
without consummation, she didn't feel married.

Had he already changed his mind? Would he
send her home in disgrace, with nothing to help
her family?

No, she was letting her imagination run away
with her. He didn't know her well enough to decide such a thing, not after just one day. But
maybe he was biding his time, waiting for her to
prove if she was worthy of him. Then she had a
chilling thought—was this how he had treated
Elizabeth? Was Gwyneth's marriage destined to
follow the same pattern as her cousin's?

She fell asleep with that awful thought making
her restless and haunting her dreams.

Edmund stood leaning against a tree in the courtyard, staring up at the tower where his new wife
slept. He could tell when she blew out the last candle, for the window darkened, although because of
the fire, the gray emptiness still glowed. As a chill
wind hinting of autumn swirled around him, he
told himself not to imagine what she was doing.

If Gwyneth was anything like her cousin, she was probably relieved and already sleeping peacefully.

He wondered if she would confront him in the morning. What would he say? Not the truth, for that would lose him the dowry fast. Perhaps he would say he was respecting her feminine sensibilities, letting her get to know him first before forcing intimacies on her.

What rot. Perhaps he should just avoid her.

But still he remained in the courtyard as the moon rose high above him, looked at her window, and imagined being between her warm thighs, holding her in his arms.

Once he was in bed, he couldn't sleep, of course. There was a woman waiting for him, and everything in him rebelled at staying away from her. He finally flung the blankets off him and paced before the hearth, but he could not erase the image in his mind of Gwyneth in that big bed. He wondered what she looked like, and before he understood his motives, he pulled on breeches and wandered up through the levels of the castle.

He carried no candle; he knew every corridor and chamber. It was all his, and he had walked it with pride for so many days and nights. When Elizabeth was alive, he had walked it to remind himself of the only good that had come from his marriage. After her death and his recovery from his wounds, he had walked it to heal himself, to understand and accept that Wintering was all he had left. He had vowed to make it a success, no matter what he had to do.

The earl's challenge had given him a second chance, he thought, as he began his limping climb up to Gwyneth's chamber. He stood outside the door for a moment, listening, but hours had passed since she'd blown out the candles. She had to be asleep.

Carefully he lifted the latch and leaned his head inside. The fire had died to a few glowing sticks, but he could still see well enough. On silent feet, he approached the bed and stared at his bride. She lay on her side facing the hearth, her brown lashes half-moons across her cheeks as she slept. Her lips were slightly parted, and her cheeks seemed to glow with that healthy color he'd thought so remarkable when he'd first seen her. Her golden curls were scattered behind her across two pillows, and he had to clench his hands into fists to keep from testing the silkiness with his fingers.

She was all soft loveliness, testing his vow of celibacy as his imagination never had. He wanted to slide in beside her, to see if she was as brave as she'd seemed.

But he would not touch her. Turning away, he limped to the door, then out into the corridor. If anything, this visit had proved his resolve.

* * *

Gwyneth awoke so suddenly, she thought someone must have startled her. She sat up, hoping to see her husband, but she was alone. She'd never slept alone in her life; she'd always had her sister Caroline to confide in as they drifted into sleep. The fire had gone out, the sun was already rising in the morning sky, and she had slept too long.

What would Sir Edmund think of her lying abed so late? Though her mind was back to wondering and worrying over why he had not come to her in the night, she could not allow her thoughts to be distracted now. She would be a pleasant, helpful wife in hopes that he wouldn't change his mind about their marriage. Somehow she had to prove he'd made the right decision.

She flung back the blankets and jumped to the cold floor, ignoring the little stairs. She dressed quickly in a brown homespun gown that had little rolls at her shoulders and a starched collar that angled out from her neck. She thought it flattered her and could only hope her husband approved. Lastly she pinned an apron to her skirt, then set off to learn about her new home.

When she left the tower, she tried Lucy's bedchamber first, but the girl must have been awake long before now—the morning was half gone. Gwyneth took only one wrong turn on the way to the great hall, but she found it soon enough.

The first servant she saw was a maid, who was

diligently cleaning the large oak table. The girl looked up with wide eyes when Gwyneth entered, but she relaxed and gave a stiff curtsy.

"Lady Blackwell?" the girl said hesitantly.

Gwyneth gave her a friendly smile. "Aye. And who are you?"

"Nell, milady."

She started to curtsy again, but Gwyneth shook her head. "There is no need for such formalities here, Nell. I am pleased to meet you."

"I'm to take ye to Mrs. Haskell, milady. Would ye come with me?"

That was the housekeeper's name, Gwyneth remembered. She followed Nell down another corridor to a large open chamber filled with spinning wheels and looms. A single girl was carding wool by hand, with an older woman standing over her.

"Mrs. Haskell?" Nell called, "The new lady is finally awake."

Gwyneth wanted to close her eyes and groan. What must they all be thinking? Probably that she'd had an exhilarating and exhausting wedding night, she thought with an inward sigh.

Mrs. Haskell was easily her mother's age, with a crown of gray braids and deep lines about her mouth. Maybe that indicated she laughed a lot, but right now her smile was perfunctory and her eyes assessing.

"Lady Blackwell," she said coolly, "I wasn't sure when you'd be down. Allow me to assemble the servants to meet you."

"No, please, that will not be necessary. I don't wish to interrupt their work. If you don't mind giving me a tour of the castle, you can introduce me to everyone as we come upon them."

That seemed to be the answer Mrs. Haskell wanted to hear, for her smile became more genuine. "Thank you, my lady. It would be a pleasure."

Gwyneth spent the next several hours in the dawning realization that the castle was much larger than it had seemed but little was actually being used. There were roughly a dozen servants working inside, and most seemed nervous, as if they'd rather be anywhere else. But all were friendly enough once she smiled at them. She knew from personal experience that her cousin had not treated servants well. And then there was the rumor about Elizabeth's death. How had such nonsense spread this far from London? It seemed suspicious to her.

Never once on her tour did she see Sir Edmund. She kept expecting to run into him when she turned a corner or held up a candle in a dark room, as if he were hiding from her. It was a foolish thought. Mrs. Haskell casually informed her that the master went about his estate duties every morning and usually returned for dinner, which he took alone.

"Alone?" Gwyneth asked, as they stood in the kitchen and watched the cook and scullery maids work.

"Though I shouldn't be saying so," Mrs. Haskell said in a low voice, "Sir Edmund is a private man, my lady, not given much to socializing."

"But I have been told there's a village nearby, and surely Castle Wintering's tenants visit."

The woman shook her head. "It is not done, my lady," she said with finality in her voice.

Gwyneth couldn't imagine not entertaining neighbors, especially when one had the means to do so. For a moment, she imagined her social cousin being told she could not give parties. Surely that must have caused a huge problem in the marriage. She wished she understood her new husband, but that was not going to happen if they continued barely exchanging sentences—and not sharing a bed.

But dinner came and went, and she ate alone in the winter parlor, her husband's private dining chamber. It was the first full day of her marriage, and she was trying not to feel alternately angry and confused at how Sir Edmund ignored her.

But she could only do her best as a wife, so after she finished eating, she found Mrs. Haskell in the pantry, where Gwyneth dodged strings of onions and garlic hung from the ceiling.

"Aye, my lady?" the housekeeper said as she looked up from counting barrels.

"I'm sorry to disturb you, but I was wondering who I should see about a tour of the rest of the estate."

Frowning, Mrs. Haskell made a mark on the paper she was carrying, then glanced again at Gwyneth. "The old steward, Martin Fitzjames, would be the man I'd suggest, but I understand that Sir Geoffrey Drake will soon be taking over those duties."

"Where would I find Mr. Fitzjames?"

"In the steward's office. Ask Nell to guide you."

But in the steward's office, which was in a corridor off the great hall, she found an angry Mr. Fitzjames confronting Geoffrey. Mr. Fitzjames was a small, wiry man, with gray hair that circled his bald head like a horseshoe. Both men turned and stared at her when she knocked on the open door.

Gwyneth walked boldly into the room, though she felt anything but bold. "Hello, Geoffrey." She turned to the other man. "And you must be Mr. Fitzjames."

He subdued his anger enough to take her hand and bow briefly over it. "Lady Blackwell."

"I'm looking for someone to guide me about the estate for the afternoon."

Mr. Fitzjames jammed a cap on his head. "Since I am no longer the steward, it would be inappropriate, my lady. 'Twas nice meeting you." After a heated glare at the other man, he skirted her and went out the door.

Gwyneth turned back to Geoffrey. "I hope my interruption did not made things worse."

The knight gave her a smile. "You have given

no offense, Lady Blackwell. Martin was the Langstons' steward, and there are still bad feelings about him among the villagers. Edmund thought it best if I took over."

She had so many questions about what went on in this castle when Elizabeth was still alive, but she would not embarrass her new husband by questioning his friends behind his back. "And are you a steward as well as a soldier, Geoffrey?"

He grinned. "I'm also a very good guide. I'd be happy to show you everything about your new home."

They spent a pleasant afternoon out in the sunshine, walking through the orchards and looking out across pastures full of grazing sheep. Some of the farm fields seemed neglected, and Geoffrey explained that this was one of the areas Sir Edmund was working on. There would be more money for grain now. The unspoken conclusion was that this was because of her marriage, and Gwyneth was grateful to have helped. But was her husband perhaps angry that he couldn't help his estate without her dowry?

Within the broken-down walls of the courtyard, she walked past the kennels where her husbands' dogs now lazed in the sunshine. Mrs. Haskell must have sent them from the castle first thing in the morning. The dairy seemed especially busy, and plenty of men moved about the stables and barracks. Geoffrey escorted her to the tiltyard, where the soldiers did their daily training on a long, narrow field of dirt and sparse grass. Remembering her husband's limp, Gwyneth didn't think she'd find him here. But she did see Lucy talking with Hugh Ludlow, one of the soldiers who had escorted them on the long journey to Yorkshire. He was a short, brawny man with a shock of red hair. Her friend seemed particularly happy as Hugh smiled down at her.

Geoffrey said, "Allow me to show you the fine new horse Edmund has purchased."

She shook her head and gave him a rueful grin. "You know I am afraid of horses. How many times did you try to make me ride one on our journey here?"

"I promise to be on my best behavior, my lady. Just come with me and see it."

When he took her arm, she reluctantly allowed him to lead her into the cool, dim interior of the stables. A group of soldiers clustered about one stall, and in their midst, a head taller than any of them, was her husband. He wore a black doublet and breeches this day, with just a hint of white shirt ruffle at his neck.

He turned and stared at Gwyneth and Geoffrey. She felt herself blush. The soldiers couldn't know that she was nervous and embarrassed. They obviously thought her blush was the result of the wedding night, for they elbowed each other and grinned.

All except Geoffrey, who looked from Gwyneth to Sir Edmund with a troubled frown. Mortified, she wondered what he knew.

Then Sir Edmund was walking toward her, and she noticed nothing else as his gaze swept from her face down her body. Once again, she felt strange and nervous, as he somehow affected her without even a touch.

Chapter 5

Edmund hadn't known what to expect from Gwyneth after he'd abandoned her on their wedding night. Anger? Relief? But as he approached her, she lifted her chin and smiled at him, like a pleasant, contented wife greeting her husband.

"A good day, my lord," she said softly.

Behind him, he could hear the laughter of his men as they imagined how he must have made the day good for her. He knew she'd slept late this morn, and he was sure the entire castle thought it knew why. But *he* knew she was exhausted because she'd waited up late for him, and he crushed any feelings of guilt. He was not going to remain married to her.

But he wouldn't embarrass her either, so he took her arm, which felt surprisingly sturdy, and led her out of the stables. Whatever she had to say didn't need to be said before an audience. Geoff caught his eye and frowned, but he would deal with his friend later.

He led her to the neglected lady's garden in the corner of the courtyard. Long ago it had been well planted for the enjoyment of the lady of the house, but his first wife had never stayed here long enough to see it replanted. He showed Gwyneth to a bench overgrown with ivy, but she shook her head and looked up at him.

"Did you need something?" he asked.

She hesitated, her gaze searching his face. They stared at each other, and he fought the urge to caress the smooth skin of her cheek, to brush back the blond tendrils that clung to her temples.

"My lord, I wanted to thank you for the gifts of clothing you left in my chamber."

Gifts? And then he remembered Elizabeth's gowns, and he suddenly wished he'd burned them all, for he did not want to see them on Gwyneth.

She clasped her hands before her, and her words came tumbling out. "I hope it does not offend you, but I do not wish to wear them. Elizabeth and I are—were not gifted with the same shape, and besides, such garments are for a court lady."

"But you will go to court some day."

Her eyes widened. "Are you sending me there?"

"Nay." He watched the relief come over her face. Was she glad not to be sent away from her mission too soon?

Perhaps she just didn't like wearing another woman's gowns. But as he looked again at her plain ensemble, he suddenly had a wish to see her in fine garments made to accentuate her small figure. Even the gown she wore now, though subdued in color, could not detract from the lovely brightness of her hair and the healthy glow of her skin.

Edmund knew he was staring at her, which didn't help his determination not to touch her. The image of her sleeping was burned into his brain, into every waking second.

He took a sudden step away, and when hurt flashed briefly in her eyes, he didn't acknowledge it.

"I shall have Mrs. Haskell put the garments in storage," he said. "Someone might have need of the fabric or trim some day."

"Thank you, my lord. Also you might want to examine the precious stones sewn on the gowns. You could use the small wealth for other things."

Precious stones? He had not even imagined that Elizabeth's gowns might help feed the estate. He tried not to look too approving as he said, "That is indeed a good thought, and I shall investigate the matter." He started to step around her. "If that is all, my lady—"

But she surprised him by catching his elbow

and letting her touch linger as their gazes met. She felt warm even through his clothing, and he knew perspiration was breaking out on his forehead. If this was how he reacted to her every look, every touch, he would have to stay far away from her.

"Nay, my lord, I have one more question."

He wanted to shake her hand off, but she sent almost a pleading look at him. Would she ask when he would come to her? What would he say?

But with a soft sigh, she said, "I need to know what my role is here."

"Your role? You are the lady of the castle. Do as you wish."

"As you may know, Sir Edmund, I have never been a lady of the castle." Her smile shone with healthy, white teeth and hint of teasing.

"Then ask Mrs. Haskell."

"You would not be . . . embarrassed that she would think me ignorant?"

He frowned down at her. " 'Twas not long ago that the entire estate knew of my ignorance where land ownership was concerned. I was not raised to this life."

"And I neither," she said softly.

He looked into her grateful eyes and knew he'd made a mistake by showing her that they had things in common.

"But I am learning," he continued gruffly, deliberately sliding his arm out from under her hand. "You will learn as well. I find Mrs. Haskell to be a reasonable woman, and I'm certain she'll gladly teach you."

"I thank you, my lord."

As he limped away from her, she called out, "Will you be joining us for supper?"

"If I can," he answered, relieved to get away.

Gwyneth remained still, absorbing the peaceful sounds of insects in the garden, trying to let the calm suffuse her. She watched her husband hastily leave her presence as if she were a demon sent to torture him instead of a wife who only wanted his company.

He walked through the courtyard, and she saw the bowed heads of each servant he passed. He didn't have their respect, only their fear. When the soldiers greeted him, it was obvious they had known him longer and trusted him, which was good to know.

But at least he had answered some of her questions. She could decide her own course here, whether to be heavily involved, or allow the capable Mrs. Haskell to command. Gwyneth thought she would try a bit of both at first, so as not to offend the woman. It was comforting to know that her husband could understand her ignorance, for he had suffered the same and freely admitted it.

But as to the question of her marriage, she was still as confused as before. He was allowing people to think they had a normal marriage, judging by the way his soldiers acted. He didn't look sick with the effects of a night spent drinking, and he had given her no other excuse. She so wanted to blurt out her questions. *Why didn't you come to me? What have I done?* They'd been in her thoughts constantly, but embarrassment had finally won out.

She would just have to hope that she'd made a start to their marriage by conversing with him, by acting as normally as she could. She would force herself to be patient. And if she discovered things about his first marriage that helped her understand him—all the better. After all, maybe he was just giving her time to get used to him, and he would come to her tonight.

She kept that thought with her for the rest of the day, even as she went to the weaving chamber to take stock of how much fabric they needed for the coming winter and discover why there weren't more girls spinning.

When Sir Edmund didn't arrive for supper, she asked Lucy and Mrs. Haskell to eat with her, and Geoffrey joined them later.

From the depths of the castle, Edmund found it was easy to keep track of where Gwyneth was and avoid her that evening. Anywhere there were cheerful voices raised and laughter heard was where Gwyneth could be found. He stood at the end of the corridor in the vacant wing of the servants' quarters and listened as she took her evening meal.

Afterward he stood high on the battlements, although still below Gwyneth's tower, watching the servants slink away by ones and twos almost secretively, as if they thought he would stop them. As long as they played their part in bringing Castle Wintering back to prosperity, he didn't care where they lived. As the darkness deepened and the wind picked up, he inhaled the rich smell of the Swaledale valley and was thankful.

Up in the tower, a glow grew steadily brighter as someone lit candles against the night. Soon he saw the shadow of a woman cross in front of the window. She stood there a moment, as if she was looking out, searching for something in the darkness, before she finally drew the draperies closed.

Edmund suddenly remembered to breathe. He put a hand on the wall to steady himself, as if without such an anchor he would again go to Gwyneth's chamber and this time ease the lust that had kept him awake most of the previous night. He was used to unfulfilled desire. But now a woman waited for him. He knew it was just her duty or deceit, but still the knowledge of her there, perhaps naked beneath the coverlet, burned a hole inside him.

He left the battlements and descended through dark stone corridors into the great hall. There was still a fire in the hearth, and Mrs. Haskell had left a pitcher of wine and a goblet on a low table next to his chair. In their corner, the dogs whined and lifted their heads in greeting, but were too tired from a day chasing chickens through the court-yard to do anything about it.

He poured himself some wine, then almost knocked it over when a voice said, "Pour me an-other, will you?"

Geoff leaned out from his cushioned chair and grinned up at him, holding out his goblet.

Shaking his head, Edmund filled it to the brim, sat down in the other chair, and stretched his feet toward the hearth. With a sigh, he sipped his wine and closed his eyes.

"So, what game do you play?" Geoff asked.

He didn't open his eyes. "Game?"

"With your new bride."

"I am not playing a game. I married her; now she's here."

"Considering that all I heard about this mar-riage was your order to escort her up from Lon-don, I'd really like to know more."

Edmund swallowed his wine. "There is noth-ing much to tell. The Langstons offered her to me. I accepted her and the dowry."

"You swore you'd never marry a daughter of a noble house again," Geoff said in a low voice, as if someone could be listening.

He found his own voice dropping. "I was about to lose Wintering, and the dowry was attractive."

"Of course it couldn't have been Gwyneth's at-tractiveness, because you'd never met her."

He glanced at Geoff, wondering if that was sarcasm in his voice. But his friend seemed merely weary as he stared into the fire.

"Geoff, do you have something to say?"

"I saw you out in the courtyard last night."

Edmund sighed and drained his wine. "What of it?"

"You didn't go to her, did you?"

He gave no answer.

"I saw you watching her when her coach arrived yesterday afternoon. You made sure that no one was there to greet her, and you deliberately remained hidden. Edmund, what is going on?"

"You need not concern yourself with this. I mean the girl no harm, if that is what worries you."

"You don't mean to do *anything*, do you?"

Geoff turned and looked directly at Edmund, who met his gaze impassively.

"I spoke to her often on our trip north," Geoff said. "She's a good woman, Edmund, far superior to your first bride."

"But she is still a Langston, is she not?"

Geoff let out a low whistle and sank back in his chair. "So that's it. She's related to your first wife—"

"And her family," he interrupted.

"—so you've decided not to give her even a chance."

"That's too simplistic, Geoff."

"Then please explain it to me. I can only imagine how she felt on her wedding night when you didn't come to her."

"Probably relieved," he said mildly.

"Don't be a fool. I spent the afternoon with her. I saw how desperate she is to be accepted here."

Edmund surged to his feet and set his goblet down hard. It teetered onto its side and crashed to the floor, wine soaking through the rushes. "Maybe only you think so. Or maybe she's doing a damn fine job acting that way."

Geoff stared up at him. "You think she has some wild plan you don't know about?"

Edmund took a deep breath and raked a hand through his hair. "I know for certain that the Langstons do. When I negotiated this marriage, the earl deliberately challenged me to best him. He said if I accepted Gwyneth and the dowry, I would have to be on the watch for his manipulations and plots. He means to see me humbled and even ruined, because he thinks I'm the reason Elizabeth died."

"And you went along with this?" Geoff demanded.

Edmund shrugged. "I could not resist such a challenge. And I needed the money above all else. He enjoyed seeing me in no position to refuse him," he added dryly.

"So that's why you had me be on guard for strangers."

"Aye."

"But surely you don't think Gwyneth—"

"She was given to me by the earl, Geoff. She could be a spy—or the means of my destruction. I certainly won't trust her."

"Just promise me you'll give Gwyneth the benefit of the doubt. She could be innocent."

His words were proof that Edmund needed to keep his own plans secret from his friend. "I shall try," he said, bending down to pick up the shards of his goblet.

"There is one other matter," Geoff said. "Remember that man at your wedding, the one who made you so suspicious?"

"Aye."

"I think he was here on your land today."

Edmund stiffened. "Why was I not informed earlier?"

"Because I didn't connect this incident with the man at your wedding until you mentioned your worries about the Langstons. I received a report about a stranger wandering through the uplands of the dale above the northwest cattle pasture. I thought it was just a traveler, but the description of his garments, especially that fur hat he wears though 'tis summer, are too familiar to ignore."

"Was there any mention of his activities?"

"None—and he's probably gone by now, because this was after noon."

"Send some men up there. Have them take a

couple of days to look around. I want to make sure that man has not hidden himself away on my property."

"Why would he do that?"

"Only a Langston might know," Edmund answered with an uneasy sigh. "And speaking of Gwyneth—"

"You cannot think she knows this man."

"I know not what to think. But I have to be vigilant."

Shaking his head, Geoff smiled. "Very well. But I'm going to make the girl feel welcome, just in case."

Edmund only shrugged and turned away. "Good night, then."

He strode off down a dark corridor toward the servants' quarters. When he found his own chamber, he closed the door firmly, wondering why it bothered him that Geoff wanted to be Gwyneth's friend.

In the dead of the night, Edmund found himself outside Gwyneth's door again. As he lifted the latch, he told himself he would not come here again. As he walked softly to stand beside the bed, he swore he was just relieving his curiosity.

This time she lay on her back, the coverlet at her waist. Her night rail, though plain, lovingly hugged her curves and more than displayed the duskiness of her nipples. He stood above her and stared, as if that would somehow ease the fire that was in his groin instead of inflame it further. Her halo of hair, spread out across the pillow, drew him. He touched one curling lock, rubbed its softness between his rough fingers.

With a sigh, she suddenly turned her head, and if he hadn't let go, she would have felt the tug on her scalp. He backed away from her bed and left the chamber before he could touch anything else. At the base of the tower he stumbled, and his foot hitting the wall made a soft echo. He hurried on.

Gwyneth opened her eyes and sat upright, startled awake. Dawn had not yet touched the sky, and beneath her the castle was still a silent presence.

That was what had awakened her—she'd thought something disturbed the stillness. She was so far removed from the rest of the castle up here in her tower that for a sound to reach her meant someone was within the tower itself. Had Sir Edmund come to her then changed his mind?

She flung off the blankets and lit a candle at the hearth. Holding it over her head, she leaned out the door and looked down the staircase, which circled around into the dark. Cautiously she went down. In the corridor, she paused at Lucy's door but heard nothing. No fires burned in the great hall itself, and it seemed a black, cavernous void spread out around her, with no ceiling and no end.

But she could have sworn she'd heard the soft rustle of the rushes just before she entered the room. It had been toward the back, where the two suits of armor stood guard at a corridor.

She felt a draft of cool air, and her skin prickled with gooseflesh. What was she doing here in the dark with no protection? The only soldiers were out in the barracks; the servants lived in the village. Somewhere in this entire castle, only Lucy, Geoffrey and Sir Edmund had chambers.

Trusting that the rumors of her husband's supposed crime gave his home protection of sorts, she decided to follow the sound she'd heard. She remembered that the corridor she was following led to the servants' wing, but only one door, the last one, showed a flicker of firelight beneath it. Holding her breath, she pressed her ear to the wood and listened. Who slept here?

Certainly not Geoffrey. Mrs. Haskell had mentioned that he'd chosen one of the barren chambers up on Lucy's corridor. The housekeeper had had to have pieces of furniture moved there quickly.

So did one of the servants actually stay in the castle unbeknownst to Edmund? And why would one of them be roaming the corridors at night?

Making up her mind, Gwyneth lifted the latch and slowly pushed the door open. She couldn't see much of the room, except that it was dark with a low ceiling. When her gaze fell on the bed, she smothered a gasp.

Sir Edmund lay there on his side, blankets pooled about his waist. She couldn't see his face, just the broad width of his bare back. For one moment, she had the insane urge to climb up beside him, to touch him. Would he continue to ignore her then?

Her face burned with embarrassment as she quickly yet quietly shut the door. What was her husband doing in the servants' quarters, when he could have had any chamber, including hers? Had he and Elizabeth kept separate chambers, as she'd begun to suspect? Was it him she had heard roaming the castle or only her imagination?

She picked up her pace as she moved through the great hall, suddenly worried about what he would think if he found her creeping about at night.

But as she returned to her tower room and closed the door behind her, she couldn't stop wondering what it would mean if Sir Edmund had actually come to her chamber.

At dawn, Edmund was dressed and striding down the corridor to the winter parlor, where Mrs. Haskell usually had his bread and ale waiting. He opened the door, the castle accounts awkwardly balanced under his arm, and came to an abrupt halt.

Gwyneth sat at the table in the chair next to his, wearing a plain gray, high-necked gown with a white kerchief about her shoulders and small ruffles at her throat and wrists. She gave him a smile of greeting, but he saw the faint smudges beneath her eyes that bore testimony to how little she had slept the previous night. He remembered barely making it back to his room before she did and feigning sleep. He'd felt her stare for endless moments, as though someone had branded him. After she'd gone, he'd lain awake and thought begrudgingly that she was brave, traipsing through a dark and nearly empty castle. And of course he tortured himself imagining her in the sheer night rail because she wouldn't have had time to don anything else.

"A good morning to you, my lord," Gwyneth said in a bright voice.

He nodded, waiting for her to mention the night's escapade, but she didn't.

"I hope you don't mind that I am joining you without asking your permission. I don't normally sleep in as late as yesterday," she said, blushing, although her gaze remained locked with his.

"You may eat anywhere you wish," he answered, reluctantly sitting down at the head of the table, with Gwyneth to his left.

She poured him a tankard of ale from a pitcher, then another for herself. When he reached for the loaf of bread, she murmured, "Allow me," then used a knife to cut him a slice instead of pulling it apart with her hands.

She pushed a small crock toward him. "Butter?"

"My thanks."

For a few moments they ate in silence.

"I would have had porridge made for you, but Mrs. Haskell told me you preferred a simple meal to break your fast."

"Aye." He looked longingly at the account book. He was desperate to think about numbers instead of her nearness.

"If you do not mind, my lord, I have a small favor to ask you."

Although her voice was soft and pleasant to his ears, his tension increased. He met her gaze and felt himself redden beneath her steady regard, as if she knew everything he was thinking about her.

"I am accustomed to bathing in the evening," she began, and he noticed that she could no longer meet his gaze, "but there are no servants at night. Would you mind if I bathed during the day?"

He stared at her, feeling utterly dull and stupid, as he imagined the sun across her wet nakedness. He licked his lips, then almost winced when her gaze dropped to his mouth.

Chapter 6

~~~OO~~~

Gwyneth felt a little shock crackle through her as she stared at her husband's lips. She had not been so close to him since their wedding meal, and even then he'd sat at her side, where she hadn't been able to look directly into his eyes. But now they looked at each other face to face, only an arm's length apart. She saw again the pale, pure blue of his eyes, the hard, masculine lines of his face.

More and more she looked at him and thought *Handsome,* although that had not been her first impression. And just a glimpse of his tongue made her mind have strange imaginings. He was wearing a well-worn leather jerkin over a loose white shirt, which emphasized his dark hair and tanned skin.

"I have already told you, my lady, that you may do as you wish. Bathe any time it is convenient."

His voice sounded gruff and stern, but his face did not seem angry. Could he be . . . embarrassed? Or just unsure of how to deal with her? That could explain so much.

"Thank you, my lord," she murmured, still watching him.

Sir Edmund's gaze seemed to search hers for a moment, and then he buttered another piece of bread and took a bite. She wanted to ask when *he* bathed, for the scent of his body did not offend her.

She could barely keep her questions down. With her gaze, she begged him for answers. Why didn't he come to her and make a true marriage of whatever was between them? And could it have been he who had been haunting her tower last night? Why do such a thing, if he meant to remain so remote? She had so many questions and was too embarrassed to ask them. He seemed oblivious to her turmoil.

She took a bite of her own bread, chewing in silence, wishing he would begin a conversation so she didn't seem to be the only one trying to start this marriage.

"I have never lived on such a large estate," she began awkwardly.

He frowned at her, but she was determined to press on.

"How do you busy yourself during the day?"

He swallowed a mouthful of ale, and she watched the movement of his throat with surprised fascination.

"I thought I said you could discuss this with Mrs. Haskell."

"I don't mean me," she countered, smiling, "but you. What do you do all day?"

Again that frown, and she wondered if he ever smiled. If his sober face made her heart beat faster, she imagined his smile would affect her very breathing.

"I keep the estate running smoothly. I was going to go over the account books while I ate."

She heard the reproof in his voice and tried to ignore it. "Is that what you're going to do *all* day?"

"No. I will be visiting all the fields and pastures and outbuildings this morning as well, to speak with my tenants."

"Oh, might I go with you? I would enjoy meeting everyone."

"I am too busy to play the lady's companion, Gwyneth."

Though the words weren't what she wanted to hear, it was the first time he'd called her by her Christian name. She liked the sound of it said in his deep voice. And she hadn't really expected him to agree, not right away. It would take much effort on her part. And she had something else she felt the need to do today.

"Forgive me if I have offended you . . . Edmund."

She watched him from beneath her lashes,

saw how he glanced at her sharply then back to his meal. But he didn't forbid the familiarity. It was enough for a beginning, so she let him eat the rest of his bread in silence. He could eat a lot of bread.

After a while, even he must have felt awkward, for he said, "I hope your chamber is comfortable."

"Oh, yes, Edmund, it is quite astounding in its luxury. And the view is everything you promised. I had heard Yorkshire was a wild, barren place, yet its beauty quite amazes me."

"I thought much the same thing before I came here," he said slowly, and seemed to be really looking at her.

She looked back.

Abruptly he surged to his feet. "I will leave you now, my lady."

"Will you be back for dinner?" she asked.

"I am not certain."

He busied himself lifting his account book instead of meeting her gaze, and her good humor faded a bit.

"Have a pleasant day, Edmund."

He nodded and limped from the room, while she watched his awkward stride thoughtfully, biding her time. She looked out the large mullioned windows that spanned one wall and saw him stride to the stables. A few minutes later, he and Geoffrey rode out of the courtyard. Her last glimpse was of them racing again.

Mrs. Haskell came into the parlor. "Might I get you something else, my lady?"

"No, thank you, Mrs. Haskell."

The housekeeper put the dishes on a tray and took them away. Gwyneth waited a few more minutes then darted down the corridor, through the great hall, and into the deserted servants' wing.

Before her courage fled, she opened the door to Edmund's bedchamber and closed it quickly behind her. Her guilt, although bothersome, faded compared to her curiosity. She'd only had the briefest glimpse of this room, and she wanted to see more.

The hearth was cold and bare this summer morn. A large window had recently been cut into the stone wall, but there were only shutters, not draperies, to cover the glass. There were no rugs for warmth, no tapestries to keep out the drafts, no cushioned chair as befitted the lord of a castle. Except for a single chest, a crude wooden table, and a chair, there was only the bed.

As she'd seen only a few hours before, it was big enough for a man his size. There was room for her too, and she ran a hand across the wrinkled coverlet.

She tried not to let memories of her family haunt her dreams. She missed them and worried for them. Every hour her husband treated her remotely was another hour of worry about whether she could gain his help someday, which wouldn't happen if they didn't have a real marriage.

When the door suddenly opened, she flinched and found herself stepping back. Her legs hit the bed.

Edmund stopped on the threshold and stared impassively at her.

She bit her lip and tried to think of something to say, but all she felt was dread that she'd damaged their already fragile relationship. Why had he returned from his ride so quickly?

He closed the door behind him, set the book on the paper-strewn table, and started walking toward her. She thought he meant to frighten her, but she wasn't frightened. She felt a thrill of danger, an awareness of him as a man—and the big bed that pressed into her thighs.

"If you meant to wait here for me," he said in a deep voice, his brow heavy with a frown, "you should have informed me."

"I was merely exploring, Edmund." Her voice sounded too brittle. Should she have called him "sir"? She arched her neck to look up at him as he finally stopped in front of her. "I hope my curiosity does not offend you."

He put his hands on his hips as he looked down at her but said nothing. Gwyneth had the strangest sensation that he was trying to frighten her away but could only make the attempt with his appearance. How could she tell him that his face, his body, hardly made her want to run away?

"Curiosity can be a dangerous thing in such an old castle, my lady," he said slowly, "for I've not yet had time to see to all the repairs that need my attention."

She heard his words, but she paid more attention to his eyes and the way his gaze strayed to her mouth twice. Without thinking, she reached out and touched his arm, felt the solid strength and warmth of him through his shirt. He seemed almost frozen.

"Edmund, is it not cold down here in the winter?" she whispered.

He took two steps back from her. With disappointment, she let her hand fall to her side.

After clearing his throat, he said, "I have seldom been here during the winter."

"Then where did you go?"

"London, as Elizabeth wished, then France most recently."

He turned his back on her, standing at the table with one hand on the account book. She longed to question him about Elizabeth but knew that would put up a wall of ice between them.

"And you fought with the army there?" she asked, moving closer.

He nodded, and she wished she could see his face. She took a step at a time nearer the hearth. His profile looked dark and troubled. When he saw her watching him, all expression was wiped from his face as he gazed at her with his ice-blue eyes.

"I did what I had to to survive."

She tried to soften him with a compassionate

gaze. "Of course you did. I—I understand that that was how you raised money for Castle Wintering."

"Did Geoff say that?"

She nodded, wondering if he would be offended that she'd spoken about him with his friend. But it had been a long journey, with little else to say in the evenings.

Strangely, he seemed to relax. "Bringing a place like this back from near ruin requires more than just the money earned from a good harvest. And we haven't had many of those lately."

Hesitating, she asked, "What was it like?"

"The harvest?"

She smiled and shook her head. "Being in the army. Living away from home so much."

With a shrug, he leaned back against the table. "I've only ever been a soldier before now. What could I compare it to?"

"Did you not miss your family?"

His direct eyes seemed to cloud over. "My mother died birthing me, my father only a few years later. What was there to miss?"

Her chest tightened with sorrow for him. "I am so sorry. I cannot imagine such a lonely life."

"I did not grow up alone in the woods," he said, with a touch of sarcasm. "A friend and his family took me in. They were almost a real family to me."

"I am very glad." The pain in her heart eased. "Was that where you learned to fight?"

He nodded.

"Yet the last time, you were not so fortunate."

"Nay," he said shortly, still watching her. "Does it bother you that I am lame?"

"Lame? You seem to do everything you want to, with that small limp. Why should it bother me, when it doesn't bother you?"

But did it bother him? she wondered, reading nothing in his eyes. Of course she didn't know how extensive the damage truly was or if the pain still lingered. A cold, sick feeling of pity washed through her. Was that the problem? Was he wounded in ways she didn't understand, ways that would make him feel that he could not be a real husband to her?

"How did your injury happen?" she asked, then winced at how hoarse her voice sounded.

"A simple attack, from more men than I could handle alone," he said unemotionally.

Geoffrey had told her that Edmund had gone against five men in defense of his squire. He must be brave and certainly did not boast about himself, as some men did. She found herself feeling very proud of her new husband, even as she worriedly looked down again at his leg.

"How recently did this happen?" she asked, searching his face.

"Four months." He picked up his account book with obvious impatience. "You are full of questions today, Gwyneth."

"Why don't you let me look at your wound?"

She dropped her gaze, feeling embarrassed heat sweep over her. Quickly she added, "I am accounted a good healer, and I brought my medicines from home."

Edmund could think of absolutely nothing to say, and the very air about them was filled with tension that had nothing to do with healing and everything to do with sex. She expected him to strip off his garments and lie quietly beneath her ministrations? All he wanted to do was lean her back on the bed, on the table, on the closest thing he could find, and taste every part of her. He had an excellent imagination, and it was filled with how she would look naked. She was a bold thing, coming to his chamber like this, and he wondered how else she would be bold.

Yet—why was she in his chamber? Surely curiosity couldn't be the only reason. He thought again of Earl Langston's smug triumph when Edmund had signed the marriage contract.

He tried to put his mind back to their conversation, but it was a moment before he could remember. All he could do was look into her deceptively beautiful face and wonder what she was lying about. "My wound is well healed, my lady, but I thank you for your offer. Now I have business to attend to. Do you need help finding duties to occupy your day, something to keep you . . . busy?"

He knew she understood the unspoken order not to return to his chambers. He watched the blush turn her skin from the color of peaches to the palest strawberries. He starved for her as a hungry man in need of food.

"I was going to work in the garden today," she said softly. "We could use more servants, now that the harvest is approaching."

"Hire whomever you wish."

" 'Tis difficult to do that when I haven't met anyone yet."

She spoke with cool necessity, not a whine, as Elizabeth would have done. And she had so easily manipulated him out of his anger at her spying.

He glanced at her, saw how her eyes bravely met his, and he almost let himself smile. "Be patient, Gwyneth. Now if you please—"

"Aye, my lord," she said, walking calmly around him and out the door.

Edmund closed it firmly behind her.

Gwyneth spent much of the day in the lady's garden, letting the memories of her early childhood on the family farm wash over and soothe her. She'd been a child the first time her father had sickened, when he was no longer able to work as a farmer. Though the move to London had been jarring, she'd adapted easily enough. But she hadn't realized how much she missed the country.

She kept her hands in the warm earth, pulling weeds and cutting back some of the overgrowth. Anything to forget the embarrassment of having practically begged to see her husband's naked body. Even now she groaned and covered her face, not caring where she spread the dirt. She had meant only to look at his injuries, but somehow that was not what the words had conveyed once she'd said them.

But was it such a bad thing to be misunderstood? She did not yet have the courage to ask Edmund why he did not come to her bed, so letting him know that his injuries did not bother her might ease this awkwardness between them. Patience, something she was normally so good at, now seemed to be stretching thin. She needed this marriage to succeed, and not only for herself.

During every good meal she ate, she wondered what her family was eating. How were they getting along without her help in the kitchen and without her selling their baked goods to the local bakeries? She'd handled the business side of their baking, and she knew her sister Caroline, her replacement, was shyer than she was. Athelina and Lydia were more than competent to help their mother bake. And then there was her father, who'd seemed even thinner during their final embrace. How grateful she would be if she could make things easier for her family. She would not give up trying to push her way into her husband's life.

If there was one way she could please a man, it was by her baking skills. Before supper, she invaded the kitchen and asked for a small space to work in.

Mrs. Haskell looked down on her with a frown, and the cook, Mr. Throckmorten, a sandy-haired man only a few years older than Gwyneth was, gave an affronted gasp.

Gwyneth went to him immediately. "Mr. Throckmorten, I assure you I mean this with no disrespect. Baking was what I did in London, and I thought to make my husband something . . . special to eat."

She glanced at Mrs. Haskell, whose anger had melted into a sympathetic smile.

"Lady Blackwell *is* a new bride, Mr. Throckmorten, and I remember well how that felt."

"I have never been married," the cook said, nodding, as he seemed to think it over.

"Were you not conversing with a certain young woman in Swintongate?" Mrs. Haskell asked.

Gwyneth was stunned when the usually dour woman actually winked at her. She smiled back.

Mr. Throckmorten cleared his throat. "Now, Mrs. Haskell, I cannot possibly imagine what you mean." He turned to Gwyneth. "My lady, let me remove these pans from the table."

Relieved and happy, Gwyneth pinned her apron on, rolled up her sleeves, and began to work on her famous ginger cake.

Edmund was at the kennels, overseeing the feeding of his hunting dogs, when he heard Geoff call out his name. He looked over his shoulder to see the man bearing down on him.

Edmund smiled and held up a hand. "Surely I did not forget a chess match. 'Tis all you reserve your ire for."

Geoff gave a smile to the groom and pulled Edmund aside by the elbow. "I've been sitting in your dining room, having dinner alone with your wife. How do you think that looks to the servants?"

"Then don't eat with her," he said, turning away.

Geoff blocked his way. "You promised you'd give her the benefit of the doubt."

"I said I'd try."

"Try harder. Your wife subtly asked me if your wounds were more extensive than she knows about."

"She wanted to look at my leg today," Edmund said, shaking his head.

"Of course she did. She's probably wondering if you can perform as a man."

"What the hell does that mean?" Edmund practically growled the question. "Do you believe I should bed her if I have no trust in her? I couldn't use her like that."

Geoff opened his mouth as if to respond, then sighed and shook his head. "I guess that would be a lie on your part, wouldn't it?"

"I know what I am doing."

"So you keep saying." He suddenly put a hand on Edmund's back and pushed. "But tonight you're going to keep up appearances by eating supper with your wife, who baked you something to please you."

"Baked? Whyever would she do that?"

"Because that's what she knows. Did you ever ask what she and her family did to survive?"

"But they're cousins to the Langstons. She was the earl's ward."

"Then that old man doesn't know the meaning of 'ward.' She never stayed with him. The house lived in by Gwyneth, her three sisters, and their parents is smaller than your stables. Gwyneth has spent years walking London's dangerous streets, selling their baked goods to local bakeries."

Edmund let himself be pushed toward the castle. "So she says."

"I saw how she lived," Geoff interrupted. "Did you even notice the poor quality of her clothing?"

"Even more reason for her to succumb to the earl's pressure." Edmund strode across the courtyard. The sun was setting and the servants fleeing the castle for the night, giving him guilty nods, which he returned. He glanced at Geoff's angry expression and spoke in a lower voice. "If you must know, I never see her clothing when I look at her body, I only imagine what's under—" He broke off at Geoff's assessing gaze.

His friend gave him another push, which made him stumble. "Now go eat with your wife and give her my regrets."

Chapter 7

When Edmund first glimpsed Gwyneth in the winter parlor, she hadn't seen him. He watched her sitting by herself in front of windows which glistened with the setting sun. She steadily ate her food, but her face betrayed distant thoughts and a subtle melancholy that made him feel uneasy.

For the first time, he truly looked at her gown, at the plain, even rough fabric, and the lack of decoration. Not that she needed frills to look beautiful. He imagined her walking city streets, prey for every unsavory criminal—even a nobly born rake. When he sent her back to her family, he would make sure she had money to make her independent of the Langstons.

Gwyneth looked up with a bright smile. "Good evening, Edmund."

He nodded and pulled out his chair. "Geoff asked me to tell you that he had to . . . that he forgot an appointment in the village."

The lie was so clumsy that he waited for her to look suspicious. But her smile only softened as he sat down near her.

"I don't mind," she said quietly. "Allow me to prepare your plate."

He watched as she served him from platters of mutton and beef then added a small meat pie. As she leaned forward to hand him his plate, he again only noticed her gown as it tightened over her breasts. He had not forgotten the sight of her in her revealing wedding gown and the sheer night rail, and if he wasn't careful, he'd show her how undamaged his vital parts were.

They ate in silence for a few minutes until the awkwardness began to unsettle even Edmund.

"I've told you about my family," he said gruffly, "but you have never mentioned yours." As if they'd had dozens of conversations. *Idiot.* He didn't want to make her suspicious as he pried for information.

She gave a happy blush. "I did not want you to think all I do is talk."

"I don't think that."

"Tell me when I start saying things that Lord Langston must have told you about me."

The earl had never said anything except that Gwyneth was related to him.

"My parents are both still alive. When I was

young, we lived on a small farm in the country-side north of London, but we moved to the city many years ago."

"Why?"

"My father became ill and could no longer do the physical labor a farm requires. In London he became a personal guard for a wool merchant."

He knew from experience how little that paid. Where was the dowry her Langston mother must have brought to the marriage?

"Do you have brothers or sisters?"

"Three sisters," she said.

To his fascination she laughed, and he tried not to stare like an unseasoned squire at her lovely face.

"So you can imagine my father's relief that one of us married. It gives hope to the others."

He wanted to say that if her sisters looked anything like her, they wouldn't have a problem. But such words would only encourage her.

"Caroline is three years younger than I am, and she is a very composed lady compared to me."

"How old are you?" he suddenly asked.

"I have twenty-three years," she said, her voice more subdued. "Does it bother you much that I am so old?"

"Old? I am one and thirty. Does it bother you?"

She grinned, and he regretted adding to the conversation, because just looking at her made him think of what he wanted to do with her.

"Of course it does not bother me. A girl expects

her husband to be older. Caroline is twenty, and I do worry about her sometimes."

"Why?"

"She has never been the healthiest girl, and it makes her seem so fragile. But we are the dearest of friends, and I miss her terribly. Athelina, who has seventeen years, is quite intelligent and borrows books from her friends whenever she can. I do worry that she's more interested in reading than in men. Lydia has fourteen years and is almost a son to Papa with her boyish ways. I fear she does not wish to grow up. But she has time yet."

He listened to the love in her voice, her worries, and he wondered how much of it was true. "And what did you do before you married me?"

She smiled and eyed him. "You do not think I was waiting for a husband, do you?"

"And why not?"

"I was too busy," she said with a shrug. "There was much baking to be done. It is how we help Papa. Our tarts and cakes and breads are very popular in the city."

"Not many women would do such a thing."

"Why wouldn't they?" she asked in a puzzled voice.

God above, how could she even be related to Elizabeth? Or was her goodness part of the earl's plot, with some hidden purpose he had yet to discover?

Edmund looked down at the food he hadn't begun to eat because he'd been so fascinated watching Gwyneth's face. He took his fork and eating knife out of a pouch at his waist and cut himself a piece of mutton.

She leaned toward him, her eyes wide.

"What is wrong?" he asked, frowning. He wanted to back away, as her very nearness tested his restraint. Smelling her scent would be his undoing.

"That is just like the large serving forks we use in the kitchen, only smaller," she said. "I have never seen such a thing before."

"I purchased it in France. 'Tis very useful."

"Might I try it?"

"I have only one."

"If you don't mind, I shall try yours."

His mind stumbled to a halt as she took the fork from his hand, pierced her meat and raised it to her lips. Watching her mouth touch what had been in his mouth sent a shudder through him, but he didn't look away—couldn't look away. Her gaze rose to lock with his as she slowly slid the fork from her mouth. When she smiled, there was a touch of gravy at the corner of her lip. He imagined licking it away, thrusting his tongue inside her mouth for the real taste of her.

When she handed the fork back to him, he deliberately made sure not to touch her.

She smiled. "What a novel thing. We should have some made for the castle."

"It is frivolous. There is too much real work to be done."

Her smiled faded. "Oh, of course."

They finished eating in silence, and he told himself that this was the wisest course. But already he'd begun to wait for her smiles.

When he pushed his plate aside, she slid a small cake in front of her and cut him a piece. This must have been what she'd worked on just for him. When he bit into it, he wasn't a bit surprised to find it delicious. She was watching him.

He had to say something. "This is very good. Throckmorten never baked this before."

That small smile touched her lips. "That is because I made it."

"You could charge much for this, and a person would pay it." He was foolish to give her compliments.

She blushed again, and her eyes softened, and he knew he'd made a grave mistake. He finished the last bite and stood up.

"Good night, Gwyneth."

"Would you like another piece?" she asked, looking at him in disappointment.

"Not tonight." He made himself turn away from the promise in her eyes.

Gwyneth watched as he shut the door behind him. Mixed with her sadness were fresh stirrings of anger. How was she to reach her husband?

She continued to sit at the table long after the sun had set. Mrs. Haskell quietly came in and lit candles but seemed to sense Gwyneth's mood and said little.

"My lady, is there anything I can get for you before I leave for the night?"

The sympathy in her voice almost made tears rise in Gwyneth's eyes, but she was still too angry to cry.

"No, thank you, Mrs. Haskell. I shall see you on the morrow."

When she was alone again, she gathered her resolve and left the winter parlor. She walked across the deserted great hall, where no one feasted, no one celebrated. She felt very alone. Even Lucy was more a maid than a companion, as the girl began to forge a new life that couldn't include her mistress.

Purposefully Gwyneth entered the corridor to the servants' wing and stopped when she came to Edmund's door. She raised a hand to knock but could only freeze in indecision. What did she mean to do, demand a wedding night? This could not be the way to woo a man such as her husband, who seemed wounded by his first marriage and everything else life had thrown at him. Surely he would be offended and refuse her. Or would he be angry and hurt her in his hurry to finish the consummation? Was that how she wanted to start her real marriage?

Defeated, she was about to leave when she realized the door was open a crack. She could see the fire in the hearth, which was the only source of light in the room, and the edge of her husband standing before it. She gently touched the door and gave the tiniest of pushes. It opened another couple of inches, and she could see all of Edmund now, not quite in profile, standing still before the fire as he stared down into it. She held her breath, but it seemed that he hadn't noticed the door moving.

And then he shrugged the doublet off his shoulders, and she forgot everything else. His white shirt was loose about his neck but snug across his broad back, as if there weren't garments big enough for him. Even his breeches, which were normally worn loose on a man, seemed tight. When they sagged, she realized with shock that he was unfastening them. He pulled his shirt off over his head, then let the breeches fall until he was wearing only a scrap of linen about his hips. Beneath his garments was a body as well muscled and sleek as a work of art. She'd glimpsed such a statue at Langston House and had not imagined that a living man could look that way. Even his scars, like the ones that twisted up his right thigh, fascinated her.

Gwyneth's face felt hot, and that heat moved down through her body until it centered strangely between her thighs. What was this feeling, this yearning? She wanted to be held in his strong arms and maybe feel safe. Was this how other wives felt?

Then suddenly Edmund turned and saw her. She was so frozen by the sight of his sculpted chest that she only flinched when he threw the door wide. He filled the doorway and her view, and it seemed that she couldn't catch her breath, even as he frowned down at her.

And then she turned and fled, knowing she'd made a terrible mistake by moving too quickly with her husband. He'd only reject her again, as he'd done each night. But this time she'd have to see it in his face.

Edmund slammed closed the door so hard, he thought the hinges would break. Gwyneth had finally seen his damaged body. Elizabeth used to cower when he was naked, as if he was about to beat her instead of make love to her.

He pulled his breeches back on and sat down heavily in a wooden chair that creaked under his weight. Except for Elizabeth, he couldn't remember a time when he hadn't paid a woman for sex. And Elizabeth had only wanted the thrill of the unknown. Then she'd panicked at the thought of marrying against her father's wishes. Unbeknownst to Edmund, she'd told her brothers it was Alex Thornton, his close friend and the brother of a viscount, who had compromised her. When Edmund had realized what was going on, he forced Elizabeth to tell the truth, and she'd never forgiven him for it. Neither had her parents.

As the night aged, he thought about Gwyneth lying alone in that fairy-tale chamber. Gwyneth, who baked for him, who wanted him to accept her. Gwyneth, who ran from him.

Did it even make sense? Perhaps he was on guard against the wrong person. But he had no way of knowing. Even the stranger who'd been at his wedding had disappeared.

He didn't go to watch Gwyneth sleep that night. All the next day he avoided the castle, taking bread and cheese for his noon meal as he went from farm to farm, discussing with his tenants which fields to harvest first. He ate supper alone at the tavern in Swintongate, where he always received prompt service and wary glances. But he still had to go back to Castle Wintering, back to Gwyneth.

Gwyneth made sure her day was busy so thoughts of her husband could remain in the distance. Mrs. Haskell brought two more girls from the village to work in the spinning chamber, and Gwyneth spent many hours there. In London, she'd bought her fabric already made. She was fascinated that here she had to oversee each step of the process, from carding tufts of wool to weed out the impurities to the final weaving of yarn into cloth on giant looms. She had so much to learn and did it gladly. Better still, she was becoming acquainted with the household staff. Soon she hoped she would not feel so awkward giving orders.

When Edmund didn't come home at noon, she ate dinner in the great hall with the servants and found herself more at ease than she'd been since she arrived. She sat with Lucy, who pointed out the servants she didn't know by name and explained their duties. Then Lucy gushed about her soldier, Hugh Ludlow, and Gwyneth could only be pleased for her. At least someone was feeling at home in this old castle.

But she had to admit that the servants finally seemed to be accepting her. No longer did they act as though Edmund was the only authority on something as trivial as what the dairymaids could leave out for the shepherds' meals. She could sense a place growing for herself here, if not in her husband's heart.

When they were done eating, she let Lucy drag her out to the courtyard. Lucy wanted to watch the soldiers train and felt foolish going out by herself for a second time in one day. Together they found a bench under a shady tree at the edge of the tiltyard and watched Geoffrey lead the soldiers through their sword training. Before they'd barely begun, Hugh Ludlow, Lucy's friend, stalked off angrily, and Lucy begged Gwyneth's leave to run after him. She watched the girl take hold of his arm and say something, but he didn't look mollified.

Geoffrey turned and saw Gwyneth, waving as he strolled over.

"Lady Blackwell, it is good to see you out on such a nice day."

"There is much to keep me occupied, Geoffrey, but Lucy asked me to come. She's gone to be with Mr. Ludlow."

He looked in the direction of the barracks, where Hugh stood listening to Lucy.

Geoffrey shook his head. "It might be a while before she's soothed him."

"What do you mean?"

"He's just found out that Edmund has promoted me to lieutenant over him. He didn't take kindly to it."

"But surely Edmund's decision is all that matters."

"Hugh and I were both sergeants under Edmund's command in France, which put us on the same level. But Hugh had bad luck with the men assigned to him and couldn't control them. They were slaughtered in battle."

"How terrible! But surely that was only simple misfortune."

"Edmund gave him another squadron to command, and this one"—he looked away, his face reddening—"abused the women in a village. Hugh was away on leave at the time."

"Good heavens."

"Those men do not serve under Edmund any more."

"I'm glad to hear it." She glanced again at Lucy, who talked so earnestly to her young man. "But Geoffrey," she said, smiling, as she changed the subject, "are you not also Edmund's steward?"

He grinned, pointing his sword into the dirt and leaning on the hilt. "My lady, you force me to admit that Edmund does most of that work himself, and I only assist where necessary. After everything that happened with the Langstons' steward, I think he feels the need to keep things under his own control."

"What do you mean?" she asked, hoping that she would hear something that would help her understand her husband.

Geoffrey hesitated as he studied her, then finally shook his head. "It is not my place to tell you about Edmund's life—or his first marriage, my lady. But I will say that Martin Fitzjames was secretly under Langston control when Edmund was lord of Castle Wintering."

Secretly under Langston control? What did that mean? Had the earl done something underhanded to Edmund, his daughter's husband?

Though still curious, Gwyneth knew that Geoffrey would say nothing more. "If my husband is in command of every aspect of the estate, I am surprised he is not out here training the men as well."

She meant it as a light-hearted comment, but Geoffrey's smile died, and he gave her a meaningful look.

"My lady, since his injury, he doesn't even train with me any more."

She stiffened. "But surely there is much he can do, even with the limp."

"I've always hoped that managing Wintering will show him that he's more than a soldier," Geoffrey said softly. "I've long worried that fighting is all Edmund thinks he's good at. It was how he supported his first wife, after all."

He straightened abruptly, as if he thought he'd said too much. Gwyneth felt a cold sadness envelop her. Again she wondered how her cousin had come to be married to him. Edmund had been so good a soldier that he'd been knighted. How must he feel, having to stop doing what he'd spent his whole life on? No wonder the estate meant so much to him.

As the sun set, Gwyneth was watching from her tower window when her husband rode into the courtyard. She watched his easy mastery of his large horse and felt again the strange sensations he made her feel as she imagined those same hands touching her. She wanted him to come looking for her, to tell her of his day, to treat her like a wife, but she knew he wouldn't. And she couldn't go looking for him, not after he had caught her in his bedchamber twice.

But when enough time had passed, she still went down into the castle, making sure all the candles were out and the fires safely banked, as her mother had always stressed. In the kitchen, she ate the last slice of her ginger cake, then sat staring into the fire until she was almost dozing. She shook herself awake, then went back along the corridor, intending to fall asleep planning her next strategy for dealing with her reluctant husband.

Just before she reached the great hall, she heard an unusual sound coming from it. It was the slide of steel on steel, a sound she'd learned to avoid on the London streets, where she knew it meant a foolish fight. But here in the castle, they were supposed to be alone but for Geoffrey and Lucy.

Taking a deep breath, she walked the last few steps to the great hall, then stood in the shadows and gaped. Edmund had built a large fire in the hearth at this end of the hall. He stood in its harsh glare, naked from the waist up, his massive chest crossed with scars. In his right hand he held a wickedly pointed rapier, and in the other was a dagger, just as lethal. Before she could even understand the heat that burst inside her at just the sight of him, he began to move.

Gwyneth's mouth went dry as she watched the play of his muscles. He thrust forward with his rapier, then parried an imaginary opponent's sword with his dagger. Even with the limp, he moved with the grace of a court dancer, and the intensity on his face made her wish he'd look at her like that, as though she meant something to him.

Weak and suddenly breathless, she put a hand against the wall to steady herself. But the movement must have betrayed her, because he suddenly stiffened and looked about.

Chapter 8

Although Gwyneth thought she'd been seen, she heard a voice at the far side of the great hall, and her husband turned toward it.

"Why, Edmund Blackwell," Geoffrey said, coming out of the darkness of a corridor, one hand behind his back, "what have you been keeping from me?"

Her husband relaxed and lowered his weapons. "You need not know every detail of my life," he said with amusement in his voice.

Geoffrey was dressed more casually than Gwyneth had ever seen him in a loose shirt and breeches. The hand he'd kept hidden slid forward at his side, and a sword reflected the firelight.

Edmund nodded with interest.

Geoffrey grinned. "You don't need to tell me

every detail of your life—I already know most of them."

"You flatter yourself. But I see that you came prepared."

"Of course."

Geoffrey reached the center of the hall, and suddenly the two men were circling each other, both wearing intent but amused expressions, as if they'd done this many times before.

"I didn't think you were still training," Geoffrey said. "I'm happy to see that I was wrong."

"Then you must be happy much of the time," Edmund said.

Suddenly his sword flashed out, and Gwyneth gasped when the two weapons connected between the men.

Geoffrey stepped back and shook his head. "Insults now, eh, Edmund?"

"Why should things be different?" Edmund tossed his dagger on the table so they were matched in swords alone.

"Indeed."

This time Geoffrey attacked first, striking hard with his sword in an overhand arc. Gwyneth bit back a scream even as Edmund parried then staggered. She sagged against the wall and put a hand to her heart, as if she could keep it from pounding out of her chest. She didn't know how much longer she could watch the two men play with each other like little boys.

"Are you all right?" Geoffrey asked in a more serious tone of voice.

Edmund put a hand on the table to steady himself. "Do not concern yourself with my injury. I could defeat you with *two* lame legs."

Gwyneth couldn't help smiling.

"Then I guess 'tis pointless for me to fight," said Geoffrey, as he lifted his hands in mock surrender. "Instead, I'll go search out the last of your wife's ginger cake. I haven't had any, and I hear it's quite delicious."

Edmund frowned, echoing Gwyneth's own puzzlement.

"What is that supposed to mean?" he asked, bringing up his sword again.

The two men came together again in a flurry of thrusts that had Gwyneth wincing and covering her face, only to peer between her fingers. Geoffrey staggered back with a laugh. As Edmund went to press his advantage, his leg twisted, and he fell heavily into the rushes.

Before Gwyneth could run into the hall, Geoffrey was at Edmund's side, his laughter replaced by concern.

"Let me help you."

"Do not trouble yourself." Edmund pushed his friend's hands away, got his good leg beneath him, and pushed himself up to stand.

Geoffrey lingered near, his eyes narrowed with uncertainty.

"Now you see why I don't train with you any more," Edmund said. "You're too worried you'll hurt me."

Gwyneth thought his good spirits sounded forced.

"Edmund—"

"Go find your bed, Geoff. I'm not finished yet."

Geoffrey looked as though he wanted to say more but only nodded. "A good night to you, then."

Edmund waited for his friend to leave, and only then did he lean against the table and frown at the pain. He looked at his useless leg, and thought again how much had changed in his life from one skirmish gone wrong. He picked up the sword from where it had slid beneath the table.

Suddenly he heard a suspicious noise, but it was coming from the wrong corridor to be Geoff. Who would be spying on him?

Gwyneth.

She was there again in the shadows, *his wife*, looking at his foolishness.

"Gwyneth," he said sternly.

He saw her flinch, but she came out of the dark with a steadiness he reluctantly admired. She stopped before him, and her gaze flickered between his weapons, then moved up his body. When she lingered on his chest, he knew she only stared at his scars. But his body wouldn't listen, and he was suddenly so aroused it was painful.

"You must stop spying on me," he said, trying to rein in his anger with this whole frustrating situation.

She lifted her chin with clear defiance and stared into his face. "I am not spying on you, Edmund, although I admit it looks otherwise."

She dared to lie to him outright? He dropped his weapon, caught her by the upper arms, and leaned down into her face. Still she showed no fear, although he wanted to see it in her eyes. Maybe then she'd leave him alone—and leave his thoughts.

"What could you be doing in the shadows of my castle at this time of night?" he demanded.

"Only what I have been trained to do since I was a young girl," she said in a calm voice. "It is always a woman's duty to ensure that every candle is out, every fire safely banked."

"I do all that myself." He watched in amazement as her gaze lingered on his mouth. She wasn't fighting him either, just letting him touch her.

"Then perhaps you need to allow others to help you. Geoffrey was trying to."

Her voice had softened, and he found himself pulling her even nearer, until her gown brushed against his breeches—which she would see were concealing little if she thought to look down. So she wanted to help him. How did it help him to have her constantly putting her slender body before him, constantly tempting him?

"I need no help," he whispered.

He pulled her hard against him, and she gave a little gasp. He hoped it meant she finally understood how much power he had over her. But to himself, it only proved how little control he had. He wanted to clasp her hips and press himself against her. He wanted to take her mouth and understand the mystery of her. Her breasts were hard points against his chest, and this fleeting contact with her body was maddening.

And still she looked up at him, though now her own breath seemed to tremble quickly between her lips. "Maybe you do not need help, but I want to offer it. Will you not give me a chance?"

"I'm trying."

He was deliberately misleading her, and part of him hated the deception. He let her go, and she stumbled away from him, wide-eyed. He saw the quick rise and fall of her breasts, but she composed herself and nodded her head.

"Then that is a start," she said. "Might I stay with you longer?"

"Go to bed, Gwyneth."

It was there, the unspoken request that he join her, the request that could lead him to disaster if she was the Langstons' ultimate revenge.

But she only said, "Good night, my lord."

When she turned and walked away, Edmund was left feeling more alone than he had ever imagined he could feel. He was beginning to question his wisdom in accepting the earl's challenge.

* * *

Once she was in her bedchamber, Gwyneth barely restrained herself from slamming the door. How could Edmund possibly think he was giving her a chance when he was trying so hard to shut her out of his life?

No longer could she think it was because he was injured. When he'd pulled her up against him, she'd finally understood exactly what her mother had told her about what a man's body did to prepare for lovemaking.

She sank back against the door and covered her face, still overwhelmed by the sensations she'd felt when his hips pressed into her stomach. The long hard ridge of him had made her insides burn. When his chest had touched hers, she'd almost cried out at how good it had felt. For those nights when she'd wondered if he desired her at all she was somehow vindicated. But she was still too much a coward to slide into his bed. She wasn't afraid of him but ignorant. How did she go about seducing her own husband? Her mother certainly hadn't told her that. How could she make Edmund like her?

She forced herself to calm down, to have faith that he really was trying to give her a chance. All she could do was spend more time with him, hoping to learn about his first marriage and understand his relationship with her family. Once he knew her, he'd let her into his life.

But a niggling doubt kept her awake that night.

Geoffrey had said Edmund never trained any more, but now they both knew that wasn't true. Edmund must need to keep in practice, ready to defend their home. *Home.* Had she really thought of it that way, when she didn't even feel like a wife?

Yet why did he train like this in secret, especially if he never meant to go back to mercenary work? Did this have something to do with Earl Langston and the steward who'd been under his control?

For a few days, Gwyneth backed away from her husband, wanting him to think she was sufficiently cowed by their midnight encounter in the great hall. Yet she felt better when Mrs. Haskell presented her with yards of fabric from the castle stores, saying that Sir Edmund had reminded her of it. More pleased than she could have imagined, Gwyneth spread the fabric out and thought of the new gown she could make. She and Mrs. Haskell exchanged triumphant smiles and went to work.

Edmund remained away much of the time, whether in his fields or at the village, Swintongate, which she still hadn't seen yet. She was going to have to remedy that soon, for how could she make a place for herself here if she was always isolated at the castle? And how else could she help the villagers be comfortable with her husband?

With that resolve, she questioned Geoffrey about when Edmund would next have to visit his tenants, and he told her that in two days' time, the rents would have to be collected. He was certain Edmund would once again insist on doing it himself.

So Gwyneth laid her plans.

Edmund spent several days free of mysterious visits from Gwyneth, and he told himself this was a good thing. He must have sufficiently scared her, and she was letting him take their marriage at his own pace. This meshed perfectly with his plans.

Yet he'd never been as lonely as he felt now, something he wouldn't have imagined possible. He knew Gwyneth was captivating his servants with her sweetness and smiles. She and Mrs. Haskell were apparently forming a friendship, and the fabric he'd offered seemed to make them both happy. He was not looking forward to seeing her in her new garments, though they certainly couldn't make his desire any more painful than it already was.

He was forced to watch from the shadows as Gwyneth wove her spell about Castle Wintering. She was a regular visitor to the tiltyard, bringing ale and cakes and laughter. She worked alongside the maids with a natural authority but easy friendship. The wild lady's garden became a serene place under her ministrations, and he had secretly indulged in its peacefulness. He even saw her feeding scraps to his dogs as they gathered worshipfully about her skirts.

Much as his household seemed more harmonious, he didn't trust it. Instead of living his life, he was becoming endlessly suspicious over the possibilities of what could bring about his downfall.

When Earl Langston heard that the bailiff from his Durham properties had arrived, he ordered the man shown into his private withdrawing chamber, anxious to hear his report on Blackwell's wedding. George Irwin entered, looking about him hesitantly, and his travel-stained boots trailed dust across the polished floor.

Langston frowned as the man pulled a ragged fur hat off his balding head. "I have waited far too long for this report."

"It took me but a week of travel, my lord," Irwin said, bobbing his head. "And that was through a fierce rainstorm!"

"Give me no more excuses. Tell me about Blackwell."

Irwin clutched his hat, and Langston imagined infected fur trailing from his fingers.

"My lord, I found them all in Richmond, and it was there they were married."

"You're certain he did not change his mind?"

"I watched the ceremony from just outside the church courtyard."

Langston sat back in his wooden chair with relief. His plan had begun. "Did you travel to the lead ore site?"

"Aye, my lord. 'Tis undisturbed. Blackwell doesn't realize its value."

"You had better pray that no one saw you."

His eyes went round. "Nay, my lord, I swear it!"

"Did you meet with my agent at Castle Wintering?"

"Aye, my lord, though it was difficult. But no one saw us. The person is as yet undiscovered and assures you that all is going as planned."

Langston nodded slowly, allowing his eyelids to drift half closed as he mused on his successes. For a soldier, Blackwell was easily duped.

"Go back to Durham, Irwin. I shall send for you when I need you again."

The man's eyes widened. "Perhaps my report to you could come by messenger next time."

Allowing his eyes to blaze, Langston surged to his feet.

Irwin gasped and jumped back, giving a quick bow. "I'll do whatever you need, my lord," he called as he fled out the door.

Langston allowed his satisfied smile to return. Then he sent for a maidservant to scrub Irwin's dirt off the floor. Now, if only Gwyneth were pregnant with a girl child, then even the marriage contract would be against Blackwell.

At dawn on the eighth day of their marriage—rent-collecting day—Gwyneth packed a basket with all the baked goods she had prepared the previous afternoon. Each small cake or tart was wrapped individually in a small cloth and tied with string. She wanted to have something to offer Edmund's tenants when she was introduced.

And she vowed to meet them this day, although she hadn't informed her husband yet. She'd decided that surprise was the best course of action—in front of witnesses too.

To that end, she ate in the kitchen while he broke his fast in the winter parlor. When he went outside, she lingered in the doorway and watched him limp across the courtyard, admiring the way his doublet stretched tight across his back and his breeches clung to his thighs. He was a fine figure of a man.

When he reached the stables and greeted the grooms and soldiers gathered nearby, Gwyneth lifted her basket in both hands and walked awkwardly to join them. The sun was already blazing low on the horizon, and not a cloud marred the lovely blue of the sky. She wore a new gown she had made with Mrs. Haskell's help. All in all, she felt confident.

As she approached Edmund, whose back was turned, she watched the soldiers straighten and smile. Alerted, Edmund glanced over his shoulder and saw her. She gave him her brightest smile and adjusted the heavy basket in her grip.

"My lord, if you don't mind, I would like to come with you on your errands today."

As he began to frown, she rushed on. "I've baked some gifts that I would like to hand out." Let him try to turn her down now.

He didn't. The frown intensified, but she had plotted well, and he was neatly caught. In his eyes was the knowledge that she had done this with deliberation. She smiled more sweetly.

" 'Tis too long a day to walk, my lady," he said as he approached her. "We shall have to ride."

Her smile faltered as her gaze shot to the stall where his large warhorse waited, pawing at the ground and eyeing her. "Could we not ride in a cart?"

There was laughter all around her, and Edmund shook his head, a look of triumph rising in his eyes.

" 'Tis too steep a course through the dale."

He was already turning away to his horse, dismissing her. He lifted a huge saddle onto the animal's back, and she thought for certain there were few men who could have done it without standing on a stool. Everything about that horse frightened her—but she couldn't let fear stop her. She took a few deep breaths, already feeling light-headed.

When he had the girth cinched, she stepped forward. "I'm ready." She forced herself to smile.

He glanced at her, and those clear blue eyes were dazzling as they swept over her. "You still mean to go?"

"If it's all right with your horse," she said doubtfully, eyeing the beast.

Laughter broke out again, and she thought even Edmund's frown showed signs of cracking.

He sighed. "Then pick a horse and I shall saddle it, my lady."

"But I don't know how to ride. I thought I might ride with you."

He shrugged and looked about him until he spotted one of the grooms, a boy close to manhood, who flinched when Edmund looked at him.

"Boy, where do you keep the pillions?"

"A pillion?" she echoed, aghast. "You mean that little seat that perches on a horse's rump, with no support, no—"

"Then what do you wish?" he interrupted with exasperation.

"Could I not ride—*with* you?" A blush shot through her as she imagined saying, "in your lap" or "in your arms." She simply couldn't say the words.

There wasn't even the ghost of a smile on his face now. "Very well," he said softly, as he led his black horse out into the sunlight.

Gwyneth followed him, still grappling with the basket. Geoffrey appeared at her side, and she smiled up at him when he took it from her and set it on the ground.

"First I'll hand you up, my lady," he said as Edmund mounted.

Gwyneth leaned back to look up at her husband, and the little tremors of panic in her stomach were rapidly expanding. He was as high above her as a mountain overshadowing a meadow. How would she even get up there?

"What—what is his name?" she asked in a choked voice.

Edmund looked down at her. "The General."

"Because he's in charge?" That made sense with a horse this size.

Geoffrey smiled, but her husband didn't, even as he gave an abrupt shake of his head.

"I shall tell you why, my lady." Geoffrey placed a stool by her side and took her hand, urging her to step up. "Because it makes Edmund feel that he's leading the army generals around by the bit."

She managed a smile as she balanced on the stool.

"Ignore him," Edmund said.

He reached for her, and she took his hand.

"Put your foot on top of mine, and then I'll lift you up across my lap."

"Do you want me to ride astride?" she asked.

Edmund only blinked at her, and she heard Geoffrey give a muffled cough. She looked from one to the other frowning, but then Edmund was pulling on her, and after a step up, she found herself turned about and sitting sideways across his lap. The pommel pressed with little discomfort into her right hip.

She looked into his face, just above hers, felt his hard thighs supporting her and his arm about her back, although she did her best to sit up straight and not be a bother. He took the reins in both hands. And then she foolishly looked down.

The ground seemed to waver at an impossible distance below her. Her muscles stiffened, and she clutched his arm where it rested across her thighs.

"Easy, Gwyneth," he murmured, lowering his face until it brushed her hair. "I shan't drop you."

His breath across her ear distracted her, and she unclamped her fingers from his arm. "I hope I didn't tear your garments."

"I can handle it."

Was that humor in his voice? She wanted to look up again but couldn't tear her gaze from the horse's massive head as it arched its neck and shook its mane.

"Edmund," Geoffrey said.

They both saw the basket he was holding.

Edmund's frown deepened. "Can we not put the contents into saddle packs?"

"They'll be crushed," she said. "I shall carry the basket in my lap."

Geoffrey handed it up to her, and she gripped it tightly, glad to have something to hold instead of foolishly clutching her husband. Edmund gave a little grunt.

"How heavy is that, Gwyneth?"

She smiled up at him, trying to relax and enjoy the close-up view of his face. "I'll manage. Will you?"

"I think you weigh less than my armor," he said gruffly as he urged The General forward.

She couldn't answer that, because she was too busy bouncing with the horse's trot. They left the courtyard and rode northwest, deeper into the dale. Nearby pastures and fields fell behind them and soon they were traveling where she had never been before.

Edmund had been right about the cart. The driver would have had a difficult time following the meandering road that wound steeply up the hillsides and sometimes on the rocky banks of the river. At first she did not try to converse with him; she was pleased that she'd gotten her way and intent on conquering her fear of her rocking perch.

After a while she trusted her husband and tried to relax. He adjusted her position once, pulling her a little more toward one hip.

Soon they arrived at the first small house of gray stone and gray slate roof. Although chickens and geese roamed the yard, no one was in sight.

"Shall we return later?" Gwyneth asked uncertainly.

Edmund just sighed. "They're here. Hardraw is probably out in the barn, so his wife will remain inside until he's here."

"Can you put me down, so I can try the door?"

He looked at her for a minute, and in his eyes was that assessing expression that she'd seen so much recently. She had asked for a chance for their marriage, and he'd said he was trying, but always skepticism lurked inside him. She tried to imagine what it must have been like married to Elizabeth. Had it changed him, made him the distant man he was?

With the pressure of his thighs, he guided the horse to a low stone wall that separated the road from a cow pasture.

"Hand me the basket," he finally said, and when she did, he continued, "Grip my hand with both of yours, and I'll lower you until you can reach the wall."

Contemplating pushing herself off The General with nothing but one of Edmund's hands for support was even more frightening than mounting had been. She gave a little gasp as she leaned off the side.

"I have you," he said patiently. "Go ahead and take the step."

He had her firmly in one hand, and she clutched him. For a moment she felt as though she was swinging in midair, but the stones were suddenly beneath her feet and she achieved her balance. With a breathless laugh, she looked up at Edmund, still holding his hand. He was leaning over her, motionless, with an expression she couldn't read. Then he released her hand, and she lightly jumped down from the wall.

"It is good to be on solid ground again," she said, as she reached up for the basket.

He only gave a noncommittal grunt as he dismounted, then turned to pull his account book from his saddlebag. "I'll be at the barn."

Wistfully she watched him walk down the hillside. She had hoped he would introduce her. "Edmund?"

He looked over his shoulder.

"What are their names?"

"Ian Hardraw. I know not his wife's name."

He continued down the sloping, rocky path, and she watched him negotiate it carefully with his limp. She took a moment to admire his impressive speed before turning to face the house. Except for the clucking of chickens and the distant lowing of the cattle, there was no sound. Surely Edmund was wrong about someone being home. She approached the wooden door and knocked.

"Hello? Mrs. Hardraw?"

No one came to the door, but she heard a child's cry quickly hushed.

"Mrs. Hardraw? I'm—" She was about to say "Gwyneth Hall," remembered "Lady Blackwell" with lingering disbelief, and finally settled on "Gwyneth Blackwell. I recently married Sir Edmund, and I wanted to introduce myself."

There was definite movement inside, and she leaned closer to the door. "I've brought a gift," she called sweetly.

The door opened a crack, and out peered a

woman's face wrinkled by exposure to the sun and wind, if not age. "Ye're Lady Blackwell?" she asked suspiciously.

Gwyneth smiled. "I am. Are you Mrs. Hardraw?"

"I never saw the other Lady Blackwell. Didn't know he managed to catch another wife."

She fought to keep her smile from faltering. "Might I give you a small gift?" She reached into her basket and offered a wrapped cake.

The woman stepped beyond the doorway to take the package, keeping the door closed behind her. She was dressed in a plain, sturdy gown, and she was obviously well fed, which said much about the success of the farm. She eyed Gwyneth, and Gwyneth smiled back.

"Do you have children, Mrs. Hardraw?" she asked, wondering what else she could talk about with such a reluctant woman.

She nodded slowly. "Three."

"How wonderful! How old are they?"

In the few minutes they talked, Gwyneth pulled only a few facts from Mrs. Hardraw and only glimpsed a child's smudged face, but she was thankful that the woman's suspicion seemed to be retreating.

Until Edmund walked back up the path with Mr. Hardraw.

His wife pushed the child back, ducked inside, and firmly shut the door. Gwyneth stood there feeling foolish as she stared at the closed door, then back at her husband.

Edmund's look asked, *What did you expect?* Aloud he said, "Hardraw, my wife Lady Blackwell."

Mr. Hardraw clutched his hat between his hands and gave her an embarrassed nod. "Milady."

Gwyneth smiled back at him. "Good day, Mr. Hardraw. Please tell your wife that I enjoyed our conversation and look forward to seeing her again."

Edmund nodded to the farmer and turned toward his horse. Gwyneth quickly caught up.

"Can you use the wall to mount?" he asked.

She nodded and received a pleasurable surprise when he put his hands on her waist to boost her up. She was back in his lap in no time, and the height did not seem as frightening. As they trotted away, she waved toward the house in case someone was watching.

Feeling thoughtful, she rode in silence, leaning against his chest with a bit more confidence than she had before.

"Did she actually talk to you?" Edmund asked.

"Aye, she did, though it was a strangely coerced conversation."

"I have never seen her before."

She glanced up at him sharply, but he was staring over her head at the path that angled beside the river.

"Some women are shy," she offered, watching his reaction.

One corner of his mouth tilted upward, but it wasn't a smile. Was he implying that it was fear of himself that kept Mrs. Hardraw in her house when he came by?

Chapter 9

They spent the morning visiting farm after farm with varying degrees of success. Gwyneth met all the wives, while her husband collected the rents. Most women did not cower in their homes as Mrs. Hardraw had when Edmund approached, but their wariness was ever present, although they gladly accepted her gifts.

Children never made an appearance.

At each house, there was always a stone wall or stair-stoop for her to step on to mount The General. Only once did Edmund have to lift her straight up from the ground until she could reach the stirrup. She felt like a sack of wheat suspended in midair, and in her embarrassment, laughed up into his face.

He was not angry; in fact he seemed almost bemused. To Gwyneth's amazement, she heard chuckles from the couple they were visiting and thought that the wife gave her a fond smile such as one would bestow on a blissful bride and groom.

She leaned sideways against Edmund and thought that that was an accomplishment of sorts.

"And what is our next destination?"

"Swintongate is just around the hillside," he said. "Unless you have a meal in that basket, we shall eat at the tavern."

She should have thought of that, Gwyneth berated herself. She could have spent precious time alone with her husband. At least there was one good point to his notoriety—not many people would be bothering them at the tavern.

To see the village, she turned in the saddle to face forward. Tentatively she leaned back against her husband an inch at a time. When he didn't object, she let herself relax fully against him, enjoying the feel of his hard warmth behind her. With her arms still wide about the basket, they rested along his as he held the reins.

It was a pleasant if wishful fantasy to imagine being in his embrace for reasons other than supporting her on the horse. He felt so warm, so safe. He seemed to be an honorable man, a quality she held very dear, and dealt well with his people, even though they were afraid of him. She let her mind drift as she wondered how different things would be if he smiled.

Edmund suddenly put a hand on her shoulder

and shook her a little. Surprised, she tipped her head up to find him looking down. Their lips were inches apart, and she felt the warmth and pleasant sensation of his breath across her mouth. Her own breath caught on a gasp at the strange shock moving through her. Couldn't he feel this new awareness between them?

He cleared his throat. "I thought you were falling asleep and didn't want you to slide off."

"Thank you for your concern. I guess my mind was wandering." She smiled at him, at her own silliness. What did she think he would do—kiss her passionately out in the open dale when he wouldn't kiss her in a bedchamber?

As he lifted his gaze back to the road, she looked forward and saw Swintongate. The village was a collection of gray stone houses built into the hillside near the Swale. An ancient bridge with three arches spanned the river, which sparkled in the sun.

"How lovely!" she exclaimed, leaning forward with excitement. "This village truly *belongs* to you?"

"The land does," he said, but she thought she heard a note of pride in his voice. "The villagers rent from me."

Behind each house she could see spacious garden plots that gave way to pastures and fields.

"Are all the people farmers?"

"Some. Others are in trade. There's a tavern, as

I mentioned, with a few rooms to rent above it. The smith who works for Wintering has his business here."

The lane ran between two houses and opened up on a small village green with a well at the center. The tavern was almost indistinguishable from the rest of the houses, except for the small, crude sign showing a drawing of a full tankard next to a meat pie.

On the green, Edmund dismounted first, leaving Gwyneth to clutch the saddle tightly. Would The General bolt with only her on his back? But Edmund reached up and caught her about the waist. She practically jumped toward him and ended up falling against his chest.

She grinned as she found her footing. "Forgive me. That beast frightens me."

He seemed to search her eyes, even as he allowed her to remain leaning against him. "I didn't think anything truly frightened you."

Deciding to press him a bit, she placed her hands flat against his chest. "Certainly you do not frighten me, Edmund, though you might make everyone else cower with that voice of yours." She felt the strong beat of his heart under her palm.

His eyebrows lowered as his gaze drifted from her eyes to her mouth. "You think it is only my voice that affects people?"

She shrugged and patted his chest. "I have seen no other reason."

His frown intensified, and his voice became a low growl. "You are very naïve, Gwyneth."

He stepped away from her and went to the well, and she felt chilled without his warmth. After dropping the bucket in and listening to the splash, he pulled it up again by the rope. Spilling the water into a trough, he led The General over to it, and as the horse drank, he loosened the girth, then tied the reins loosely through a ring nearby.

"You're not afraid someone will take him?" she asked in surprise.

He gave her an ironic look. "This isn't London. Everyone knows who owns him."

"He certainly is distinctive," she said with a laugh.

She caught up with him as he limped toward the tavern. Suddenly a group of children came running between two houses onto the green. Laughing, they tossed a ball among themselves until they caught sight of her and Edmund. She smiled and waved, but one by one they stopped short, and their little faces reflected horror. Without even touching her husband, she knew he stiffened, and she gripped his hand firmly in her own.

As if suddenly unfrozen, the children turned and ran back the way they'd come, casting anxious glances over their shoulders. One little girl even had tears streaming from her eyes, and Gwyneth prayed that Edmund hadn't seen.

But one look into his expressionless face let her know he had. She wanted to bring his cold hand up and press kisses to it, warming it with her mouth.

"Edmund," she whispered, "they know no better."

He looked down at their joined hands, then back into her eyes. "Perhaps they know better than you."

He pulled away and kept on walking, while she followed behind more slowly. Her heart could have broken in pity for him, because she could not imagine being so feared. She knew now that she was the only one who could make things different for him.

Edmund felt more than saw Gwyneth fall into step at his side. He was walking too fast for her, but she quickened her pace without complaint.

He had known this day was bound to happen, but he'd never imagined the shame of it would feel like a kick to the stomach. Did one ever become accustomed to striking terror in eight-year-olds? All his protestations had never stopped his tenants from believing he'd had a hand in Elizabeth's death.

Yet Gwyneth had taken his hand, offering comfort.

Suddenly he felt her hand slide between his body and his arm. Stunned, he bent his elbow without thinking, and they were linked as they walked. She didn't look up at him, just wore her usual smile as she studied everything around her with interest. He told himself to push her away, but the tavern door was before him, and he opened it instead, then released her arm to put a guiding hand on her lower back. She glanced over her shoulder and smiled at him like a woman in love.

Then he knew her game, and he helplessly watched her play it as if she were a seasoned actor. She projected such innocence and goodness as she looked at the dozen or so assembled villagers. She wanted them all to think they had a normal, happy marriage. Was that for his benefit—or hers?

Goodman Walcot, the owner, came forward, wiping his large hands on a towel. The man's shaggy beard and mustache framed a generous smile. He was always good-natured, for he knew how to keep his customers.

"Sir Edmund," he said jovially, and his merry eyes played over Gwyneth, "a good day to you."

"Goodman Walcot, I would like to introduce my wife, Gwyneth, Lady Blackwell."

To Edmund's surprise, Gwyneth slid her slender hand back under his elbow.

"Goodman Walcot," she said, smiling that angelic smile, "I am so pleased to meet you. My husband has spoken often of his friends in the village."

Edmund wanted to roll his eyes, for surely his tenants, suspicious as always, would not believe such foolishness. But as he looked about the low-ceilinged chamber, he could see men and woman eyeing Gwyneth with interest.

Goodman Walcot gave a little bow over the large roll of his stomach. "He should have brought you here before now."

"I would have liked to," she said almost conspiratorially.

Edmund stiffened.

"But I fear I have been busy becoming accustomed to my new duties. I am only a city girl, Goodman Walcot, and easily overwhelmed. But Edmund"—and here she blushed like a well-satisfied bride—"Sir Edmund—is very patient with me."

Edmund wanted to laugh and almost bit his lip to stop himself. *Patient?*

Although there was a low rumble of laughter about the room, Gwyneth seemed not to notice. She just smiled up at Edmund serenely as Goodman Walcot showed them to a table. Unlike the long tables and benches that lined the room, this was small and private, with two chairs. Edmund set her basket beneath the table then helped her to sit, and her smile turned intimate as she reached up to touch his cheek in full view of the interested occupants. He froze, still bent over her, stunned by her gesture.

"Thank you for your kindness, Edmund," she said softly—but loud enough to carry in the stillness.

Oh, she was good at this. Even he was falling under her spell. He sat down across from her, let her take his hand as he ordered fish soup and bread for them both. But her playacting chilled him. If she was this good at pretending for an audience that they had a normal marriage, was she already fooling him as well?

Because every soft touch was torture, and every smile made him wonder how things would have been if he could have trusted her.

Two of the village women ventured forward timidly to speak to her, casting worried glances at him. As Gwyneth stood up, the women exchanged smiles. All he could do was drink his ale and watch her work her magic.

When the meal was finally over, he rose before she had even finished drinking. Yet she dutifully set down her tankard and stood up without complaint. A quick escape seemed unlikely when Goodman Walcot strolled over and smiled at Gwyneth.

"Lady Blackwell, has Sir Edmund shown you the falls yet?"

"Falls?" she echoed, looking up at Edmund with interest.

"The Swaledale Falls. Famous waterfall in these parts. 'Tis not much out of the way to Castle Wintering."

She put her delicate hand on Edmund's arm and smiled up at him. "Sir Edmund, might we?"

"If there's enough light," he said reluctantly.

While he paid for their meal, he noticed Gwyneth waving good-bye to the other patrons. She received a few nods in return and even one smile, though he thought it was a pitying one.

When she headed for The General, Edmund shook his head. "I have people to see here first."

"Wonderful!" She took the basket from him and swung it merrily at her side.

Within a couple of hours, he introduced her to the smith, the miller, and the carpenter, people who treated Gwyneth respectfully because he paid for their skill. Their wives were friendly enough, and he watched Gwyneth stoop to speak to a child who hid behind her mother's skirts and peered fearfully at him.

At mid-afternoon, they returned to The General, who regarded them impatiently.

Edmund had thought putting Gwyneth in his lap so many times in one day would stop affecting him, but it didn't. Every time she lay across his thighs, he could feel her backside rubbing into his groin, leaving him in a state of perpetual arousal. Her skirts fluttered in the breeze, making him itch to slide his hand underneath. Her lovely face was always just beneath his, and more than once they'd glanced at each other at the same moment. Her lips had been right there, parted, waiting for a kiss he could not give.

Why had he ever agreed to this excursion?

When he once again had Gwyneth in front of him, with that damnable basket blocking his easy access to the reins, he guided The General out of the village.

He spent a few peaceful moments rocking to the movement of the horse, listening to the wind pick up, and trying to forget that his willing wife leaned so freely and comfortably against him.

He could tell she looked up at him by the way her head slid along his shoulder. He didn't look down, knowing he could not stare at her lips much longer without doing something about this hunger to kiss her.

"Edmund," she said, "I forgot to thank you for the fabric."

"That is not necessary. I only reminded Mrs. Haskell about it. It was part of the castle stores, after all."

With an intriguing sideways glance, she smiled up at him. "Then my thanks for thinking about me."

This was not a place he cared to tread. Fortunately she went on talking.

" 'Tis a shame my sister Caroline isn't here."

He frowned down at her, wondering where this topic could lead.

"She is a much better seamstress than I am."

"There are good seamstresses in Swintongate."

He saw her smile fade.

"So you don't think I did a fine enough job on this gown?" she asked.

Edmund realized belatedly that the gown was new, made from the fabric he'd given her. It was grass-green, with a neckline that only hinted at the valley between her breasts, even from his perspective above her. When she raised her gaze to his, she must have seen where he'd been looking, although she gave no sign but a faint blush.

"You did a very competent job," he said in an overly serious voice.

Her face broke into a smile. "You are laughing at me."

"You are searching for compliments. And do I look like I'm laughing?"

"Not on the outside, but I'm trying to learn to read your eyes."

Frowning, he gazed at the meandering road. He prided himself on his impassive face and did not like the thought that a wife of only eight days could read him so easily.

"And I am not searching for compliments," she said with mock severity. "You implied that I needed a seamstress, and I was only countering that."

"You said that you wished you had a *better* seamstress, and I was offering a suggestion."

She leaned back even farther to study his face. Her head rested on his shoulder, and her hair tumbled down his arm, brushing his thigh.

"You can be very amusing," she said contemplatively.

What did he say to that? Aye, a long time ago he'd been considered amusing, but that had been a marriage—a lifetime—ago.

To distract her, he said, "We're almost to the falls."

A slow smile spread across her face, and he couldn't stop himself from watching it happen.

"You remembered," she said softly.

Something in her expression wouldn't let him look away, a combination of curiosity and tenderness and longing. Such sentiments called to him in a dangerous way.

Gruffly, he said, "There was nothing to remember. 'Tis on the way home."

All right, so that wasn't quite true, but he watched some of the happiness fade from her eyes and was relieved.

He guided the horse off the path and into the trees until the woodland became too thick. He let Gwyneth down first, a quick movement they'd become good at, then dismounted.

"You can leave the basket here," he said.

She shook her head. "We can have something to eat before we leave."

Now she'd maneuvered him into a romantic outing in the woods. But looking into her expressive face, he saw a spirit of adventure as she learned to live in a new place so far from her home and family. He thought that she would approach lovemaking with the same abandon and eagerness.

He stopped that thought before it could work its way in a hot flash to his groin.

Edmund led her through the woods, holding

branches for her until she could grab them herself. The ground sloped downward, and as it leveled off and the trees thinned, the River Swale appeared before them. This far up the dale it was shallow and wide and tumbled over rock formations as far upriver as they could see. Mist rose from small waterfalls cascading everywhere.

Gwyneth came up to his side, and her smile lit her face like a sunrise. "Edmund, it is so beautiful."

She dropped the basket on the dry bank, kicked off her shoes, and reached beneath her skirts to her knees. He stared at the glimpse of her bare lower legs, so delicate and feminine. He could imagine tracing the gentle slope of her calf up behind her knee, then sliding his fingers up the soft insides of her thighs.

He suddenly realized she was watching him looking at her legs, and she wore a half-smile that made her look like a woman who wanted to be seduced. Folding his arms across his chest, he frowned at her. He was doing so much frowning lately that it was giving him an aching head.

She only laughed as she pulled off her stockings.

"What are you doing?" he demanded.

"Walking in the water. I am quite overheated." She gave a saucy little lift to her shoulders as she turned and stepped into the river.

He watched her shudder, then she spread her arms wide and looked up at the sky.

"I never knew such places existed!" she cried, spinning about to smile at him. Suddenly off balance, she whirled her arms to right herself.

Edmund hurried to the water's edge, reaching for her. "Gwyneth, get back here before you fall. Moss grows on all these rocks."

She shook her head even as she stepped up onto a rock ledge where a tiny waterfall spilled. She dipped her toes in the spray and looked up at him.

"Gwyneth." He said her name with a growl.

She had the nerve to laugh. "If you're worried, then come with me."

Lifting up her skirts to her knees, she waded in even farther. He knew he couldn't go barefoot. He didn't have the balance he used to have. So, cursing under his breath, he trudged right in, feeling the cold water seep into his leather boots.

"Gwyneth!"

When she looked over her shoulder and saw him, she laughed and jumped to the next rock with the grace of a fairy sprite. He felt like an ox lumbering up the river after her.

When he was finally close enough, he ordered, "Take my hand."

She splashed between two rocks to reach him, then leaned against his side and slid her hand so naturally into his. He spread his legs wide to balance himself amidst the slippery rocks.

"What a successful day," she said, glancing up at him with a smile.

Distracted by the touch of her along the length

of his body, he managed to remember what she'd just said. "What constitutes a success?"

"That I met so many people," she answered, taking another step through the water. He followed in her wake. "I made sure to find out who had older children who could use work."

"Why?"

"We definitely need more servants inside the castle. I could use help in all the gardens, too." She glanced almost nervously at him. "You did say I could do as I wished as the lady of the castle."

"I did. Just clear all hiring with Mrs. Haskell, who knows who the good workers are."

"Everyone I met seems quite capable."

"There used to be more idlers before, but now they all seem to work well out of fear."

Her gaze was puzzled, and she seemed to stiffen. "What do you mean?"

He'd deliberately started this conversation to look for a reaction of guilt on her part, but he almost hated breaking the spell of magic she wove about this place.

"Well, I am a murderer, aren't I?"

Chapter 10

~~~OO~~~

Stunned, Gwyneth stared up at her husband. Many in the valley thought he was a murderer, and Edmund accepted it all as his due without defending himself. The water was suddenly cold as it swirled about her calves, and the brightness of the day faded. She pretended to lose her balance, and as she hoped, he quickly grabbed her other hand. She held him firmly and looked into his inscrutable eyes.

"We both know that you are not a murderer, Edmund," she said, hiding the compassion she knew he'd hate.

"Perhaps the Langstons did not bother to inform you of my scandalous deeds."

"They didn't need to inform me about this. I was the one who found Elizabeth's body."

His eyes narrowed, and he seemed to probe her honesty with a searching gaze. "You?"

Gwyneth had thought he knew all of this, and to have to remind him only gave her pain. "While you were in France, I spent the last few months of her life at court as her companion."

"Companion? She never needed anyone's company but her own."

"So I found out," she said dryly. "But when Earl Langston sent for me, it seemed like such an exciting thing to go to court with my fascinating cousin. I was an unpaid maid."

He studied her with narrowed eyes. "Did they not care for you as they did for Elizabeth?"

"If you mean did they handle the marriage negotiations, then yes. But other than that and my brief months with Elizabeth I never saw the Langstons."

"I'm sorry."

His gaze was so direct, but she could read nothing in his face.

"Don't be. It made me realize that I don't care to be part of a society where clothes and scandal are more important than making one's family happy. And even when I was angry with Elizabeth, it was easy to pity her."

Had his grip tightened? Or was it only a reaction to the water flowing between and around them, pulling them apart.

"Elizabeth knew nothing of happiness," she continued, "or how to achieve it. She pursued her vanity, because it was all she knew."

"Then you know what she did to herself," he said in a low voice.

She nodded.

"I tried to stop her. I even destroyed the potion."

"She had more made. She was determined to look like the queen, regardless of the fact that the queen came by her thin figure naturally."

"Why did she not just paint her face, as so many other women do?" he asked hoarsely.

Gwyneth gripped his hands even tighter, wishing she could put her arms around him. "Because it wasn't natural enough for her. One of her friends told her about the ratsbane, how eating small amounts made a woman pale and weak."

"From illness. God, she was such a fool."

"And she paid for it with her life. I am certain she was trying to heighten her pallor by taking even more of the poison, and that's what killed her. But Edmund, 'twas not our fault that we couldn't save her from it. And you were not to blame. You were out of the country. I don't understand why people think that you . . ." She trailed off uncertainly.

"That I murdered her."

She didn't answer.

"A loyal villager said they were told that while I was in France, I hired someone to kill her."

"And no one would say where such a lie came from?"

He shrugged. "They were too afraid. But I have other sources, and I've traced the rumor back to one man."

"Who would do such a thing?"

"Earl Langston."

She couldn't help the gasp that escaped her. "Edmund, he knows the truth. He was the first one I ran to when I found Elizabeth's body."

"The truth doesn't matter to him. I was not his choice for Elizabeth's husband. Surely that is obvious."

She hesitated, hoping she didn't hurt his feelings. "I will admit that I wondered why they did not give her in marriage to someone more influential."

As the current dragged at her feet, he hauled her close. He was as immovable as any rock formation that survived the pounding of the river.

"Did they not tell you why Elizabeth and I were married?"

Holding her breath, she could only shake her head and pray he continued. She so wanted to understand him.

"I did not court her like an honest man. I had a wager with my friend on who could kiss a maiden first. Only I did not stop at a kiss."

She stared up at him. "You are not telling me everything. I know you could not force yourself on a woman."

"You think you know me so well in but a week?" he said thickly. "I don't know you."

When he pressed her against his body, she stared into his face, seeing the pain he didn't want to show.

"You made a wager over a kiss." She kept her

voice calm. "But the attraction between you went further."

"I bedded her," he said harshly. "In the end it didn't matter that she was willing that first time."

That first time? she wondered.

"All that mattered was that her brothers discovered it. She was compromised, and I offered to marry her." He laughed harshly. "I thought we suited each other. I should have known better, since she tried to blame my friend Alex for her disgrace."

She wanted to hear more, but his eyes seemed to search the past before they settled back into impassivity, as if he was hiding something from her.

"The earl was furious that his plan for her successful marriage had come to naught. The thought of a scandal kept him from rejecting me outright, but he worked on Elizabeth during our marriage. And then he used her against me in death. There is no one else who hates me enough to see me an outcast. So you can see why her parents might want people to think I murdered her."

"No matter what the earl thinks he can get away with," she said heatedly, "we both know 'tis not true."

He stared down at her, eyes intent, his grip even more purposeful. She felt his body along every inch of her, felt the hardness against her stomach that he didn't try to conceal.

Without planning what she meant to do, she

raised herself up on tiptoes, slid her hand behind his head, and pulled. Obviously surprised, he bent, and she put her mouth against his.

She had wanted to comfort him, to convince him that she was not like other women, but she didn't know how a man should be kissed. With her eyes closed, she pressed several gentle kisses against his unmoving mouth. His lips were unexpectedly soft, moist, and a shudder moved through her with the realization that she wanted to taste him too. Could she do such a bold thing?

But before she could attempt it, he gave a mighty groan and slid his arms about her, molding her to him. Her feet left the rocks as she gladly put her arms around his neck. He tilted his head, and his mouth opened over hers. With a single thrust his tongue entered her, stroking the roof of her mouth and sliding over her teeth. The shock of it settled like a heat storm through her middle and made her body shiver helplessly against his. Her breasts ached where they were pressed hard to his chest, and she didn't know how to assuage this yearning. She could only run her hands through his soft hair and kiss him back, letting new sensations overwhelm her, even boldly stroking his tongue with her own. As his big body shuddered against her, his hand slid over her hip to pull up her knee. For the barest moment, she felt the wild pressure of him between her thighs.

Then suddenly he set her down, grabbed her

arms, and held her away from him, leaving her bewildered by the ache spreading through her. As she stared into his hooded eyes, she felt as though she was watching him board up every speck of humanity behind a fence.

He was so wounded by what Elizabeth and her parents had done to him. She understood him so much better, that he needed to feel comfortable with their marriage. She was no longer hurt that he was taking his time getting to know her. But she would still attempt to hurry the process.

Without a word, he grabbed her hand and began to walk back to the riverbank. She watched his slow step and realized that it must be difficult to maneuver over mossy, wet rocks when he couldn't bend one knee. One moment she felt guilty, and the next she was again resolute. He had kissed her, and surely the result was worth his efforts.

Ah, what a kiss it had been! She knew she should be concentrating on where she was stepping, especially now that her skirts clung sodden to her legs and hampered her. But she let Edmund pick the path and dwelt on how wonderful it had felt to be held in his arms against that powerful chest while their hearts pounded and their mouths mated.

Her mother had been right. Kissing was wonderful. And she wanted more of it.

In her dreamy state, she forgot to pay attention to what she was doing. Her foot slid down a slanted rock. Losing her balance, she tried to release Edmund's hand, but he only gripped her harder.

Both feet flew out from under her, and she landed in a small pool of water that soaked her to her hips. As Edmund fell, his elbow struck her shoulder hard enough to make her wince. He landed in a heap face down at her side.

Wide-eyed and aghast, she stared as he came up on his hands and one knee, spitting water and shaking it from his hair.

When he glared at her, she timidly asked, "Are you well?"

"I distinctly remember telling you to watch where you were stepping, my lady."

Biting her lip, she tried not to laugh. "But are you well?"

"I am wet but fine. Besides a bruise on your posterior, I think you'll have another one from my elbow."

He stood up with remarkable grace, then hauled her up as if he was plucking a carrot from hard earth.

When they reached dry land, she stumbled the last few steps to a big rock and collapsed on it, spreading her wet skirts, then leaning back on her arms to lift her face to the sun.

"Put on your shoes," he said. "We still have another stop before we reach the castle."

She lazily opened her eyes and watched her husband as he looked over the river, not at her.

Was he regretting their kiss? Saints above, they'd been married for over a week! She wanted to question him but sensed he wasn't in a talkative mood. Was he ever? she thought, trying not to smile.

"But Edmund, hunger weakens me. I made all these delicious treats. Do you not want to sample them while we let the sun dry our garments?"

She thought if his jaw was clenched any tighter, his teeth would break. Was he trying not to kiss her? What a provocative idea.

"Gwyneth . . ."

Ignoring him, she knelt down in the sandy dirt and opened the basket. She brought out a selection of tarts and cakes, removing the string from each package and spreading them before him.

"Pick what you want," she said. "I can describe each of them for you if you like. Or you can kneel down here and smell them."

And then she realized that he couldn't kneel, not with both legs. Her gaze shot to him as she wondered if her thoughtless words would send him stomping to his horse.

"Edmund, forgive me, I spoke before thinking."

With a shake of his head, he brushed her words off. Dripping with little rivulets of water, he limped to the large rock she'd just vacated and sat down. Grinning, she lifted a tart and a cake in her hands and awkwardly moved a few steps on her knees until she was between his wet boots. Boldly she rested one elbow on his bent knee to prop the food up for him.

"Which appeals to you?" she asked.

But her smile slowly died as he stared into her face, not at the pastries. His eyes had lost their distance and now smoldered with a blue flame. She was practically between his legs, and she wanted to press herself against him and demand he give her another soul-shattering kiss. Was he thinking about it too?

But she was not so brave. When he took the tart from her hand, she sat back on her heels and bit into the sweet cake. She watched him eat. He looked across the river rather than at her. He could have pushed her away when she kissed him, but he hadn't. He'd been just as swept away as she was. She would have to make sure they kissed again—soon. She could do nothing about the hurt inflicted on him by his first marriage except show him that she would not treat him that way. As for his relationship with her cousin the earl, she still sensed that there was much he was not telling her. Should she bide her time and hope he'd confide in her, or should she find someone else who would speak for him?

When he was finished, she offered him another tart, but he shook his head and got to his feet. She closed the basket, then followed her husband back through the woods, looking over her shoulder as the beauty of the falls faded between the trees. It was a wonderful place for her first kiss.

When she stumbled, he called back, "Perhaps you should watch the ground better than you watched the rocks."

That might have been an actual attempt at humor, and she smiled with satisfaction at his broad back. He was warming to her.

Once they were mounted, and the horse was trotting onto the road, she asked, "Are we going back to the castle now?"

"We have one more farm to visit," he reminded her.

She thought he sounded rather grim, which confused her. After a half-hour, he guided The General off the road. Low stone walls flanked a dirt path that wound its way up the side of the dale. The higher they rode, the more the whole valley spread out behind them. There was a beautiful symmetry to the different squares of green pastureland, broken up by the occasional checks of oat fields, all separated by stone walls. Flocks of sheep grazed like white clouds across a green sky. She held onto her husband and looked back beyond his shoulder, thinking that she could enjoy this view forever.

"Oh, Edmund," she breathed, unable to give voice to the beauty of the Yorkshire dales.

He glanced down at her, but she didn't immediately take her gaze away from the valley. When she realized he was still looking at her, she turned to him, wishing the basket weren't in her lap. Otherwise she could slide her arms about his neck in hopes that he'd kiss her again. She shivered at the thought.

Somehow he must have guessed what she was thinking, for he looked at her mouth. On either side of her, his arms stiffened, and she could feel every bulge of his muscles. She had never imagined a man's body could excite her like this. The wild, restless feeling overtook her again, burning through her, making her yearn to know where it would lead.

He suddenly looked up, then pulled on the reins to bring The General up short. "We've arrived."

She let out the breath she hadn't known she'd been holding.

Both the farm and the house were vastly different than the ones they'd seen earlier. The hillside was much steeper; there was little flat ground to grow crops. The house was small, built of uneven wood with dirt patches covering the holes. A few skinny chickens pecked through the yard.

Gwyneth looked up questioningly at her husband, but he only dismounted and helped her down. Why would he rent out such a hard piece of land to work? Surely money wasn't that important to him. She shivered at the bleakness of the place. Edmund went up to the house and knocked, and she followed.

After a moment, the door slowly opened. A wiry, small man stood there, clothed in brown homespun. When he saw who it was, he gave a nervous smile and opened the door wider.

"Sir Edmund, please come in."

"Yates, we're a little damp. We would understand if you'd like to talk outside."

The other man looked up at the sky, then back at them in puzzlement. "Did it rain and I not know it, milord?"

Edmund sighed. "Nay, we fell into the river."

"It was my fault," Gwyneth quickly offered.

Edmund glanced impassively at her. "Thomas Yates, this is my wife, Lady Blackwell."

The man bobbed his head. "Me wife'll be pleased to meet ye, Lady Blackwell. Come right in, for a little water won't hurt us none."

She smiled at him and preceded Edmund inside, knowing that he had to duck to avoid the door lintel.

There was only one room, with an earthen floor and a small fireplace. There were two beds, a table, and benches. Beside the hearth stood a pale young woman, barely out of girlhood, though with two children at her skirts and a baby in her arms.

Gwyneth smiled at the girl, whose eyes widened as she nodded in return. Mr. Yates motioned for Gwyneth to take a seat on the bench, and Edmund sat at her side, with Mr. Yates opposite. His wife stayed where she was, hushing the baby, who whimpered against her shoulder.

"How have things been this month, Yates?" Edmund asked.

The man looked at his folded hands. "Not good, milord. But they'll get better. I know ye tol' me not to take this land, but I'm workin' hard and I'm sure things will turn around."

Gwyneth glanced at her husband with relieved curiosity. So he'd tried to talk the Yateses out of renting this property.

"The sheep and goats seem to be healthy," her husband continued.

Mr. Yates straightened with pride. "That they are, milord."

"How is the farming?"

The little man's shoulders sagged. "Comin' along," was all he said. He glanced at Gwyneth as his face reddened. "I'm sure next month I'll be on time with the payment."

"You know," Edmund began in a casual tone that she hadn't heard from him before, "I have a small parcel of land near the castle set off from the rest of the field by trees, so 'tis difficult for me to work properly. It will need harvesting soon, but I won't have the time or men. Would you like to take this over? I'm sure when you bring it to market, you can get good money for the oat crop. And then it will not have gone to waste."

Mr. Yates's eyes brightened. "Aye, milord, I'd be happy to take it over."

" 'Tis a distance to walk," Edmund cautioned, "and it'll be hard to work alone. I can wait for the payment until after harvest."

As Yates pumped his hand in agreement, Edmund wished that Gwyneth hadn't been there. That soft look was back in her eyes, the one he'd seen only an hour ago, when he'd broken away from her compelling kiss.

What had he been thinking? he wondered, as they said their good-byes to the Yateses and went outside to The General. He was supposed to rid himself of this new wife, and instead he was kissing her like a besotted groom.

And she'd tasted incredible. He could have drowned in the sweetness of her, in the passion and heat of her response. He'd barely been able to keep his hands off her body and had only come to his senses when he'd realized he could have easily taken her there on the wet rocks. Then there would be no annulment, no breaking of this link between him and the Langstons.

Yet he was confused. The earl had sworn him to secrecy about Elizabeth's death and certainly wouldn't have told Gwyneth for fear the story would spread to become the scandal the Langston family dreaded. Yet Gwyneth knew all about it. She wanted his trust, but for what purpose?

He would have to play her game, pretend he was beginning to trust her, and see if she would betray him. He realized that he was hoping she wouldn't prove false, though where that would leave him he preferred not to speculate. As she continued to ride in his lap, it was all he could do not to kiss her again.

When they arrived at the castle, Gwyneth was prepared for Edmund's coldness. She knew he felt he had violated some kind of oath to himself by kissing her. But he seemed almost mellow as he let her off the horse in the center of the courtyard, handed down the basket, and then rode to the stables. She stared after him until he disappeared inside, remembering how gentle he'd been to the poor Yates family, feeling a quiet pride that such a good man was her husband.

He didn't come in for supper. Geoffrey and Lucy were interested in her journey, and she enjoyed telling them about the people she'd met.

That night, when Gwyneth was alone in her bedchamber, she told herself that she'd won a victory of sorts. But it didn't help with the loneliness, and she tried not to think of her family, so many boisterous, happy voices in one small house. She'd already sent them several letters, but she knew it would be weeks, if not months, before she heard back.

She knew better than to expect Edmund to come to her bed. She wanted more kisses. She wanted his hands on her, touching her in other places—and she wanted them both to be naked while he did it. She imagined him in the great bed at her side, whispering words of love, looking at her as if she was the most important thing in his life. She sighed at her foolish dreams.

She'd made inroads today, winning a skirmish, not the battle. It was time to begin seducing her husband in earnest, and if she had to learn as she went along, so be it.

Chapter 11

❦

At midmorning the next day, Edmund was working with the masons he'd brought from Richmond. He'd had to hire extra workers to repair a wall in an empty wing of the castle. It was heavy physical work dealing with large slabs of stone, and in only a few hours, he and the men were sweaty and exhausted.

The sun was at its zenith and he was helping to build wooden braces to hold a freshly mortared section of the wall in place when a low buzz seemed to move through the workers. The man he was working beside straightened with a smile.

Puzzled, Edmund turned around to find the whole contingent of maidservants from the castle gathered around Gwyneth. When had his household staff grown so big? Each of the women held a bowl or pan, and beside them a trestle table was being set up. Gwyneth spread out a large table-cloth, then directed where she wanted the food to be placed. The women giggled and eyed the appreciative male audience, who'd already begun to set down their tools and move toward the feast.

Edmund watched dispassionately, knowing he'd forgotten to tell Gwyneth that the workers brought their own meals. As she stood among the men piling their plates with food, she smiled at each compliment, but her gaze sought and found his. She lifted her chin a bit, as if to say, "You won't eat with me? Then I'll bring the food to you."

Wiping his hands on a rag, he limped toward her. That confident smile never left her face, and she boldly slid her arm around his waist before all the men.

"A good afternoon, husband," she said demurely, but her eyes glinted at him.

He nodded. "Gwyneth." He studied the food, trying to pretend that with a single touch of her body she was not undoing all his efforts to be objective about her. He had no choice but to let his arm drape itself across her back and his hand rest on her hip. Beside him, she seemed a shy, fragile wisp, not meant to bear well the regard of so many men—or the weight of his body. But she continued to surprise him.

She looked up at him innocently. "I hope you were ready to stop for a meal."

"How could I refuse when you've offered the men such temptation?"

She blushed, which only brought out the sparkle in her brown eyes. "I hope you mean the food."

A man nearby overheard her and laughed out loud, then ended on a cough when Edmund gave him a sharp glance.

"What else would I mean?" he asked, knowing he was challenging her.

She only shrugged and stepped away from him. "Come, my lord, rest yourself while I prepare you a plate."

"I can serve myself," he said.

"Then indulge me by allowing me to serve you."

She pushed him toward an empty bench in the shade of a tree near the garden but still well in view of all the men. Most people were openly smiling at Gwyneth's antics. He imagined not many men thought he'd let a woman be playful with him.

When he finally sat back heavily on the bench, Gwyneth stood above him, resting her hands on his shoulders. He stilled when she began gently rubbing the muscles in his neck.

"You are very stiff and tense," she said, wearing a delicate frown of concentration.

She didn't know how stiff. Edmund couldn't stop staring at her lovely face, and then lower to a bodice that was more revealing than the one she'd worn on their rent-collecting journey. It gaped away from her breasts until only their peaks escaped his gaze. He stood there stupidly staring down her gown, wishing he could touch, wishing even more that he could taste.

Suddenly she leaned toward him, and he was too stunned to avoid the kiss she pressed to his cheek.

With a waft of subtle perfume, she left him, walking back toward the table of food, her hips swaying in an ancient, alluring rhythm. She looked over her shoulder, saw that he was still watching, laughed, and gave a little wave.

He knew he should go back to work immediately, should pretend that he wasn't hungry—anything to escape this assault on his senses and on his resolve.

But Gwyneth was too quick for him. She came back with a full plate, like a courtier bearing gifts to her king.

"You'll need to spread your knees," she said softly.

With his mind no longer functioning properly, he could think of no reason not to do as she wished. To his amazement, she perched on his left knee and handed him the plate. From a pouch at her waist, she removed a spoon, an eating knife, and a napkin.

When she went to spread the napkin over his lap, he said hoarsely, "I can manage that."

She smiled up into his face. "Of course you can. Forgive me."

Knowing he had to stop looking at her and start eating, he turned to his right and began to put food into his mouth. He wasn't sure about what he was eating. It all tasted rather bland and identical, since his senses were consumed by the feel of Gwyneth's backside pressed into his thigh. Her gaze was a caress that left scorching heat in its wake. He might have finally melted under her innocent seduction if he hadn't caught sight of Geoff turning a corner of the castle and coming to a halt. His friend seemed confused at first until he looked at Edmund and Gwyneth. Then his smile turned into a broad grin, as if Edmund had openly confessed that he trusted in her innocence and was now going to follow her to bed.

"Gwyneth, stand up," Edmund said in a low voice, as Geoff began to walk toward them.

"But why? Surely Geoffrey understands that we're married."

Edmund shifted his knee as if he was going to spill her into the dirt. She rose hastily and gave him a searching glance.

"What a cozy display," Geoff said, giving a dramatic court bow to Gwyneth, one leg bent, the other straight. "Is there plenty for another hungry mouth?"

Without thinking, Edmund curtly said, "Plenty of what?"

Geoff only laughed and regarded him a little too intently.

Gwyneth smiled. "If you see nothing to your liking at the table, Geoffrey, just tell me, and I'll search out more in the kitchen."

"I'll be content with whatever morsels are here, my lady. Perhaps you could point out a good selection."

When she glanced uncertainly at Edmund, he found himself suddenly reluctant to let her go. How ridiculous.

"I'm going back to work," he said, handing his plate to Gwyneth, who took it with perhaps a touch of disappointment showing in her eyes. "See to Geoff."

For the next hour Edmund caught glimpses of Gwyneth walking among his workers. They smiled when she left them with a few simple words of kindness, and seemed to work even harder. More and more this castle seemed like a home, and it was all because of her. It made him feel wary, as though he should be looking over his shoulder.

That night, as Gwyneth walked down the corridor toward her bedchamber, Lucy opened her own door just as she passed. The draft almost blew out Gwyneth's candle, and she shielded it as she smiled at her friend.

"Milady, I'm so sorry I startled ye."

"Think nothing of it, Lucy. Could you not sleep?"

The girl shook her head, then motioned her to enter. By the light of the fire and the few scattered candles, Gwyneth could see that the room was much cozier than it had been the last time she was there. The rushes on the floor had been changed, and the bed was hung with curtains. An old chair and small table were positioned near the hearth. Lucy guided her to the chair, and Gwyneth took a seat as Lucy pulled up a stool.

"Milady, I have a question for ye, and I hope ye don't think me forward."

"Go ahead, Lucy, and please, can't you go back to calling me Gwyneth?"

"I don't want to forget meself when I'm with the other servants," she said, even as she fiddled with her skirt and avoided Gwyneth's eyes. "Milady, aren't ye . . . afraid of your husband?"

"Afraid?" she echoed, surprised.

"Well, I saw ye sittin' on his lap outside today. Ye treat him like a man ye wanted to marry. And the way ye look at him . . ."

The girl trailed off, obviously uncomfortable.

"Why should I be afraid?"

"I've been speakin' with the other servants, milady, and though I don't mean to be passin' on rumors, they say"—she lowered her voice even as she stared purposefully into Gwyneth's eyes— "that he killed his first wife."

"That isn't true, you know," Gwyneth said calmly.

"How can ye be so certain?"

"You know that his first wife was my cousin. I'm not permitted to speak in any detail, but I was with her the last few months of her life. Sir Edmund was in France when she died."

Lucy shook her head. "Still, he could have hired someone. Everyone thinks it, so there must be a reason they're all ready to believe such a thing. And milady—ye don't sleep in the same chamber."

"You don't know him as I do, Lucy. And the rest of them won't take the time to know him. He's nothing like he shows the world. I find him . . . intriguing, and I want to prove to him that he can trust me."

"Do ye love him?" she asked, wide-eyed.

"I don't know," Gwyneth said thoughtfully. "But I am willing to try."

The next morning, Gwyneth was up and dressed before dawn, unable to wait for the servants to bring her bath water. She had a busy day planned, and the first obstacle to get by was her husband. She had to catch him before he escaped the castle.

After walking into the servants' wing, she knocked briskly on Edmund's door. She heard a muffled, "Come in," so with surprise, she lifted the latch and entered.

Edmund stood with his back to her before a cupboard on the far side of the room, naked from the waist up. She stared in wonder at the broad, flexing muscles of his back as he pointed at the hearth.

"I've set the tub before the fire. You may start filling it up."

"But I haven't brought any water," she said softly, walking toward him.

He turned around very quickly for a man with a lame leg, then stood unmoving as she approached within a foot of him. She lifted a hand, meaning to touch that wondrous chest.

"Don't."

Frozen, she looked up at him, wishing she could understand whatever he was hiding. "But I want you to kiss me again."

Tension crackled between them.

"I seem to recall that I did not initiate that kiss," he said, so mildly that she was disappointed.

"But do you not want to?" She placed her palm on his chest, regardless of his wishes. His skin was hot, and she wanted to lean into him.

"Of course I want to," he murmured, leaving her hand where it was. "But we need more time. We barely know each other, and I do not want you to be hurt."

"You won't hurt me," she whispered, sliding her palm across the hair on his chest. When her touch swept over his nipple, she lingered, and she could see his swift inhalation.

He gently took her wrist and held her hand away. "Why did you come to my chamber?" he asked, his voice huskier than before.

She hesitated, still staring at his chest, feeling befuddled, before she finally shook herself and looked up into his impassive eyes. "I would like your permission to walk to the village."

He frowned. "It would take more than an hour. And the roads can be dangerous."

"I don't mind the journey. I'm a strong woman."

He lifted one eyebrow. "And what would your errand be?"

"I would like to visit the villagers that you introduced me to. Mrs. Haskell gave me a list of people who could use work. I'm rather worried about harvesting the kitchen gardens and the orchards."

"I already have men to help."

"But aren't they needed in the fields?"

He shrugged.

"Then 'tis good that I go. Perhaps you could send a groom to escort me, a lad you trust."

"I would want you to ride a pillion behind him."

"On a horse?" she said, aghast. "Without you to keep me from falling? Nay, we can walk. So who do you suggest?"

He touched her chin, and she held her breath, wondering, hoping that he might kiss her. He just stared seriously into her eyes.

"And if I ask you not to leave the castle?"

"You will confine me here?"

"Nay, but if I ever need to ask such a thing of you, will you obey me?"

"Well, you *are* my husband."

He slid his fingers up to cup her cheek. "Does that mean you will obey me?"

"Aye," she answered, wanting to rub against his palm like a lonely kitten. "But I pray you would at least tell me why."

"If I can." He lowered his hand. "Ask for Will at the stables. He's a sandy-haired lad with a good head on his shoulders. Be home before supper, so you don't lose the light."

"Thank you, Edmund." She smiled up at him, wishing she could come up with a reason to stay.

But there was a knock on the door and servants lugging in buckets of water, and she found herself in the corridor with Edmund firmly closing the door in her face.

How had he done that? she wondered with frustration. She stayed in the great hall until the servants had left Edmund's wing of the castle. She even waited a few extra moments for good measure. Then she marched back to his bedchamber, took a deep breath, knocked quickly, and walked right in.

"Oh, my," she breathed, and promptly forgot whatever excuse she'd made up for barging in.

Edmund had been leaning back in the tub, his thick arms resting on the edge, one leg bent in the water, the other resting on the rim of the tub. After she'd burst in, he sat up so straight that half the water must have sloshed out the sides and formed pools about it.

"Edmund, forgive me for startling you," she said with forced sincerity, even as she walked toward him.

"What are you doing here?"

His voice was a growl that did not scare her.

"I—I forgot the groom's name," she said, hoping that God forgave her the lie. "My, I wouldn't have believed you could fit inside that tub."

And then she was standing over him. Before her eager gaze could move lower than his damp, hairy chest, he snatched a towel off the stool and dropped it across his hips. Gwyneth could only sigh as it soaked through and sank to cover him.

"The groom's name is Will," he said. "He works in the stables, in case that slipped your mind as well. Now would you mind leaving, so I can enjoy my bath in peace?"

Not breaking their shared gaze, she dipped her fingers in the water, then splashed a few droplets across his chest. "You cannot enjoy your bath with your wife waiting on you?"

This time she was certain he hesitated.

"I have not needed help bathing since I was a child."

"I understand. But I would like to kiss you again. Therefore, in order to make me leave, you shall have to oblige me."

He frowned. She grinned. But his gaze was on her mouth. Resting both hands on the tub, she leaned over him. Edmund tipped his head back to look at her. He was not smiling, but she thought she saw reluctant amusement in his blue eyes.

"You have grown quite bold for a new wife. Allow me to explain certain facts to you. I am in command of this castle. When I call, my servants will come running."

"And they will certainly be aghast when they see the lady of the castle in her husband's bedchamber. 'How dare she?' will be the horrified comment that spreads throughout the castle."

Closing his eyes, he sighed. "Will you not be reasonable about this? I have much to do today, and the delay—"

"Is your own fault," she interrupted. "All I ask is a kiss."

He suddenly cupped his hands and splashed her. With a gasp, she backed away. When he threatened her again with the same motion, she retreated to the wall near his account books. She picked one up and held it before her, peering over the top.

"I'm still not leaving. And if you splash me again, some of your valuable work will be ruined."

He suddenly hoisted himself up to his feet, and she caught a glimpse of his white backside for only a moment before he wrapped the wet towel about his hips and stepped out of the tub. Wearing a frown that was almost mild, dripping water everywhere, he advanced on her. Her breath came rapidly as she pressed herself against the wall and waited with great anticipation. What a wonderful idea this had been!

She gave another gasp of surprised excitement when he planted his hands on either side of her head. His hair dripped a steady stream onto her face, and she blinked, but didn't stop staring at him. Should she purse her lips? She'd only had one kiss, which she'd initiated. How would *he* do it?

But he reached to open the door, grasped her underneath the arms, and lifted her off the floor.

"Edmund!" she cried as she dangled awkwardly from his hands.

He put her in the hall, then lifted her hand to briefly kiss her knuckles. "Tell Mrs. Haskell to send more hot water."

Then the door slammed shut. Pouting, she folded her arms across her chest. Why hadn't she specified what *kind* of kiss?

Will, the groom, perhaps ten years old, not only had sandy hair, but a cheerful face full of freckles. He bowed low before Gwyneth, then strode off at her side, pleased to be chosen. The walk into town only took an hour, and the boy kept up a steady stream of chatter about the plants they passed and the places he'd visited that never varied farther than twenty miles from Swintongate.

This time when Gwyneth entered the village,

people waved to her. Will introduced her to those she didn't know, and soon she had a few more young men and women ready to come work at Castle Wintering. She even talked with the seamstress, who agreed to make regular visits to the castle several days a week.

"Would ye like to meet me ma?" Will asked with excitement, when they'd left the seamstress's parlor. "We live in a room behind the carpenter's shop."

"I would love to meet your mother," she said.

On the way, Will explained that his father had died when he was young and his mother supported them by working at the tavern. "She serves the food, milady, and since 'tis not quite dinner yet, she'll be home."

They walked through a narrow alley between gray stone buildings, behind which was a small field planted with vegetables and flowers. He flung wide the only door at the rear of the building, and she winced, hoping his mother wasn't caught at a private moment.

A woman stood at the table just inside, pinning on an apron. Her hair was shiny black and her face pale and lovely. She must have borne her son when she was very young. She gave a little jump as she glanced up at them, then her eyes flickered back to her son with a worried frown.

"Will! Please don't tell me Blackwell let ye go."

"No, Mum. I'm runnin' errands with Lady Blackwell. Here she is!"

The woman's eyes widened as if she'd only just seen Gwyneth standing outside her door. "Milady! Please come in." She gave her son a scolding glance as Gwyneth entered the room. "Will Atwater, ye should have introduced us proper."

Gwyneth smiled. "Please, Mrs. Atwater, I enjoy your son's high spirits. He's a good lad."

The woman smiled back at her as the boy sat down at the table and lifted a pear from the bowl. "Thank you, milady. And call me Prudence. Will is doin' all he should?"

She got the impression that Prudence wished to ask more but wouldn't. Though the woman was polite, there was speculation in her gaze every time she looked at Gwyneth.

"My husband is quite pleased with Will's service. He was the first boy Sir Edmund recommended when I asked for a groom to accompany me."

"Do ye like livin' at the castle, milady?"

"I never thought I could enjoy it so much. I'm from London, and this is quite a bit different."

"Aye, the fresh air and all," Prudence said, as she pulled a linen cap over her head. "I have to be at the tavern, but would ye walk with me, milady?"

The two women walked across the green with Will running ahead of them. Clouds had begun to cover the sun and brooded over the village with the threat of rain.

"Is that not yer husband?" Prudence asked.

Gwyneth turned her head in surprise and found Edmund dismounting near the well in the center of the green. Will ran off to help him with The General, leaving the women alone.

"I guess ye can't get away from yer husband's eye," Prudence said dryly.

Gwyneth glanced at her in confusion.

"Ye know he probably doesn't want ye talkin' to me."

"Why?" She stared hard at the young woman, wishing she understood what emotions lingered beneath her peculiar words.

"I tried to do him a favor once. Tried to lure him away from that cold fish that was his first wife."

Gwyneth was amazed that Prudence would tell her such a personal thing—about her own husband, yet!

Prudence's smile died, and she stared at Edmund with a narrowed gaze. "Aye, the poor man looked like he needed a little comfort." She gave Gwyneth a false smile. "But he's got you for that now, hasn't he?"

Chapter 12

At first, Gwyneth could only blink in shock. "I'm not sure why you're telling me this, Prudence. Are you trying to warn me of your intentions?"

"Heavens, no, milady. Ye seem like a good wife for him. Just thought ye'd want to know what kind a woman he was married to before, so ye didn't make the same mistakes."

Gwyneth gave her a gentle smile. "She was my cousin."

Prudence's face reddened. "I—forgive me, milady."

"There's nothing to forgive." She hesitated, casting a guilty glance at Edmund before turning back to Will's mother. "I didn't know her well, and when we did speak, she treated me with a disdain I couldn't fathom."

The woman nodded fervently. "There was no respect in her for anyone, least of all her husband. I saw that he tried to treat her nice, but she wanted none of it. Never saw a man so patient with a woman."

Gwyneth patted her arm. "I thank you for the information."

After Prudence had bobbed a curtsy and hurried away, Gwyneth walked toward her husband, who was watering his horse. She watched him contemplatively, relieved to know he could be faithful, even to Elizabeth. Prudence had told her what she'd already known deep in her heart: that Edmund had done his best when married to Elizabeth. But then, she knew him to be an honorable man.

Yet it couldn't be only the memory of Elizabeth that made him so wary of her. Gwyneth herself was related to the Langstons. Whenever Edmund looked at her, did he remember how they'd portrayed him as a murderer?

As she approached, Edmund looked up. "Are you finished with your errands?"

"Aye. Are you? I assume that is why you came, and not because of me."

His eyes seemed to lighten, though he didn't smile. "It was. I promise you I did not know I'd have to come see the carpenter when you left this morning."

She grinned. "I was not accusing you of anything, Edmund."

" 'Tis good to know."

He gave a whistle, making The General's ears twitch, and Will come running. Edmund put his large hand on the boy's head.

"I'll take my wife home, Will. Thank you for the excellent care you've shown her."

"Do ye not need me back at the castle, milord?"

Edmund looked up at the overcast sky. "The weather is turning. You go play with your friends, and I shall see you on the morrow."

Wearing a beaming smile, the boy gave a quick nod to both of them and ran off.

Gwyneth studied her husband, who finally looked down at her. He must have seen her talking to Prudence, and she could only imagine what he was thinking.

But all he asked was, "Are you ready to leave?"

"I am rather hungry," she answered, glancing at the tavern.

He hesitated, and she barely stopped herself from smiling. Perhaps he did not wish to see Prudence again.

"I still have much to do at the castle," he said, "and the sky does not look good. We'll purchase meat pies and eat them on the way."

She nodded and walked at his side to the tavern. Inside, Edmund gave their order to Goodman Walcot, and Gwyneth smiled and waved at Prudence, who blushed even as she nodded in response. When Prudence was finished waiting on her table, Gwyneth told her about Will remaining in town. The woman thanked her and hurried away without looking at Edmund.

When they were riding The General out of the village, Gwyneth finished her pie and said, "You seem nervous, Edmund."

"Nervous?" he echoed. "I am concerned that the coming storm might be severe."

"Is that all? Or could it be that you're wondering what I was talking to Prudence Atwater about?"

"She is Will's mother," Edmund said.

She thought she heard a note of caution in his voice. "She is that." Leaning her head back against his shoulder, she looked up into his face. "She also wanted to tell me that she once tried to seduce you away from Elizabeth."

He winced. "She felt the need to say that, did she?"

"I think she wanted to shock me."

"Probably."

"She claimed it was because she didn't want me to make the same mistakes Elizabeth did."

"How kind of her."

Gwyneth grinned at his sarcasm. "She thought so."

"And what do you think?" he asked, glancing down at her.

"I think she confirmed for me that you can be faithful even to a wife who treats you as Elizabeth did."

She thought he clenched his jaw as he looked

back at the road. "And how would you know about my first marriage?"

"Prudence told me a little. Now, don't be angry," she said, putting up a hand as if to stop the lowering of his brow. "I admit I led her to speak by telling her that Elizabeth didn't treat me well. All she said was that you were patient and kind to your wife, things I have always seen in you."

She wanted to kiss his stoic face. It must have been horrible to have his patience and love rewarded with indifference and cruelty.

With a sigh, she finally said, "But I imagine you don't want to talk about it any more."

"Nay, I do not."

She leaned even further into his embrace, letting his arm support her back and his chest support her side. She even dared to rest her head against that very comfortable chest and allow the rocking of the horse to soothe her.

" 'Tis a shame my sister Athelina isn't here."

"And why is that?"

"Both times I've been to the village, I've seen children running about. Athelina is a very learned woman, and I'm certain she would want to open a small school to teach the children."

"This is the sister who likes books."

She glanced up at him in surprise. "You remembered!"

He raised one eyebrow. " 'Twas not difficult. There are only three of them."

"Well, Papa thinks she would do well as a

teacher, although most of the teachers in London are men."

"We have a teacher here, a woman."

"Oh," she said, then sighed.

"You are disappointed that the children are learning?"

Again she thought there was amusement in his voice.

"Of course not. I am merely relieved." How could she explain that she was only trying to interest him in her family, maybe eventually invite them for a visit? He might be more inclined to help them with their marriages if he met them.

Several drops of rain splashed across her face, and she looked up at the sky. The gray clouds had massed together into inky blackness. She sighed again. "Wet for the second time in one day."

"We need to move faster," Edmund said, "but 'tis difficult to gallop with you lying across my lap. You need to ride astride."

"But Edmund, there cannot be room on this saddle for two."

"It has a low cantle, so I can slide back."

The rain was coming faster now, and Gwyneth found her hips squeezed between the pommel and her husband. He put an arm around her waist and lifted her up.

"Slide your right leg up over the horse."

"But my skirts!" she cried, even as the rain soaked into her hair and slid down her face.

"Surely they're wide enough," he said into her ear.

Pressing back into her husband, she lifted her bent leg over the horse, then adjusted her skirt to sit on it rather than on the bare saddle. She smoothed the rest of the fabric down her legs and discovered to her relief that only her ankles and feet were showing.

"Are you ready?" he asked, raising his voice to be heard above the rising wind.

She nodded and gave a little gasp as he slid against her. His hips pressed into her buttocks, his thighs were molded to hers, and his arms came around her to grip the reins. She could only hold on to the pommel with panicked excitement.

"We're going to start galloping. Just move with the horse's gait as I do. You'll be all right."

"Edmund, I've never—"

He pressed his hand against her stomach, and her breath caught.

"Relax."

How could she relax, when his splayed fingers were barely above her spread thighs? But before she could dwell on the wicked pleasure of that, she felt his thighs tighten, and The General burst into a gallop. She could only hold on. The rain poured down on them, sheets of it, which soaked through every layer of her clothing. Edmund leaned forward over her, urging the horse ever faster to speeds she had never imagined. The countryside moved by in a rain-soaked blur.

When she got over her fright, there came a sense of exhilaration, of feeling that this was where she was meant to be, with this man whose body enfolded hers.

When the castle courtyard and the broken-down walls loomed ahead out of the gloom, she was almost disappointed.

But she couldn't be, not when she felt so free on this horse. As they slowed down, she straightened and threw her arms wide up to the sky, opening her mouth to taste the cool rain. In the deserted courtyard, Edmund didn't even wait for her approval. He just lifted her leg over the horse, and dropped her down to the ground in a maneuver they both were getting to know well.

Gwyneth leaned against his leg, laughing up at him. To her surprise, he was smiling down at her, a smile so wonderful and alive that she felt as if someone had caught her lungs and squeezed. He was such a handsome man when he grinned like that, with strong, white teeth and those blue eyes that sparkled with merriment. She wanted to see that expression every day of her life.

He flung himself off the horse and led it into the stable, and she ran behind him.

"Where is everyone?" she called, as he loosened the saddle and pulled it off The General's back.

"Probably in the great hall, waiting for the storm to pass."

"Then we're alone?"

He glanced at her and looked away, leading the horse into his stall. "Perhaps."

Gwyneth eyed the large mound of fresh hay piled between the stalls. She waited for Edmund to emerge, and then she gave him a hard push. She must have caught him unawares, because he fell backward, and she let herself fall with him. She landed on his long, hard body, and felt a thrill as their legs twined together.

She grinned into his surprised face, propping her arms on his chest. "Oops. That was an accident."

Suddenly he rolled them over until she was on her back. For a moment she thought he would leave her, but then his body covered hers, his hips holding her down. He braced himself with his elbows on either side of her.

"That was an accident too," he murmured.

Her smile died as she absorbed the overwhelming feeling of having this man's body touch every bit of hers. She didn't feel crushed, only sheltered by the pleasurable weight of him. Her restless legs wanted to part, to let him slide between them, but her skirts trapped her.

When Edmund did nothing but stare down into her eyes, then at her mouth, she reached up and framed his face with her hands.

"Will you do that again?" she whispered.

"Fall?"

"Smile."

But he didn't. If anything, his eyes darkened

with an intensity that might have frightened her if she hadn't felt so drawn to him. When he leaned down and gently kissed her cheek, she gave a little moan.

"Raindrop," he said. He kissed her other cheek. "Another one."

He pressed tantalizing little kisses all over her face until she tilted her chin and whispered, "I'm very wet."

His mouth trailed down her neck, and she felt his tongue tease behind her ear. She pressed her face into his hair, kissing him, holding him against her. Of its own volition, her body moved against his, rubbing, needing more of this incredible sensation.

He shifted, and suddenly her skirts gave a bit and she could spread her legs. His hips settled between them, and his hands caught her face only a moment before his mouth covered hers.

She was better prepared this time and gladly parted her lips to meet his tongue with hers. She felt selfish in her need to explore his mouth, to suckle his lip between her own. The kiss was hot and greedy in its speed, and the lack of gentleness only made it more wildly exciting.

Edmund couldn't get enough of the taste of her, of flowers under a spring rain. He'd spent the whole day remembering how she'd looked with bath water sparkling on her face. It had taken every ounce of his control to keep from touching her, but he could resist no longer. He had one hand grasping her ribs, and he was moving slowly higher, while she breathlessly moaned and squirmed against him. He rubbed his hips into hers, wanting to pull her skirts up and thrust himself inside her.

Instead, he rolled off her and lay on his back for a moment, breathing deeply, raggedly.

Gwyneth came up on her elbow and grinned at him. "That was very enjoyable."

Hay stuck out of her long blond hair like the spines of a porcupine he'd seen in France, and her mouth was swollen from what he'd done to her. There was even a red mark below her ear. Quickly he sat up, running his hands through his hair.

"I must dry off The General, and you need to get out of those wet clothes."

With her eyes she seemed to be imploring him to help with that task.

He turned away. "Go on."

"Shall I see you at supper?"

"I'm not sure. I've been gone too long."

She stood up, and to his surprise, leaned down to kiss the top of his head. Frustrated, aching, he watched her saunter away. At the stable door, she paused and looked up at the sky. Before she could take another step, Geoff came running across the courtyard with a cloak over his arm. He ducked into the stable, bowed to Gwyneth, then spread the cloak wide with a dramatic flourish.

Edmund found himself slightly irritated, then

grew even more so when Gwyneth giggled. She allowed Geoff to place the cloak around her shoulders. When her back was turned, Geoff winked at him.

Edmund frowned and started to say something, but Geoff was already leading her across the courtyard. What the hell was that about?

Then his mind went back to the kiss, and he sat in the hay feeling bemused and uncertain. He had only done what she'd expected. She thought he was giving her a chance, getting to know her better, maybe even courting. To her, kissing was part of that.

He was a selfish man, touching her for his own pleasure instead of the reasons she thought. He was only using her, craving the feeling of knowing she wanted him. But he wasn't going to give her anything back but heartache. Even if he found out she was innocent of the earl's plot, he would still annul this marriage.

Yet he couldn't stop himself from imagining how she'd feel naked, how she might clasp her legs about his hips.

"Edmund?"

He looked up to see Geoff leaning in the doorway, arms folded across his chest.

"The hay in your hair carries implications," Geoff said.

Edmund shrugged and got to his feet to curry The General. "Thank you for Gwyneth's cloak, although it was probably a bit too late."

"If I'd have gotten here any earlier, I might have had quite a show."

Edmund glanced at him and reluctantly smiled. "I mean that you were too late to keep her dry."

Geoff didn't answer for a moment, only studied him a bit too closely. "She's getting to you."

Edmund hesitated, then said, "I cannot allow it."

"Why?"

"You know why." He had to remind himself that he hadn't told his friend about his plan to annul the marriage. He looked about and lowered his voice. "Some things have happened that cast doubt on her connection to the earl."

"I believe she's innocent, Edmund."

He lifted a hand. "I know your thoughts, but I have to be suspicious of everyone. The earl will only be happy with my defeat. But today Gwyneth talked to Prudence Atwater about my marriage to Elizabeth. She could have kept this a secret and continued to inquire about me behind my back. But she just . . . told me. And then the other day, she said things about Elizabeth's death, things the earl swore me to secrecy over."

"And what was that?"

"I cannot tell you—and it isn't because of my oath to the earl about her death. Elizabeth deserves some peace instead of being the butt of cruel jokes."

Geoff walked toward him. "How does this re-
late to Gwyneth?"

"If she is under the earl's control, I cannot believe he would have confided in her the details he
most feared would become public."

"Then you believe she's innocent too," Geoff
said with a relieved smile.

"I did not say that. She's simply given me cause
to wonder, and I'll remember that.

"You're giving her a chance, Edmund. Maybe
that's all she's asking for now."

When Geoff left him alone, Edmund dropped
his head to the horse's flank and tried to push
away the pain and pleasure he felt when he
thought of Gwyneth. They were all mixed up inside him.

Two days passed, and whenever Gwyneth
came upon Edmund, she would give him a secre-
tive smile, and to her pleasure, he returned it. It
was time for her to step up her efforts to seduce
him beyond simple kisses. She needed this marriage to be real, for her family—but mostly for
herself.

And when a daring idea came into her mind,
she spent the night awake and trembling, uncertain if she could do such a thing. Just before dawn,
she thought she was too much of a coward to try
it. But when the sun came up and she looked out
her window over the grounds that she already

considered home, her courage reasserted itself, and she ran to find Lucy.

As Edmund strode through the great hall after breaking his fast, Lucy caught up with him.

"Sir Edmund!" she called.

He turned to face her, wondering if this had anything to do with her mistress. "Aye?"

"Have ye seen Lady Blackwell?"

"Nay. I suggest you ask Mrs. Haskell."

"I already did, and milady has not been down yet. But when I try her door, 'tis locked, and she doesn't answer."

"Knock louder."

"I did! I'm worried for her, milord. 'Tis not like her."

For a moment, he wondered if the earl's plan could be for him to fall in love with his wife—and then lose her. The thought brought a strange feeling of bleakness and a need to hurry. "Very well, I shall go up with you. The door must be stuck, and she's probably sleeping soundly."

Lucy only whispered, "But she wouldn't do that."

When they stood before the door in the tower, Edmund lifted the latch and gave it a solid push, expecting difficulty. When it gave way easily, he stumbled forward into the room before he could catch himself.

Gwyneth was taking a bath before the hearth,

her damp hair piled on top of her head. He slowly straightened and stared at her. She was obviously ignoring him, because she raised one arm to soap its length. Water and soap bubbles slid down her shoulder to her chest. His gut tightened as he realized he could see one pert nipple glistening.

The door shut behind him, and he glanced over his shoulder to find Lucy gone. Then he knew this had all been planned.

Gwyneth gave a start and, wearing a trembling smile, glanced over her shoulder. She wasn't quite as good at seduction as she wanted to be, and something inside him softened.

"Edmund, what a lovely surprise so early in the morning."

His feet were rooted to the floor, but he managed to speak. "Hardly a surprise. This is a trap."

"A trap?"

She tipped her chin and ran the wet cloth down her neck. He watched its progress, unable to look away, even when the cloth slid through her hands and landed with a plop in the water. She frowned and fumbled for it.

"A trap implies evil intent," she continued after a moment. "There is no evil intent here. I just haven't seen much of you these past days."

"And you wanted to make sure I saw *all* of you." To his dismay, his voice had gone hoarse.

She smiled tentatively. The water lapped at the upper slopes of her breasts.

"Very well, you may leave if you must," she said softly. "But I've accidentally left my towel on the bed. Could you bring it to me first? Oh, and would you throw another couple of logs on the fire? I feel chilled."

Suppressing a groan, he deliberately kept his eyes on the hearth as he walked to it. With his back to Gwyneth, he built the fire higher, all the while listening as she dripped water from the parts of her body he was trying not to imagine.

He walked to the bed, picked up the towel, and turned around to hand it to her. She looked all soft and beautiful sitting there trembling before him, soap bubbles covering her body like clouds crossing a summer sun.

She was the perfect weapon to use against him, with her large doe eyes shining with hope. More and more she seemed too honest and innocent. But he couldn't know for certain. Elizabeth had been far too good at disguising her true self when he'd courted her.

This cruel contest between him and the earl seemed more pointless than ever before. He'd needed the money, but why had he felt the need to best a cruel old man? The only escape he could see was to give back the dowry and annul the marriage. But the thought of how she would look when he told her the truth sickened him.

Gwyneth couldn't breathe enough air. She was stunned by her own audacity, trembling with wonder that it might actually work. Finally she raised her gaze to see Edmund staring down into the tub. For just a moment, she saw the desire in his eyes. Then he shuttered them and dropped the towel onto a stool beside her. He braced his hands on the rim of the tub and leaned over her.

"This was cheating," he whispered. "Don't do it again."

He gave her a quick kiss, straightened, and left the room.

Cheating? This was hardly cheating. This was desperation, and she wasn't done yet. Not when things seemed to be going so well.

When he reached the winter parlor, Edmund sank into his chair and tried to pretend the image of Gwyneth was not the only thing he could see emblazoned on his mind. He was almost glad when Nell brought him a missive that had just arrived from the constable in Richmond—until he read it, of course. Harold Langston, the youngest son of the earl, was back in Yorkshire, in the Richmond jail to be precise. Another puzzle for the plot that was his life of late.

He was perusing the message when Gwyneth strolled in. Her hair was still damp and her cheeks were still pink. They stared at each other awkwardly until Nell brought in another bowl of porridge.

Gwyneth took it and sat down near his elbow. Mrs. Haskell entered next, filling their goblets with wine before retreating silently.

"What are you reading?" Gwyneth asked when they were alone.

"A missive from the Richmond constable. 'Tis about your cousin Harold."

She put down her spoon in surprise. "Elizabeth's brother?"

"He is in jail."

"Jail?"

"Does that surprise you?" he asked dryly.

"I only met him once or twice, but you mentioned before that you were familiar with him."

"He and his brother, Kenneth, were very instrumental in my marriage to their sister. Of course they didn't mean to be."

"I do not understand," she said slowly as she scrutinized him with her golden-brown eyes.

"Elizabeth told them that my friend Alex Thornton had compromised her and refused to marry her."

"You mentioned this before, but not in any detail. I'm confused as to why she would do such a thing."

"Alex's brother is a viscount, and the family is old and noble, with plenty of land and money. I was a landless knight. Reason enough in her mind."

His voice was a little sharper than he'd intended, but Gwyneth's eyes had gone soft and sad again, and she laid her hand on top of his.

"How did the truth come out?" she asked.

"They tried to kidnap Alex, steal from him, humiliate him for what he supposedly did to their sister. When I finally realized it was they who were following Alex about, I told them the truth. 'Tis how her family found out about me, and though they were angry, they had no choice but to agree to my offer of marriage." He slid his hand out from beneath Gwyneth's to eat, though his appetite had vanished. He hated having to tell her such a humiliating tale.

"Then why would Harold have the constable send news of his whereabouts to you?" she asked in surprise.

That was a perceptive question, one he couldn't give his true thoughts on.

"Perhaps because he is only twenty miles away and hundreds from his family. Perhaps he was coming here because his father sent him. I don't know. I only have to decide if I shall have him released from jail."

Gwyneth picked at her food. "Do you know why he's there?"

"The letter does not say."

"Then I should go with you."

He narrowed his eyes. "Why?"

"Because not only am I his cousin, it sounds like you might need me to help restrain your temper after all he's done to you."

He cocked a brow at her and leaned closer. "Do you think you could stop whatever I mean to do?"

"I can try. I certainly have no wish to visit you in jail."

"Gwyneth—"

"Oh, please allow me to come. Richmond seemed lovely, and perhaps I could look at some of the shops while you talk some sense into Harold."

He was about to refuse when he remembered where he was in their supposed relationship. He was giving her a chance, wasn't he? Getting to know her. This trip would even allow him to further his scrutiny of her.

And besides, why would she need to talk to a cousin she barely knew?

"We shan't spend the night," he said. "We can make it there and back between dawn and dusk. You might have only an hour to wander the town."

She smiled and lifted a spoonful of porridge. "That's fine. What are you going to do with Harold?"

"Send him on his way. I harbor no good will toward him."

When he rose to his feet, Gwyneth put a hand on his arm. "Edmund, I meant to ask you who I should see if I've discovered some"—she lowered her eyes and blushed—"linens missing after the laundry was done."

For a moment, his mind pictured the linens she was implying, and he wondered how intimate they were. His voice was husky when he spoke.

"The laundry maids, of course."

"They hung them on racks to dry in the laundry and haven't seen them since."

"Mrs. Haskell?"

"She's as baffled as I am."

"Question the rest of the servants, I guess."

"I shall do that," she murmured, looking almost worried. The she brightened. "When do we leave?"

"In the morning. Langston can spend another night in jail."

Chapter 13

⁓⌀⌀⁓

Gwyneth dressed in the morning still unable to believe she'd persuaded Edmund to take her with him. Her heart felt light, and she tried to think up other ways to maneuver him into kissing her. Sometimes it was easy to forget that she had another reason besides happiness to want a good marriage.

After breaking her fast, she took a basket of food for the journey out into the courtyard, only to see two saddled horses outside the stables. Edmund was adjusting the girth on The General.

Her steps slowed as she eyed the much smaller brown horse with a lovely white star on its forehead. Although she was nervous at the thought of riding solo, she was even more disappointed not to be riding in her husband's lap. Such closeness could only further their intimacy—which Edmund had seemed to realize. She gave a heavy sigh.

He must have caught her response, because he held up a hand. "You have to attempt this some-time. This is not an easy country to walk in."

"Can I not ride with you?" she asked.

"But then what will you have accomplished?" *Another kiss?*

He walked around to the other horse. "You've ridden The General at a hard gallop. Trotting this little pony will seem easy."

"'Tis not a little pony." She stiffened as the horse nudged her arm.

"She wants you to pet her."

Gwyneth awkwardly rubbed the animal's nose.

"She's a very gentle old girl," Edmund contin-ued. "She has birthed many a prize horse, and she does not startle easily. We'll take our time."

"'Tis a shame that Lydia's not here."

"Who?"

"My youngest sister. She's quite fond of ani-mals, and they used to follow her home. I am cer-tain she'd find some way to make me feel at ease."

"I can make you feel at ease." He finally noticed the basket and frowned. "Gwyneth, we shall be in Richmond before noon."

"I'd rather be prepared," she said quickly. "And I remembered to bring food you could put in a saddle bag."

He gave her a little half-smile that made her heart warm.

"Start handing things to me."

When they were all ready, he turned to help her mount the mare, but she backed away.

"Gwyneth?"

"I know I am being foolish, Edmund," she said, wearing a shaky smile.

"Try petting her."

He showed her how to stroke the horse's nose and the special place she liked between the ears.

"What is her name?"

"Star."

"Just what I would have picked." Gwyneth watched his gentleness with the animal and felt a sense of peace steal over her. She was so lucky to find a man like him to marry. It felt strange to owe Earl Langston her gratitude.

After having her feed a carrot to Star, he said, " 'Tis time to try mounting her. It would be easier for you to learn to control the horse when riding astride instead of perched on a sidesaddle." He smiled gently. "Trust me."

She used a stool to reach the stirrups and get up into the saddle. She was taller than Edmund like this and could see many people in the courtyard as they stopped to watch her. With a low groan, she closed her eyes.

"Hold onto the pommel," he instructed her as he adjusted the stirrups. "You won't fall."

" 'Tis not that. I just . . . feel very foolish learning to ride a horse at my age."

"Don't. I am proud that you're trying."

She couldn't imagine feeling better if he'd told her she was the most beautiful woman in the world.

He gave her some basic instructions about using her legs and the reins, then led her slowly about the courtyard as she became accustomed to sitting in the saddle.

"Do you know why horses frighten you?" he asked as he walked beside her.

She gripped the reins tightly. "I'm not sure. My father tells me that when I was a little girl, he used to put me up in the saddle, and I would ride about our farm."

"And you do not remember?"

"I had only seven years when we moved to London. But my mother thinks the true reason for my fear is really a sense of loss. She claims I cried for days when they had to sell that horse before we moved." She felt herself blushing, and she risked a glance at her husband. "Foolish, aye?"

"Nay, I do not think you're foolish at all."

They had stopped in the middle of the courtyard, and Edmund stood with his hand on Star's neck, looking up at her solemnly. She couldn't think of a thing to say, unless it was that she might be falling in love with him. And he certainly wouldn't want to hear that.

He finally stepped away from the horse. "Are you ready to try? I promise we'll start slowly."

She nodded and resolved to make him proud of her.

When they were finally on the road, with the castle dwindling in the distance, she began to let herself relax. The mare seemed content to travel at The General's side, with little guidance required from Gwyneth. It felt awkward to have her legs spread so wide, but she was certain she'd become used to it. Even when Edmund picked up the pace, she only clutched the pommel for a moment until she felt she wasn't going to fall off. She was beginning to feel quite proud of her new skill—and relieved.

They stopped to rest only once on the journey, and she felt a little stiff but otherwise fine. They reached Richmond just before the noon meal and entered through the town gates. Again she was struck by how pretty the town was, with its gray stone houses side by side on curving lanes running up the hillside. The streets were cobbled, but there was a line of sewage running down the middle of them.

At the tavern where they had dinner, Edmund asked for directions to the jail. On their way, they even passed the church where they were married. Gwyneth glanced at him, but he seemed not to realize the significance, and her shoulders drooped. But she was in this battle until victory was declared, and she would fight on.

The jail was a small, single-story building on a back street. There were bars in the window that they passed, and she shuddered when she heard two men yelling at each other from within. When they stopped out front, Edmund gave her a searching glance.

"You should visit the shops," he said. "There are some nearby, so you won't be too far away."

"Edmund, Harold is my cousin, and I might deal with him better than you can," she replied, holding onto the pommel. "The two of you have an unpleasant history."

"You do not know what he's capable of, Gwyneth. I'm not sure I want you exposed to his anger."

"You think he'll be angry that I married his sister's husband?"

He glanced at the jail. "I don't know."

"It is sweet of you to want to protect me, but I can handle this."

"I am not being sweet." He studied her for a moment, then shrugged. "Very well. But you must promise me that if I tell you to leave, you will do so immediately."

"I promise."

They found stables behind the jail, where they left their horses contentedly munching on hay. Gwyneth moved a little stiffly, but walking loosened her muscles. After they knocked on the front door, it was opened by the constable himself, a burly man wearing the red coat of his office, with a long black truncheon tucked into his belt.

"And who do ye be?" he asked in a growling voice.

"I am Sir Edmund Blackwell, lord of Castle Wintering. You sent me a missive about Harold Langston."

The man's grim expression lightened, and he gave a weary shake of his head. "So I did, Sir Edmund. Do come in."

"This is my wife, Lady Blackwell," Edmund said.

He put his hand on her lower back to guide her in, in that possessive way she so enjoyed. She looked about her at a bare room, with a scuffed wooden floor, a cupboard, several chests, benches, and a table scattered with paper. There was a faint, unpleasant smell she couldn't quite define.

The man doffed his cap to show a head of gray curls. "I'm Constable Bayler, milady."

"A pleasure to meet you, sir."

"Could you tell us what Langston has done?" Edmund asked.

"Causin' trouble in the local taverns mostly. In the last week, I've put him behind bars to sleep off a couple drunken revels, but he's begun damagin' property. The tavern owners banded together, and I was forced to bring charges."

"Has he seen the Justice of the Peace yet?"

The Constable nodded. "Sentenced him to a public flogging, which he's already had, and a few more days in jail, which end tomorrow."

Gwyneth was suddenly elated; they would have to stay the night in Richmond!

"That cannot be all," Edmund said, "or you would not have written to me."

"There's a fine to be paid for the damages."

"What happens if I choose not to pay?"

"He stays in jail until someone does. I admit, Sir Edmund, I'm hopin' ye'll take him off me hands. His temper is not an easy one."

Before her husband could say anything, Gwyneth touched his elbow. "We should pay it, Edmund. I would feel very guilty leaving my cousin in this place. It could take weeks for his parents to send money."

He looked at her with disapproval, but all he said was, "Constable Bayler, can you take me to see him?"

When the man nodded, Edmund looked down at her, but before he could speak, she quickly said, "I should like to come too. He is my cousin, and my presence might . . . soften things."

He sighed. "Are there other prisoners, Constable?"

The man shook his head.

"Very well, Gwyneth, but jail is not an easy thing to see."

Even with that warning, she was unprepared for the dreadful stench and the poorly lit cells with filthy straw covering the floor. She was certain that the straw was moving as things scurried beneath. Each door had bars for a window. When the constable stopped at her cousin's cell, all she could see was the corner of a rickety pallet.

Edmund felt himself getting angry as he neared Harold Langston. He didn't like the whole situation, especially Gwyneth being there. If he'd come alone, he would have left Langston to rot, but now he had to worry about her feminine sensibilities.

When Langston jumped to his feet and gripped the bars, his lank yellow hair fell into his eyes. "Are you releasing me?" When he saw Edmund, his jaw sagged for a moment before fury twisted his features. "Why didn't you just send money, you bastard? That's all I wanted from you."

Edmund folded his arms across his chest. "Have a care with your words, man. My wife is present."

Langston looked disdainfully at Gwyneth. "So you found a wench to marry you after you killed my sister."

Edmund was able to ignore the constable's sudden interested look, but Gwyneth didn't.

"Harold, what foolishness! Edmund did not kill your sister."

"And you believe everything he says?" Langston said with a sneer.

"I was there when she died. I am your cousin, Gwyneth Hall—now Blackwell. We met in London."

His gaze narrowed as he studied her. "I might have seen you before."

"I was your sister's companion, and I found her

body. It was an accidental death, as your father must have told you, but regardless, Edmund was in France when it happened."

Edmund wasn't sure how he felt about Gwyneth defending him. He took her hand and pulled her back to his side. "Gwyneth, allow me to handle this."

She nodded, although she didn't release his hand.

"Langston, the constable has told me of your crimes and your punishment. There is the matter of the fine before you can be released from jail."

"It will take weeks to contact my parents and have money brought here," Langston said sulkily, his face pressed against the bars.

"Aye, it will. If *I* pay the fine, you'll have to return to Castle Wintering to work off what you owe me." And Edmund could keep close guard over him.

"Work off—" He stopped and spat into the straw. "I'm not working for you, Blackwell."

"Harold," Gwyneth began in a reasonable voice, "I do not see that you have much choice. Edmund treats his servants fairly, and he would treat you the same."

Unlike the earl, Edmund thought, remembering how downtrodden the village had been when he'd first arrived with Elizabeth as his bride. "Langston, I certainly do not want you at the castle, and it suits me fine to leave you here. Enjoy the accommodations."

"All right, all right!" Langston yelled, when they headed to the door. "So pay it and release me."

Constable Bayler opened the door. "You have one more day of your sentence, Langston. You better hope Sir Edmund decides to come back for you on the morrow."

As they left the jail cell, Edmund could hear Langston cursing and thought the pallet might have hit the door.

"Beggin' your pardon, Lady Blackwell," the constable said. " 'Tis a shame ye had to see such a thing."

Gwyneth shook her head. "I come from London, constable. There are whole streets much worse than your jail."

She turned to look at Edmund, and he could see the excitement she was trying to repress. "Is there a nearby inn where we can spend the night?"

So that was it, he realized with dismay. He was going to be subjected to another attempt at a seduction he had to refuse, something that was getting more and more difficult. Pretending to give her a chance was making his life hell. He made arrangements to bring the money in the morning, then escorted Gwyneth outside.

She took a deep breath that ended with a relieved sigh.

Edmund gave a reluctant smile. "It is good to get away from the stench."

"I fear it is clinging to my garments."

He leaned down very near her ear and inhaled the scent of her hair. "I think you're safe."

She blushed and smiled up at him. "Shall we find an inn before we shop?"

"Shop?" he echoed with distaste.

Edmund could have kicked down the door to the bedchamber Gwyneth had rented at a small inn below Richmond Castle. He'd allowed her to make the room arrangements, while he stabled the horses. Naturally she'd taken only one chamber instead of two, and he knew he'd humiliate her if he went down and insisted on separate rooms.

So now he had to spend an entire night in the seductive company of Gwyneth, a woman using all of her ample capabilities to make this marriage real in every way. He'd encouraged her purchase of ribbons, fabric, and even a few spices for the kitchen, hoping she'd be distracted. But nothing had distracted him from the memory of her wet and naked in the tub.

After she followed him into the bedchamber, she set the packages on the table. "Is this not lovely?" she cried, looking about.

Edmund knew there was other furniture in the room, but all he saw was the massive bed with curtains hanging from the canopy for privacy. He began to perspire. "We should go down and have supper."

"I've already asked the innkeeper to send some up," she replied.

She wore a sweet smile that he knew must mask her triumph.

"Why don't you remove that travel-stained doublet?" she said, already reaching for the buttons on his chest. "I can brush the dirt out for you."

He backed away, and when he hit a chair, he sat down heavily. "I can manage to remove my own garments, Gwyneth."

Would you? her sparkling eyes seemed to say.

He tried to remember that he intended to find a new wife, but his current one was unlacing the small lace ruff about her throat. When she removed it and rolled her head with a sigh, he couldn't stop staring at how the delicate muscles of her throat met in the hollow between her collarbones. He wanted to press his mouth there and suck the sweetness of her, feel her pulse quicken to match his own. His heart seemed to roar within his chest, and already his loins felt afire after he'd been alone with her for only minutes. He would be dead by morning.

Someone knocked on the door, and when Gwyneth went to open it, Edmund slumped back in his chair with relief. A cheerful maidservant bustled in, setting a heavy tray on the table beside him. The aroma of good food spread through the room, and he tried to resurrect his appetite for something besides Gwyneth.

While they ate, she kept up a steady patter of

conversation that he only occasionally had to answer. He kept looking at the bed and hoping the floor was comfortable.

Gwyneth berated herself for talking so much, but didn't seem to be able to stop it. Edmund was barely a part of the conversation, and she felt that she had to do something to fill up the awkward silences. He hadn't been so uneasy with her in days—but she could guess why.

They were spending their first night alone together, and there was only one bed. She was alternately exhilarated and frightened. She didn't have the first idea how to make him consummate their marriage. If she came right out and asked him and he refused, it would be even worse than not knowing. So she decided to just carry on with her usual nighttime routine and see what developed.

When they were finished eating, she set the tray in the corridor beside their door and slowly straightened, rubbing an ache low in her back. Her legs were mildly sore, and she hoped the morning would not find her worse. When she turned around, Edmund had removed his black doublet and tossed it on the end of the bed. He knelt on one knee at the hearth to start a fire. Picking up his doublet and draping it across the back of a chair, she used her hands to brush out as much of the dirt as possible.

Then she stood in the center of the room, awkward and shy again, knowing all that was left to do was remove her clothing and climb into bed.

Chapter 14

For a wild moment, Gwyneth wondered what Edmund would do if she removed everything, then decided she couldn't bear the rejection. She would just have to wear her smock as a night rail and hope that he wished to remove it for her.

She wore a feminine version of a doublet, snug to her waist and ending in a point at her stomach. Though the sleeves were tied on at the armholes, she merely unbuttoned the front to remove it. Just as she was shrugging it off her shoulders to reveal her smock, he stood up before the fire and turned around. They both froze, staring at each other, and it took her a moment to remember what she'd been doing.

He didn't look away.

Lifting her chin, she unbuttoned her skirt and let it drop before picking it up and draping it over

228

the same chair. She removed the padded roll about her waist and followed it with two petticoats. She was wearing only the long-sleeved smock, which fell to her ankles. Edmund stared at her, making her unsteady from the warm languor stealing over her.

Not breaking his gaze, she sat down on one chair and propped her foot against the other chair. She pulled her smock back until her leg was exposed from the knee down. After untying her stocking from her garter, she slid it the length of her calf and off the end of her foot. When she turned to her other leg, this time she daringly let the folds of her smock slide toward her hips.

When she dropped the second stocking and both garters, she glanced up to find her husband staring at the floor, his hands fisted on his hips. Slowly she rose and started walking toward him. Would he allow her to touch him?

"I'll let you finish preparing for bed," he said in a hoarse voice, as he limped around her and out the door. "There is no need to wait for me."

As the door closed, Gwyneth felt a painful ache of defeat build in her chest before she overcame it with a renewed sense of determination. She crawled into the cold bed and pulled the blankets up, wiping away a single angry tear. She affected him, but that was only slight consolation. Somehow she had to make him forget Elizabeth—and the Langstons—and learn to trust her.

* * *

When it was past midnight, Edmund softly opened the door to their chamber. He had been careful not to drink too much, so the room only wavered instead of spun in the dying light of the fire.

Taking a deep breath, he turned and looked at the bed—and then wished he'd slept on a bench in the taproom. Gwyneth lay curled on her side facing the door, her arms clutching a pillow beneath her head. As he neared, he saw the faintest glistening of tearstains on her cheeks, and pain clenched tight about his heart. He hadn't meant to hurt her, had hoped she would be relieved to go home to her family. He had never imagined she could have feelings for him, feelings that seemed so real.

Torturing himself, he removed his boots and slid into bed beside her. He lay on his side so he could look into her slumbering face. With a shaking hand, he slid her hair back from her cheek, then gently caressed her soft skin. She murmured something, then rubbed her cheek against his hand.

Edmund pulled away and lay still, watching her, and felt that it was hours before he slept.

A rooster crowing in the courtyard beneath the window awakened Edmund. Still half asleep, he was warm and comfortable and at peace.

And then he felt the soft body burrowed into his side. Stiffening, he opened his eyes and glanced down at Gwyneth, whose head was tucked beneath his chin, her arm thrown across his chest, her breasts pressed into him. Her bent knee rode against his erection, and if he hadn't been fully clothed, he probably would have been inside her in an instant.

He pressed his free hand over his eyes and tried to think about anything else—calculations for the wall braces he was working on, the acreage of fields to plow in the coming weeks. But in her sleep, Gwyneth moaned and squirmed against him, and he held his breath to keep from groaning along with her.

Slowly he began to inch toward the edge of the bed. Her head slid from his shoulder to his arm, and suddenly she was awake. With a gasp, she lifted her head and looked the length of his body up into his face. Her hair was gloriously tousled about her face, and her wide eyes, framed with thick brown lashes, were almost golden in the low light. Her lips were parted, and he didn't even move his head when she leaned down to kiss him.

Stop! his mind cried, even as he caught her face with both hands to turn her head and deepen the kiss. With a swift movement he rolled her onto her back. His rational mind had succumbed to the onslaught, and all he could do was feel.

Caught in the passion of his kisses, Gwyneth lay still and marveled at her husband as he rose above her. His lips and tongue stroked and explored her mouth, then he was kissing her neck and biting her earlobe and suckling a path down to her shoulder. Somehow she knew his hand worked at the buttons between her breasts, and she thrilled to the knowledge that he desired her as much as she did him.

She felt a draft of air across her chest at the same moment that Edmund stopped kissing her. He looked down at where he'd pulled open her smock. Though her garment still covered everything else, she felt naked to his gaze, strangely shy, though he'd already seen much of her.

"Sweet Gwyneth," he whispered, and with the back of his hand, he stroked across the peak of one breast.

She quivered helplessly as her nipples tightened and ached.

"You are too beautiful," he whispered.

Then he lowered his head and took the tip into his mouth. She cried out and arched her back, pressing herself up to a wondrous sensation she'd never imagined feeling, hugging his dark head against her. While her hands stroked through his hair and down his shoulders, he rasped his tongue along her breasts, teasing each nipple until she shuddered and squirmed against the bed. This was magic and ecstasy and passion, and she pulled his shoulders down so that he might rest his body on hers. But he resisted.

As he licked slow circles across her breasts, she felt his hand sliding the smock up her legs. Though she quivered in longing for his touch, still she wanted to press her legs together in embarrassment, especially when he lifted his head to look at what he'd revealed.

He whispered her name again as he came down on his side and gave her a deep kiss before returning to her breasts. With his mouth tormenting her with slow strokes, she felt his hand sliding up her inner thigh, then brushing lightly across her curls. Any thought in her head was drowned out by sweeping passion and need. When his fingers slipped deeper, parting the folds of her flesh, she could only cry out and push her hips hard against his hand. He stroked and teased and caressed, even sliding a bit inside her, though that was slightly uncomfortable. And then his fingers found a spot that seemed to start a fire racing out to make every part of her body even more sensitive. He continued rubbing it and licking her nipples at the same time, until she was aching and wondering how she could find what her body was seeking.

Suddenly she froze as her feelings reached a violent crescendo that shuddered through her and made her rock under him. She said his name over and over again until the passion inside her lulled with contentment. Breathing hard, she opened her eyes and found him watching her with a soft gaze, his palm resting on her bare stomach, his upper body braced on his elbow.

"Edmund," she whispered.

He gave her a crooked grin that was so endearing, even as he slid her smock back over her knees, then closed her bodice.

"I have never felt anything like that." Tears pricked her eyes as she was overwhelmed by how much pleasure he'd given her. She started to sit up so that she could take him into her arms when a sudden twinge low in her back caught her by surprise.

His smile faded as he watched her face. "Gwyneth?"

She tried to bend her knees, and sharp pain made her muscles clench. "Edmund, forgive me, I'm suddenly . . . very sore. I was stiff yesterday, but I never thought—" She bit her lip.

He helped her to sit up, and it was all she could do not to moan when she lowered her legs over the side of the bed. She watched his gaze dip to the open front of her smock, and only then did she remember what they had not finished.

"Edmund, you—you didn't—we didn't—"

She reached for the buttons on his shirt, but he clasped her hands between his.

"No, Gwyneth, I wasn't sure either of us was ready for the next step anyway."

"But—"

"Do you not see? You rode a horse for the first time in a long while yesterday. I should have realized you'd be sore. I'm surprised you felt nothing earlier."

She blushed. "My mind was on . . . you."

"I shall go have a hot bath sent up. It will make you feel better for the trip home."

She couldn't help wincing at the thought. He laughed, a deep, wonderful sound that made her realize she *must* be falling in love with him.

"Do not worry so. You can ride home with me."

She gave him a trembling smile as he strode to the doorway. "Thank you, Edmund—for everything."

After a last searching look into her eyes, he left the room.

While Edmund watched two servants haul up a wooden tub and fill it with hot water, he couldn't keep his gaze from straying to his wife. Gwyneth had overwhelmed him with a passion he'd never imagined a woman could truly feel. He was incredibly thankful that she was saddle sore, because he'd almost made love to her and demolished every plan and suspicion he'd built for himself.

When the servants had gone, Gwyneth dropped the blanket she'd been holding about herself and struggled to her feet. She took a few painful-looking steps toward the tub, almost stumbling when she tried to pull her smock off. He crossed the room, quickly pulled the smock up and over her head, then swung her up into his arms. Before she could do more than gasp his name, he gently lowered her into the steaming tub. When the water didn't quite cover her breasts, he knew he had to leave.

"I shall go order food," he said. "Take your time." He moved a chair next to the tub, then piled it with towels and a ball of soft soap.

He made the mistake of looking at her, seeing her soft, grateful smile and the beaded moisture that clung to the curves of her breasts. He left as quickly as he could, then stumbled to a halt in the corridor and leaned back against the wall.

His determination was crumbling in ruins about him, and he tottered on the edge of abandoning it all. He couldn't imagine another wife in place of Gwyneth. Was this just what the earl wanted? Had the man known how irresistible Gwyneth would be to him?

And then he felt a cold sense of horror. Could *she* be in danger if he fell in love with her? The earl would easily go that far to make him suffer. He wished the man would just send an assassin, someone he could fight instead of having to play this shadow game that made him question everything.

When he returned an hour later, she was already dressed, though sitting in a chair, as if the process had taken a lot out of her. When she saw him, she smiled sweetly and blushed. Her long, golden hair hung free, the way he liked it, and he resisted the urge to touch it. Instead, he tortured himself by watching her eat.

"Did the bath help?" he finally asked.

She nodded. "I feel better, though I will admit that even the thought of riding Star makes me wince."

He smiled. "I shall not force you."

They left the inn and walked to the jail, holding their horses' reins. Each step was painful for his wife, so Edmund kept his pace slow. He paid the fine, then left Gwyneth with the constable while he went in to talk to the prisoner.

He pointed out the futility of trying to escape and was reluctantly impressed by Langston's anger that he should question his honor. Edmund refrained from asking if Langston had conveniently forgotten his honor the last time they'd tangled.

But that the man professed himself honor-bound to pay his debt did not make him a pleasant companion on the journey. Though he had already lost his horse in a wager, he grumbled about having to ride Gwyneth's mare.

When he discovered the reason that she was riding in Edmund's lap, he gave a superior sniff and said, "My sister, Elizabeth, was an excellent rider."

Edmund felt Gwyneth stiffen in his arms, but she made no response, and he was determined to follow her example. Traveling with Langston made him miss the pleasant conversation he and Gwyneth had shared the day before. She was easy to be with. But in their silence, he was free to remember the touch and taste of her, to imagine himself fulfilled inside her. Even her hand on his arm was erotic, and her backside rubbed repeatedly across his groin. Surely he was losing his mind in lust.

When they arrived at Castle Wintering at midafternoon, Edmund was distracted from his feverish thoughts seeing Prudence Atwater entering the stables. It had only been days ago that the woman had told Gwyneth she'd tried to seduce him. It was brave—or foolish—of her to visit her son here rather than in the village.

But he forgot about Prudence in the process of helping Gwyneth inside and finding Langston a decent chamber to sleep in. By the time he remembered the widow, she'd already been seen leaving the castle. Mrs. Haskell had not spoken to her but assured Edmund that the widow had friends among the servants that she could have been visiting, besides her son.

"Sir Edmund," Mrs. Haskell continued, as they stood alone in a corridor, "might I ask you another question?"

"Of course," he said, though his mind was already dwelling on what work he'd assign Langston.

"Did Lady Blackwell talk to you about the missing linens?"

"Aye."

"I've never been able to find them, which is a bit peculiar. And now I've discovered that some of the money I'd set aside for foodstuffs is gone."

That earned his attention. He narrowed his eyes as he looked at her. "Are you saying that we have a thief?"

She held up a hand. "I cannot imagine such a thing being so, my lord. Perhaps it is my own memory at fault."

"You've never struck me as the kind of woman with a faulty memory, Mrs. Haskell."

He thought she might actually be blushing.

"Thank you, my lord. I shall see what I can discover."

After she walked away, Edmund's first thought was that petty crime seemed beneath Earl Langston. The man went for something more elaborate and devious. But there was Prudence's visit. Damn, but he couldn't believe she'd be foolish enough to make mischief because of something that had never happened between them. And she'd come right out and told Gwyneth the truth. Not something a person with plans of revenge would do. But he'd keep an eye on her all the same.

Yet how many people could he keep watch over without missing something crucial?

That night, Gwyneth stood in the corridor outside Edmund's chamber, waiting for him. She'd taken another bath after supper to ease the continued soreness from horseback riding and felt ready. She tried not to pace with anxiety, but she didn't know what else to do. She had spent the entire day reliving how her husband had touched her that morning—every gentle caress, every demanding kiss. He knew how to awaken her body to what could exist between a man and a woman, feelings she'd never imagined. She blushed even remembering what he did to her—but not out of embarrassment. Never that. She wanted him to make her feel alive again, and she wanted to do the same thing for him. If only he'd allow her to touch him, to see everything beneath his garments. With a shudder, she closed her eyes and hugged herself as she imagined being held in those strong arms.

"Cold?"

Her eyes snapped open to find Edmund frowning down at her. He must have just followed her from the great hall.

"Nay, not cold," she whispered, then cleared her throat. "I—I wanted to talk to you. Might I come in?"

She saw his hesitation, the way his glance darted to the door and back to her. Then suddenly he cupped her face in his hands and made her look up at him.

"It was a mistake to move so quickly this morning, Gwyneth."

Her eyes widened in dismay.

"You won't be joining me in bed tonight."

She gripped his arms. "But Edmund, I want to be with you. Did I do something wrong? Did I make too much noise, or was I supposed to do more?"

"My God, it was nothing you did," he said. "You were . . . perfect. We both need more time, though you may not realize it. I have been married before, so trust me, I know what I'm talking about."

"I am not Elizabeth!" she said, with more anger than she'd known she felt.

He smiled and gently pushed her hair behind one ear. "Believe me, I know. Can you do this for me, Gwyneth? Trust me?"

"Of course I trust you. I just wish you'd trust me."

His smile faded, and as he cupped her cheek, she thought he looked almost wistful.

"I don't know if I can. A good night to you."

She stood still, even as he closed the door in her face. If it wasn't Elizabeth, then what made him distrust her so? Had bringing Harold Langston here only brought back even more memories of what the Langston family had done to him? First Elizabeth, then Harold, then the earl himself. Could Edmund only think of them, her relatives, when he looked into her eyes? How could she make him see only her?

She ran back up through the castle, stumbling because of the tears that burned in her eyes and only releasing them when she was safely in her chamber, in this beautiful room that felt cold and lonely without Edmund.

Chapter 15

*T*rust her?

Edmund wiped a hand down his face and continued pacing before the hearth. Gwyneth wanted his trust, as if it were something he could easily hand over. He braced his arms on the mantel and stared down into the fire.

Was this so difficult because he really *was* beginning to trust her? After all, he had only the deadly challenge from the earl to make him suspicious of everyone. What had Gwyneth ever done to make him doubt her?

Just the thought made his head hurt and his mouth go dry. Hadn't he learned his lesson by now—especially where her family was concerned?

He remembered her lying almost naked in bed that morning, willing to let him do whatever he

242

wanted with her. She wore goodness like a garment. And she seemed to trust him.

And he wanted to trust her, no matter how it would open him up to even more danger. More and more he wanted her in his bed and in his life. Saying no to his desires where she was concerned was becoming impossible. He couldn't think without his passion for her clouding his thoughts. He felt he was losing his judgment, his pride, and his sanity. He was at war with himself, because when he allowed himself to believe in her, he would be at the mercy of the earl, who could use this new weakness against him.

Edmund was awakened by a pounding on his door that did not sound as if it could be made by his dainty wife. He pulled on his breeches and flung wide the door, only to find a disheveled Geoff standing in the corridor.

"Edmund, you'd better come."

As his stomach clenched, he grabbed a shirt and pulled it over his head as he followed his friend. "What is it? Is Gwyneth all right?"

" 'Tis not Gwyneth but her cousin Harold."

Edmund almost groaned. He'd brought a Langston home and only had him watched by one guard. "Damn, what has he done?"

"Mrs. Haskell and a few of the kitchen maids decided to spend the night to get an early start on some baking project that they had planned for the workers tomorrow."

"The women actually decided to spend the night in *my* castle?" Edmund asked.

"I'm sure 'tis Gwyneth who makes them feel safe," Geoff said with a grin.

"Of course."

"I just caught Harold chasing one of the maid-servants through the great hall, trying to steal a kiss, or so he claims. She claims he invaded her bedchamber."

"And where was the soldier I had watch him?" Edmund's anger began to simmer.

"In the privy. I guess we'll need two men from now on. The girl said she wasn't touched badly. She's just afraid it will happen again—or something worse."

"The fool," Edmund said as they entered the great hall.

They found Mrs. Haskell, wearing a heavy dressing gown, with her arm around a girl dressed only in her smock. Harold Langston was sprawled in a chair before the fire, looking as if he was about to doze into a peaceful sleep. Behind him a sheepish-looking soldier whitened when he saw Edmund, though he came to attention. His jerkin was still caught in his breeches, giving evidence that he'd been interrupted.

Edmund ignored him and nodded to Mrs. Haskell and the maid. "Your name is Nell, is it not?"

The girl nodded and shyly ducked her head away from him.

"I am sorry this happened, Nell. Can you tell me your story?"

Before she began, he kicked Langston's legs, and the man bolted upright.

"Wha—" he yelled, then settled back when he saw who stood around him. "Nice staff, Blackwell."

Edmund knocked the chair out from under him, then hauled him up by the shirtfront until the man's toes only trailed through the rushes. He smelled strongly of ale. "You will listen to this recitation of your deeds, Langston."

Edmund nodded to Nell, who haltingly repeated what Geoff had already told him.

"Put me down, Blackwell," Langston said in a choked voice, his face reddening above Edmund's fists. "I did not harm her."

"Aye, but you intended to, and I will not stand for it. I'll take you back to the jail at dawn."

His eyes widened even as they started to bulge. "Nay! I p-promise it shan't happen again!"

Edmund shook him like a puppy before setting him roughly on the ground. He hauled him by the arm to Nell.

"Now say something to her."

Langston gulped air as he straightened his clothing, and his eyes showed a flash of immature anger. "I'm sorry, girl. It won't happen again."

Nell bobbed a nervous curtsy to the man who'd tried to attack her. She shot a quick smile at Edmund before running back into the servants' wing.

"Do you need me for anything else, Sir Edmund?" Mrs. Haskell asked.

As Langston shook off his hand and turned toward the fire, his shoulders slouched, Edmund shook his head. "Go find your bed, Mrs. Haskell. My thanks for your help. I shall see you in the morning."

Geoff followed the housekeeper out, turning about to grin at Edmund before leaving the great hall. When they were alone but for the soldier, Langston tried to walk away.

"Not yet," Edmund said. "I can see now that I made a mistake in not setting out the rules immediately."

"What rules? I work until the money is paid back—or until my parents send you the sum. I'm sending them a letter first thing," he said smugly.

"You do that. The sooner I have my money, the sooner I can be rid of you. But until then, you're to work for me for three months."

"Three months!" Langston said with belligerent defensiveness. "That fine was paltry, and surely my work is worth more than that! I say one month."

"Unless you are a skilled craftsman, you have no worth to me except as a strong back."

"I could train your soldiers."

"I have lieutenants with war experience for that. Have you even been in battle?"

His face reddened.

"I thought not. So what do you know how to do, besides chase helpless, frightened girls?"

"I thought she wanted me to!"

For a moment, Edmund saw shame and bewilderment in the young man's eyes. How old was he—had he even seen twenty years? And what else should he have expected from the son of Earl Langston?

"Then I have your word that this will not happen again?"

Langston nodded sulkily.

"Very well, I'll give you another chance. And you will work for three months. But if you cause trouble again, you shall live in the barracks with the soldiers."

He shuddered.

"Tomorrow I expect you up at dawn ready to work."

"What will I be doing?" he asked with fading bravado.

"For now, hauling masonry. We're repairing the castle walls."

"But—"

"Do not protest, or I'll set you to scrubbing privies."

He nodded hastily. "Might I return to my bedchamber now?"

"You may," Edmund said, watching as the man hurried from sight, followed by the guard.

* * *

Gwyneth was waiting for her husband when he came down to the morning meal. She gave him an easy smile and sat down at his elbow as if he had not upset her last night. She made some casual remarks about their journey to Richmond, hesitated, and then finally took a deep breath.

"Edmund, I received a letter from my family yesterday, the first since I've been here."

"You must have been relieved to hear from them."

"At first, yes. But I am so worried about them—especially for their future. My father's health is not good, although he always insists he is fine." She tried not to let her stinging eyes give way to tears. She was a failure as a wife and she did not want to be so as a daughter. "Edmund, might I ask you a favor?"

When he nodded, she wet her lips. "My sisters and I never had luck finding husbands because my father could offer no dowry. Well, that is not quite true, because there was a merchant interested in me."

He frowned. "You had a suitor?"

"He was as old as my father and felt he could use our noble connections to make his business more prosperous. He even offered money to my family."

"And the Langstons took this away from you."

She touched his arm and leaned toward him. "No, Edmund, you misunderstand. I didn't want to marry him. He only wanted me because of the earl and for my work in his shop and for—" She broke off, knowing she was blushing, but unable to stop herself. "And in his bed," she continued in a softer voice. "I almost married him for my family."

"And instead you were forced into a marriage with me."

"But I chose to accept," she said, seeing how remote his expression had become. "I was fortunate. That is why I'm asking for your help. If you could see your way to offering a small dowry to each of my sisters, then they, too, might have a chance to have good lives."

A few moments passed before he spoke. "Gwyneth, believe me when I say that if I could help, I would."

She felt her stomach clench, and the last of her hopes began to fade.

"But the only money I have is your dowry, and I have already spent most of it on the castle. The remainder I've set aside to help my people survive the winter."

"But . . . you've had this castle for several years. Why is there no other money?"

His expression hardened. "There was—once. And I trusted my steward with it. I thought he would want what was best for the future of the estate. But while Elizabeth was my wife, unbeknownst to me the Langstons controlled the steward."

"You mean Martin Fitzjames. You had Geoff replace him." She was almost afraid to talk, for fear he wouldn't explain.

He nodded. "Last year they funneled two years' worth of profits through him to their daughter. They pitied her, since she was married to me. By the time I returned from France, she had already spent it. I was forced to continue my mercenary work to keep the villagers fed after several years of bad harvests. The next time I returned, she was dead."

"And you were injured."

"Aye. And now I can do nothing but be a landowner and hope that the harvest is good."

Another part of the mystery of her husband was revealed, and it frightened her. She looked into his cold face, his remote eyes, saw the way his hands were clenched where they rested on the table. "Do you wish you could still fight?" she whispered, feeling the hatred inside him as a physical presence in the room.

"Every day. 'Tis all I know. 'Tis what I excel at."

"You've done good things here, Edmund," she said, taking one of his fists between her hands. "And you've done it all without violence. You just have to be patient. I know you'll succeed."

He looked down at their clasped hands, then back into her face.

"Perhaps your faith is misplaced," he said. "I cannot help your sisters."

"Aye, but you are already helping everyone

here. Did not Mrs. Haskell and a few of the maids spend the night? 'Tis a good sign."

"But staying here still put them in danger. Your cousin was found chasing Nell through the castle."

"Harold? Edmund, you don't mean—how could he possibly—"

"He claims he thought she was attracted to him. I told him the rules he must abide by, and he apologized to the girl. In fact, since he has not made an appearance, I shall have to roust him out of bed."

"Perhaps he has already risen and is hard at work."

He only grunted his response.

She smiled at him, then returned to a thought she'd had earlier. "What about Martin Fitzjames?"

"I asked him to leave, but he claims to have nowhere to go. Where Elizabeth was concerned, he says the Langstons threatened to kill him, so he had no choice but to follow their orders. Now he claims that if he leaves the safety of my lands, they'll follow through on their threat."

"You are generous to allow him to stay, even though he seemed angry about losing his steward position to Geoffrey."

"He was, which seems foolish, considering I could have banished him. But I put him in charge of organizing the foodstuffs and supplies that are already within the castle. He *seems* content."

"Seems?"

"I find it hard to believe that losing such a position of power is so easy for him."

Edmund listened to his own banter, the way he was delaying having to leave Gwyneth. He had barely slept the previous night. No matter how he resisted trusting her, he realized that he no longer believed she knew anything about the earl's plots. The revelation eased something deep inside him. She was a genuine, loving woman, and he didn't like seeing her sick with worry over her family. She was picking at her food absently, and when she looked at him, she seemed distant and preoccupied.

And the thought of her married to someone else had suddenly seemed intolerable. He was actually jealous of a man in her past. He could never send her back to London, where she'd once again be under the earl's control. He put away his notions of annulling this marriage, of finding another wife. He would defeat the earl another way, perhaps by exposing him for what he was when the old man finally revealed his intentions.

Gwyneth would remain married to *him*.

"Gwyneth?"

It took her a moment to focus on him, but when she did, her smile warmed him. "Aye?"

"I cannot help your sisters with money, but I could help another way. If your father is ill, he will not be able to work much longer, will he?"

Her smile faltered and her eyes glistened.

"He'll do what he needs to. And my sisters and my mother are very strong."

"If they are anything like you, then I have no doubt of that."

She was watching him closely now.

"Ask them to come here," he said simply.

The eyes he could lose himself in now went wide and uncomprehending—then full of so much hope that it was painful to watch.

"You—you want them to visit us? You would not mind?"

"They could live here permanently, if you would like them to. I could send several of the soldiers to deliver your letter and escort your family back here."

Her tears spilled over, and with a glad cry she flung her arms around his neck. Edmund sat back in his chair and let himself enjoy her body pressed so tightly to his. He patted her back awkwardly when he heard her breath catch on a sob and then tightened his arms about her.

"I have been so worried about them," she whispered against his neck.

"Then worry no more. When your letter is written, my men will be ready to leave."

Immediately she pushed herself to her feet. "I shall be finished in less than an hour."

He laughed. "I think it might take them a bit longer than that to prepare."

Pointing to the door, she said, "Then go tell

them!" She clapped a hand to her cheek. "We're starting to harvest the kitchen garden today—but we'll need to prepare chambers for my family. There is so much to do!"

She gave him a swift kiss and ran out of the room.

After she'd gone, the cold reality of what he'd done hit him. Was he putting her in danger by keeping her with him? Surely if he let himself fall in love with her, the earl would use her against him. He couldn't let that soft emotion touch him. It was better for her—and him.

As Gwyneth walked quickly through the great hall on her way to the kitchen, she took a moment to enjoy her wonder at Edmund's change of heart. She had begun to fear he would never banish the ghosts of the Langstons that seemed to hover between them. It was such a wonderful sign that he wanted her family to join them. Surely he was beginning to trust her at last.

And the relief of knowing that her parents and sisters would never know hunger or uncertainty again made tears of gratitude spill from her eyes. She wiped them away, feeling as if the shadows that had lurked around every corner were now banished. Castle Wintering was coming to life again.

If Edmund had any worries about experiencing tender feelings for his bride over the next fortnight, they were quickly dispelled. He only saw her at supper, when she was so tired she sometimes fell asleep with her head on her arm. She was opening up chambers that hadn't been touched in decades, since more and more of the servants needed rooms. She had them all busy preparing the castle for new residents. A constant hunt was on for furniture and more often than not, she was full of dirt and cobwebs from her searches through the undercroft below the main floor of the castle.

Edmund spent his days in the orchards overseeing the harvesting, and his nights frustratingly awake, trying to tell himself that if he actually managed to sleep with his wife, he wouldn't fall in love with her, that he wouldn't be the cause of even a moment of suffering for her.

At least the harvest was progressing on schedule, and he was pleasantly surprised at how well Harold Langston had begun to blend in. The accusations from Nell seemed to have changed him for the better, as if he'd never thought of his own arrogance before.

When a cold spell threatened and Edmund moved all the workers to the orchard, he often found Langston in the highest branches of an apple tree, doing the hardest, most dangerous work. He'd developed a legion of admirers, girls who probably liked his courtly manners and the proper way he talked. When dinner was called, he had companions on both sides of him.

Geoff informed him that Langston had even asked to spend a few hours training with the soldiers when he was able to find the time. With a sigh, Edmund allowed him an hour here and there.

While the harvest continued, Geoff occasionally took a few men out to explore every parcel of Edmund's land, searching for opportunities before winter arrived. Farther up in the Pennines, other landowners had discovered that mining could enrich a castle's coffers, and there was a chance Castle Wintering could benefit from the same.

Edmund wished he could enjoy the land's resurgence, but always he felt the need for vigilance. He made certain Geoff was training the soldiers harder than ever. They could not afford to be unprepared for an attack by Earl Langston.

It had begun, and there was no returning to safety. Being a traitor made one feel as if everyone were watching. Sir Edmund and Lady Blackwell had been the most generous of souls, and their repayment would be betrayal. The guilt was almost too much to bear and made the nights long and sleepless. But it was too late to stop—too dangerous to stop. The earl's instructions outlined the plan, and all that was left to do was follow it, but the fear was crippling and the risk of discovery ever nearer. Things were going to get worse.

* * *

On Sunday morning, when her family was due to arrive any day, Gwyneth persuaded Edmund to go to church with her. Mrs. Haskell had told her that there was to be a celebration on the village green afterward to give everyone a rest from the hard work of harvest. Gwyneth thought it would be good for her husband to make an appearance—and she convinced him of the same. She had realized that in her excitement over her parents' pending arrival she'd neglected him. Her plan to seduce him had given way to exhaustion, something she wasn't proud of.

The villagers stared in surprise when he limped into the church, but Gwyneth held his arm and smiled at all her new friends as they found their pew. After the service, everyone adjourned to the village green, where trestle tables and benches were being set up. The musicians were tuning their viols, the brewer was setting up a table to sell his ale, and another long table was turned into a banquet, the best dishes from every house in Swintongate.

Gwyneth had Edmund bring her basket from where she'd left it tied to Star.

He watched dourly as she pulled out pies and cakes. "I should have known you had something planned."

She smiled and patted his arm. "I only had plans for amusement. And is this not enjoyable?"

She slid her hand in his arm and gave him a little squeeze, leaning her head against him for a moment.

"Hmm," was all he said.

She looked around and was glad to see that the villagers were watching their intimate conversation with interest. She would make her husband a popular man by any means possible.

When the music started up, she stood at Edmund's side and clapped her hands. When he frowned down at her, she only grinned. "My mother taught me to dance, but I'll admit I have never done so except with my own sisters. They did say I was exceptionally talented at it."

She thought he would laugh, but his mood seemed to darken, and he swallowed a rather large mouthful of ale before giving her a short bow and walking away. Her gaze followed him, but she didn't allow her worry to show. If it was dancing that worried him, she would convince him later that night that a limp mattered little to her.

Gwyneth gladly accepted Geoffrey's offer to dance, and soon she was traded from one partner to the next song after song. When even Martin Fitzjames, the old steward, claimed her for a dance, and then her cousin Harold, she hoped Edmund was watching. Maybe he would see that his people were learning to put the past behind them.

When she finally sat out a dance, she saw her husband standing at the brewer's table, listening to something Prudence Atwater was saying.

Gwyneth wished she could hear what was going on, especially when the merry widow gave an angry toss of her head and walked away. Gwyneth couldn't help being curious, but she would not have Edmund think less of her by questioning him. But when Geoffrey sauntered over to Edmund and they both turned to watch the widow's departure, Gwyneth allowed herself to wander closer under the guise of examining the peddler's wares.

Edmund was shrugging. "I know not what she was thinking, Geoff. As if I would dance with her when I will not dance with my own wife."

"But now she's angry," Geoffrey said, smiling as he accepted a tankard of beer.

"I've angered her before."

"And you didn't feel the need to share it with me?"

"'Tis not something you need to know." Edmund drained his tankard and reached for another.

Gwyneth strolled away, relieved about Prudence but worried by how much her husband was drinking. She had hoped he would be drawn in by a country party, but still he kept himself on the fringes, talking little and wearing his ferocious frown. He wasn't going to make friends with the villagers like that.

Hugh Ludlow, the soldier Lucy had befriended, wasn't helping either, as he stood with a group of villagers. Gwyneth saw him deliberately turn his back to avoid having to talk to Edmund, and then when Edmund passed by, he seemed to be whispering something to his friends. Gwyneth strolled over to stand in their midst, and at least Hugh had the decency to seem embarrassed. After a moment of awkwardness, she pulled Lucy aside.

"Milady?" Lucy said uncertainly.

"Can you tell me what is going on with your Mr. Ludlow?"

"*My* Mr. Ludlow?"

"Is he saying unkind things about Edmund? If he is still angry that Geoffrey was promoted over him, I do so wish he would not involve the villagers."

"I swear to you, milady, that I'm makin' him see reason. And it *is* workin'. Just give me more time."

Gwyneth studied her friend's pale face. "Of course, Lucy. Thank you for your help."

But she watched her walk away and could not stop her nagging sense of worry. Was Hugh perhaps not the man Lucy should be with? Surely the girl would tell her if he were harming her in some way?

That evening, the servants all remained in Swintongate. Geoffrey and Harold disappeared rather quickly, leaving Gwyneth alone with Edmund in the great hall. She watched suspiciously as he swayed before the hearth. She'd never seen him overcome by drink before.

Walking up to his side, she slid her arm through his and looked up. "Edmund, I could teach you to dance. No one would care that you had to limp."

He smiled and shook his head. "I already know how to dance. I used to be quite good."

"Really?" she asked with delight, knowing he had to be drunk to compliment himself like that.

He arched a brow. "Do you doubt me?"

He caught her about the waist and whirled her out into the center of the great hall. Though his lame leg was awkward, his grace in fencing carried over into dance.

When they stumbled to a halt, she laughed and clutched his waist.

"I cannot do the leaps with a leg that won't bend," he said ruefully. "Such things were probably strange from a man my size anyway."

"I would have liked to have seen it," she said softly, not releasing him. She was thankful that he didn't seem too depressed by the party. In fact, he hadn't even pushed her away, which started her thinking about a drunken man's lack of inhibitions.

When he staggered and clutched the table for support, she said, "Let me help you to your bedchamber."

Chapter 16

"I am perfectly capable of walking," Edmund said.

He probably was unaware that his words were starting to slur together. Gwyneth noticed he didn't protest when she held him around his waist and pulled his arm over her shoulders. Together they walked down the corridor into the servants' wing, where she pushed open his door. He moved slower and slower, and she staggered under his weight once inside the room. Guiding him to the bed, she propped him against it. He sat on the edge, blinking at her, while she studied him.

"Let us begin by removing your garments," she said firmly.

When he said nothing, she allowed herself to relax and enjoy the chance to touch him as she'd always wanted to. She remembered their morning at the inn, when she'd been naked beneath his caresses. If she did the same thing to him, surely he wouldn't resist consummating their marriage then?

Working his boots off was difficult, but he managed to help by lifting his legs when she requested it. The stockings came next, and she saw a rough-looking scar that snaked down from higher up his leg. Although the room was lit only by firelight, she knew he watched her, felt his gaze never leave her face. After unbuttoning his doublet and pushing it back off his shoulders, she let her hands slide down his arms. He felt so big and warm and safe that she wanted to bury her face in his chest and smell the clean scent of him.

She settled for unbuttoning his shirt and spreading the neck, letting her fingers graze through the hair on his chest. He was too tall for her to pull the shirt over his head. Feeling brave and even seductive, she put her fingers on the buttons of his breeches then slowly opened them one by one. Her face felt hot, and she couldn't meet his eyes until the breeches sagged down his lean hips. Then she glanced at him, only to find him watching her hands instead of her face.

"Stand straight, Edmund."

He almost fell, but she caught him around the waist, even as his breeches dropped to the floor.

"You're still too tall," she whispered, sliding a stool closer and pushing him down onto it. He kept his right leg straight out to the side.

Their eyes were almost at the same level, and he watched her as she pulled his shirt up over his head. Her breath caught as she took a step backward to look at him. She'd seen his naked chest and arms, massively muscled and so impressive, and the small linen undergarment at his hips. He had long, heavy legs, well shaped until that last dreadful battle. Though the room was mostly shadows, she could see his misshapen knee and the painful-looking scars that cut across it.

When she touched the hard ridge of one scar on his thigh, he flinched and fumbled for her hand.

"Gwyneth, nay." His words weren't slurred so much as too slow and careful.

"I want to touch you," she whispered, evading his hand. Stepping between his spread thighs, she let her fingers trail up his skin ever closer to his hips.

Suddenly his head dipped, and he rested his forehead against her shoulder. "I don't want to hurt you," was his harsh whisper.

He'd said such words before, all in an attempt to elude her. But this time she heard a wealth of pain he was too drunk to disguise.

"You won't hurt me," she answered softly, sliding her hands up his neck and into his hair, stroking him.

He slung his arms about her waist and pulled her closer until his face was pressed between her breasts. "Whenever I came to Elizabeth's bedchamber, she cried."

Gwyneth cradled his head tighter against her, feeling an aching lump lodge in her throat. "What do you mean?"

"She never wanted me to touch her." He broke off, his voice muffled. "I stopped going to her. And she was happier."

She kissed his soft hair and then rested her cheek there. "I am not Elizabeth, as I keep telling you."

"I don't want to hurt you." It was a desperate whisper.

"My mother told me that as long as I relaxed and enjoyed your touch, it would hurt only the first time. I trust her, Edmund." She tilted his head up so that she could look into his eyes. "And I trust you. After how you touched me and cherished me in Richmond, I want nothing more than to give myself to you, to prove that you're wrong."

"But if I let myself love you, you'll be in danger." His voice suddenly grew hoarse, hesitant, and he again dropped his head to her shoulder. "I refuse to be the cause of that."

She frowned and stared down at him. Before she could ask him to explain what he meant, he slumped against her, and she staggered beneath the weight of his upper body.

"You're right next to the bed," she said into his ear. "Help me. I cannot do it alone."

She groaned as he seemed to press down on her in an effort to stand. Then he collapsed back on the bed, and she was able to help him swing his legs up. He lay on top of the coverlet, snoring softly now, but she found a blanket inside the chest at the foot of his bed. She looked at his body one last time, amazed at how well made he was. She imagined spending every night pressed against him, before with a sigh she covered him up to his chin.

Her plan to seduce him this night no longer mattered. She leaned against the edge of his bed and brushed the hair back from his face. Pressing her lips against his cheek and then his forehead, she berated herself for her selfish plan to make their marriage work only to help her family. There were so many more reasons why she wanted to have a good life with this man. She wanted to make him happy, she wanted to bear his children. She wanted him to love her as much as she loved him. She was certain he was falling in love with her; he had almost admitted it.

Surely his words about her being in danger were only the drink talking.

In the darkness before dawn, Edmund left his room, dressed in leather breeches, jerkin, and a heavy shirt for another day of backbreaking labor harvesting his crops. He was the master of this castle and controlled the bounty of all its lands— but he was trying to avoid his dainty wife.

He didn't remember exactly what he'd said to her the previous night. Words had seemed to pour out of another man instead of him, and now were unintelligible. But he knew she'd removed most of his clothing and put him to bed. He had a vivid memory of his face pressed between her breasts and a terrible suspicion that Elizabeth's name had come up. What had he said?

But he wasn't about to ask Gwyneth. All he could do was inwardly curse himself for getting drunk.

Yet she was there at his table in the winter parlor, smiling gently at him, warming the start of what was going to be a long day.

"A good morning to you, husband," she said.

The softness in her eyes pulled at him—yet made him uncomfortable too. "The same to you, Gwyneth."

He sat down and watched as she cut him a large slice of bread, then pushed a crock of butter toward him. He took a sip of ale and then began to speak before she could.

"I do not remember how I got to my bed last night. I hope I did nothing to embarrass myself."

He saw the flash of her disappointment, but she hid it quickly behind another smile.

"Edmund, you were ever the gentleman. I was the one who helped you to bed."

"I seldom drink like that." He spoke words, but all he was thinking about was that his wife had undressed him and he didn't even remember it.

"I know."

"Did I—what did I—never mind." He picked up the bread and pushed himself to his feet.

She reached for his free hand and held it. "You talked a little about Elizabeth."

Appalled that his memory was accurate, he stared down at her.

"But you won't want to talk about it again, will you?" she continued with a sigh.

He shook his head.

When he continued to just stare at her, worried about what he'd said and done, her smile grew broader and she stood up. She leaned lightly against him, her breasts so soft, her hips slight but rounded, and reached up to touch his cheek.

"I'll miss you today," she murmured.

Enthralled by her scent, by her touch, he leaned forward and brushed a kiss against her cheek; her fingers played in his hair. He almost groaned as he imagined swiping everything off the table and spreading her atop it as his feast. He turned his head and captured her mouth with his, hauling her up against him. He kissed her deeper and harder, memorizing the taste of her, saying with his need and frustration everything he didn't know how to say aloud. How had he thought he could ever give her up? Though he would have to guard his heart, he would take pleasure in her body and give her pleasure in return.

Though he was bound by a marriage contract to the Langston family, at least when a male heir came along, the land would not leave his descendants. That clause in the contract would be easily fulfilled, since he planned on keeping Gwyneth abed with him much of the time.

Only when he was having trouble breathing did he break the kiss and lean his forehead against hers, staring into her warm, gold-flecked eyes.

"I shall see you tonight," Edmund heard himself say in an unrecognizable voice.

Her smile widened, and she caressed his face. With a groan, he leaned down to kiss her again.

They both heard someone discreetly cough. Though Gwyneth started to push herself away, he held her against his side. They turned to find Geoff watching them, wearing a satisfied grin.

"Excuse me for the poorly timed interruption," he said, pulling out a chair and sitting down.

"It had better be important," Edmund answered, trying to sound stern, while still bestowing light caresses on Gwyneth's waist.

She squeezed his fingers and then broke away, saying breathlessly, "I'll allow you gentlemen to talk. I have so much to do."

She gave Edmund another brilliant smile as she left. He stood there staring after her, unable even to remember what he should be doing.

"Please tell me you've bedded your wife already."

He shot a frown at Geoff. "What did you say?"

"Any fool can see that she's in love with you."

Edmund gaped at his friend, then back at the door where Gwyneth had just disappeared. *In love with me?*

"That must mean you didn't bed her, right?" Geoff laughed at his own joke.

"Must I show you the way to the orchard?" Edmund pulled him up by the front of his doublet.

He only laughed harder. "My duty is to the soldiers, remember?"

"You have to eat this winter, remember? We're all picking fruit today."

After a long morning overseeing the harvesting of apples and pears, Edmund sat in the great hall with his aching feet stretched toward the fire. Behind him, the servants bustled between the kitchen and hall, preparing dinner for the weary laborers. Gwyneth hovered over him occasionally, but he sent her off to help Mrs. Haskell. Men and women slouched with exhaustion at the trestle tables, talking tiredly amongst themselves. When the harvest was all over, there would be a joyous celebration of relief.

Before he could sit down to a much-welcomed meal, he saw Geoff stride in, wearing a grim expression. Edmund stood up, even as the voices in the hall were lowered to murmurs, and Gwyneth came to his side.

"Geoff, what is it?"

His friend gave an angry shake of his head. "We've discovered holes in the roofs of a couple of the grain storage sheds. The rain a few days ago ruined some of the grain."

Edmund felt his gut tighten at this new threat to the health of his people. "How much did we lose?"

"Not too much. We should be all right."

Martin Fitzjames came over to the fire. "Sir Edmund, surely you knew to have the sheds examined before harvest."

Edmund felt his face redden even as the friendly eyes of his servants became suspicious. Though he'd worked hard here the past few years, he knew some people would always consider him a soldier, not a landowner.

"Be still, Fitzjames," Geoff said angrily. "Just a week ago Edmund ordered every shed examined for repairs. Those holes weren't there before, and I don't think they accidentally appeared."

Edmund ignored his old steward as well as the rumblings of dismay from the servants. "Geoff, I cannot believe someone would do such a thing deliberately. More likely an accident happened and the culprit is too ashamed to step forward. We shall set guards patrolling the sheds and barns. Come talk with me about scheduling it."

He drew Geoff closer to the hearth and lowered his voice. "You know what I really think, do you not?"

Geoff nodded, and the two of them looked casually over the great hall. Most people had gone about their business. Gwyneth did not hide her interest in their conversation, but she didn't attempt to join them.

"Such a thing doesn't happen accidentally, Edmund. Why would someone do this?"

"There's more you might not know about. Some linens and garments disappeared after laundry day, and then household money."

"A thief?"

"I thought so at first, but now I don't know."

"You cannot think the great Earl Langston would stoop to something so trivial."

"I never would have thought so, but the incidents are intensifying, are they not? And I'm worried about Gwyneth."

Geoff rolled his eyes. "I saw you kissing her. You can't still think she's involved."

"She *is* involved—because she's married to me. I'm worried she's in danger from that fact alone. Do not think the earl would hesitate to harm her just because they're cousins. Let us just be ever vigilant, even if it means more soldiers patrolling. I'd rather the villagers wonder what was going on than be left unprotected."

"Very well."

Geoff's smile was forced, and Edmund had never seen his unflappable friend so uneasy.

Gwyneth watched Edmund and Geoffrey until they separated to approach the tables laid out for dinner. She didn't know what they'd said, but she knew neither of them thought the holes in the sheds appeared by accident. Was Edmund's pride too great to allow him to show his worries to his wife?

She sat down beside him at the head table, pleased that he was eating with his people. The servants brought platters of meat for his choosing, and she waited to speak until he'd filled his plate and begun to eat.

"Edmund, 'tis a shame my father has not arrived by now. He could help."

"What?" he said distractedly.

When his eyes finally focused on her, she was pleased to see that he was staring at her mouth. She moistened her lips with her tongue.

"My father has spent many years guarding the wares of merchants in London. He has great experience in matters such as these."

"Such as what?"

"Whoever is chopping holes in sheds and stealing money."

He took another bite of lamb and chewed as he watched her. "Let it go, Gwyneth. Nothing is deliberate here."

She was almost angry that he was shutting her out, but all she said was, "Is it not?"

He smiled, and the pleasure of looking at his face mollified her. She leaned closer to him.

He sipped his beer. "So you think your father can ferret out some kind of truth here?"

She nodded with confidence.

"You seem to believe everyone in your family is skilled in some area."

"They are," she said slowly, not quite sure where he was going with this conversation.

"So what are you good at?"

She suppressed a little shiver at the way his low voice moved through her. In her mind she relived his kiss that morning and the way he'd promised to see her that night. "I am competent at many things."

He leaned closer. "But is there not one thing that gives you special pleasure?"

She opened her mouth, but could think of nothing clever to say. "Well, not just one thing," she murmured.

He rested his arm on the table, his shoulder brushing hers, his mouth near her cheek. "I think you're exceptionally good at kissing."

Chapter 17

— ✤ —

Gwyneth's breath caught and her heart sped up like a galloping horse. She knew everyone was openly staring, and still Edmund flirted with her.

"Children give me pleasure," she whispered.

His eyes widened, and wearing a half-smile, he straightened to continue eating. When his hand settled on her thigh, she quivered.

She knew he did this deliberately to make her forget her suspicions—and perhaps to make their marriage look real for his people. But oh, how such things gave her hope!

The double doors at the entrance to the great hall were suddenly flung open, and two soldiers strode in, throwing damp cloaks back from their shoulders to drape down their backs and catch on the swords at their waists.

"We've returned, Captain Blackwell," the one said with a smile. "We had good weather."

As Gwyneth realized what was happening, she pushed her chair back so quickly that it fell to the floor. Edmund smiled and nodded toward the main doors. She ran across the hall and out into the courtyard, where a gentle mist had begun to fall. She saw a covered cart piled with baggage and then a single coach behind, its doors swinging open as people jumped out.

"Mama! Papa!" she cried, waving her arms and jumping across puddles to reach them.

With shrieks, her sisters reached her first, and she was enveloped in warm, grateful hugs. Two months had not passed since she'd seen them, but she could not stop the happy tears that ran from her eyes.

Lydia, the youngest at fourteen, escaped the group embrace and stared up at Castle Wintering. "Why, Gwyn, 'tis just like the story of the princess! Has he rescued you yet?"

She laughed along with her sisters and then exchanged a fond smile with Caroline, the one closest in age to her. "I guess he did."

Caroline's smile was filled with relief, and Gwyneth put her arm around her.

"Truly, you are happy?" Caroline whispered.

"Oh, yes," Gwyneth breathed softly. "I think I love him already."

"I cannot wait to meet the man who put such

happiness in your eyes, Gwyn. Truly he must be wonderful to invite us all to live with you."

"Where are Mama and Papa?" Gwyneth asked.

Her smile faded. "Papa did not do so well on the journey. Mama must be helping him."

Gwyneth walked farther out into the courtyard where Athelina waited for their parents. The seventeen-year-old frowned up at the coach with the impatience of a girl who believes she can do everything quite well and wonders why others can't. She gave Gwyneth a distracted smile.

"Are they all right?" Gwyneth asked.

From the front bench, her mother leaned out of the coach window, wearing a relieved smile. "Gwyneth!"

"Mama, let me help."

"Nay, I am well. Help your father."

Athelina held open the door, while Caroline and Lydia came to help. Gwyneth reached up with both hands. Her father's head and shoulders emerged first as he peered out. Was his hair whiter than when she'd left? He was a tall man, once so broad-chested and strong, but now that was only a memory, as the outline of his bones seemed to slowly emerge from what used to be muscle. But he looked about the courtyard with his usual intent expression and then smiled down on her.

"Ah, Gwyneth, do move aside before I accidentally knock you down."

"Papa, you must be stiff from the long journey. Please take my hand."

"Allow me," said a deep voice behind her.

She felt Edmund's hand settle on her shoulder. She was able to watch her sisters turn as one and stare up at him with wide eyes and open mouths. Remembering how dark and frightening he'd appeared to her at first, she gave them all a reassuring smile and patted her husband's hand.

"Edmund, meet my family, especially my parents, Chester and Alyce Hall. Papa, Mama, this is my husband, Sir Edmund Blackwell."

Her mother, whose head was still at the window, smiled politely. "Good day, Sir Edmund."

Her father sat on the rear bench, though he could still lean out the door. "Sir Edmund, good to meet you. I am glad my daughter looks well."

Gwyneth laughed and leaned back against her husband, then glanced up at him. He wore a small smile, and perhaps only she could tell that he seemed almost . . . nervous. She was rather touched by that.

"He has taken good care of me, Papa. Now let him help you."

She stepped aside and watched her very tall husband put his hands inside the coach to steady her father. Papa took hold of his arms and managed to reach the ground easily. She'd once thought her father the tallest man in the world, but Edmund rose many inches above him.

"Edmund, allow me to introduce everyone to you."

He glanced up at the overcast sky, and only then did she realize that the mist was starting to soak through to her skin.

"Let us step inside first," he said, offering his arm to her mother.

She'd always known he had the manners of a nobleman, Gwyneth thought with delight as she watched her mother smile and walk at his side. Her father must have noticed Edmund's limp, but he said nothing. She held his arm and moved more slowly to accommodate his hesitant pace.

"How are you feeling, Papa?" she asked softly.

"Better now that I've seen your face. This is lovely countryside you live in, though the castle seems a bit . . . in need of work."

She laughed. "And Edmund is doing it. Wait until I show you all the things he's done."

He stopped and studied her. "I admit that you were often in my thoughts, but you look content, Gwyneth."

She squeezed his arm and leaned against his shoulder. "I am, Papa. He is a wonderful man."

"Then he has grown to love you?"

Her smile faltered. "I don't know. I can only hope so."

With the rain beginning to come down harder, Edmund knew he could not spend any time that

afternoon with Gwyneth's family. He left them to
their tours of the castle and his wife's pleasure in
settling them in the rooms she'd prepared. When
he returned that evening for supper, the frantic
pace of their arrival had settled into what he could
see was the relaxed routine of people who knew
and loved each other well.

He had supper surrounded by Gwyneth's family, and he found that conversation wasn't really
required of him. They had so many questions
about what her life was like, and he enjoyed listening to her responses. He had dreaded their arrival these past few weeks but found they were
not the kind of people who sat in judgment.
Gwyneth's happiness seemed enough for them,
and he wasn't quite sure how he'd earned the approving glances they gave him.

Her sisters were as lively as she was. Caroline
had pale blond hair and even paler skin, suggest-
ing that she was not always as healthy as she appeared now. Hadn't Gwyneth praised her sewing
skills? Lydia, the youngest, still had the energy of
childhood, and he often caught her staring at him.
He stared right back, and she only raised her eyebrows before looking away. He had the feeling she
wanted to stick out her tongue but considered
herself too old for that. Athelina, the middle sister,
seemed as though she could easily disappear between the winter beauty of Caroline and the in-
quisitive vibrancy of Lydia. She had the air of a

prim spinster—and hadn't Gwyneth thought she'd make a good teacher?

Lady Hall was plump and practical, ever watchful of her daughters—and the servants too. This was the woman who'd taught Gwyneth everything she knew and now seemed to be quietly rejoicing. He could only imagine how worried she must have been when Gwyneth had to leave them all for the harsh north and a stranger for a bridegroom.

Edmund did not mistake Sir Chester's frailty for weakness. He questioned Edmund about Castle Wintering's holdings and how far along they were with the harvest until Gwyneth, embarrassed by her father's directness, changed the topic of conversation. But Edmund found himself glancing at Sir Chester throughout the evening. There was a peacefulness about the man that was enviable. Edmund tried to tell himself that Sir Chester's contentment was because Edmund had now taken on the burden of the Hall family, but deep down he sensed that love had always been enough for them.

When the four sisters retreated to benches before the fire, Edmund decided to let the newcomers hear about Gwyneth's adventures in private. He said good night to everyone and then went out to the stables. He wasn't at all tired but needed some distraction. He had meant to go to his wife's bed and had spent the day imagining the ways they'd pleasure each other. But this night she would be preoccupied with her family. He could tell that her sisters were her closest friends, and they all had much to talk about.

He curried The General for a long time, then fed and watered him. He leaned his shoulder against the door frame and looked up at the castle, watching as lights went out in the many windows.

He'd never be able to sleep, but he might as well try.

In the great hall, a few servants lingered after they'd finished cleaning, talking in small groups. Edmund still found himself amazed at the smiles he now received, all since Gwyneth had come. She'd changed how everyone thought of him.

The servants' wing was lit by torches now that so many rooms were occupied. His own chamber was the last, and he approached it wearily. He pushed the door open, then stopped in astonishment.

Gwyneth was sitting in his tub before the hearth, her damp hair piled up on her head, one foot raised as she washed it. The drip of water off her fingers filled the silence.

She tilted her head to look at him and then gave him a smile. "Edmund, won't you close the door?"

He did so as if in a daze, then leaned back against it.

"I have nowhere else to sleep," she said softly.

He must have stared at her with stupid incomprehension, because her smile became tentative.

"I gave my chamber to my parents. I shall have to sleep here from now on."

As if in a dream, he walked to her and stopped at the edge of the tub. Although soap bubbles floated on the surface, he could see beneath the water easily. He stared at the lush roundness of her pink-tipped breasts, her delicate waist, the slim curve of her hips framing a triangle of golden-brown curls.

"I'll be done in a moment," she said.

"You're done now."

Gwyneth gasped as Edmund reached down into the tub and lifted her out of it. Water from her body soaked him, but he didn't seem to notice as he stared into her eyes.

This was the night, she realized with relieved delight. She was almost glad that they'd waited, because she felt only desire for her husband instead of fright. She looped her arms around his neck, watched as his gaze dropped to her wet breasts. With a gentleness that reassured her, he set her on the bed, and she dropped back on her elbows to look up at him. He put both hands into her hair and began pulling out the pins until the mass of wet hair fell about her shoulders and down her back. He looked at her, unmoving, for so long that she felt her whole body blushing. She shook her hair forward, meaning to cover herself.

"Nay!" He said the word almost harshly, and then whispered, "Just let me see you."

While she lay there naked, he began to remove

his garments with such haste that she heard a button pop at his neck. He threw them on the floor, never taking his gaze off her. As more and more of his skin was revealed, she felt her breathing become more difficult, knew her heartbeat had accelerated to a dizzying speed. When he was wearing only the narrow undergarment at his hips, he seemed to hesitate. His eyes locked with hers, and he let the last garment drop.

Gwyneth couldn't help staring at his penis, surrounded by dark, curling hair. It was larger than she had thought it would be, very different to look at, and it did seem rather amazing that it would fit inside her. Then she remembered how his first wife had behaved and knew why he hesitated. Smiling, she lifted her arms up to him.

With a groan, he came down on top of her, and she whispered his name in joy at the wonderful feeling of his hot skin on hers. Bracing himself on his elbows, he held her head while he kissed her hard, entering her mouth, sucking her tongue, nibbling at her lips. She felt his erection against her thighs, and in her fevered excitement, she parted her legs so that she could experience again what it felt like to have him touch her there. But instead of his hand, she felt his hips slide between, felt his heavy erection rub against her. She shuddered and cried out beneath his kiss, clasping him hard against her.

She was amazed to hear him chuckle.

"You are going too fast, Gwyn. We have all night."

"But I want—I need—"

He shushed her with kisses. "Right now I want and I need to taste you."

She lifted her head up and kissed him, then arched her back when his mouth traced her jaw and her neck.

Into her ear, he whispered, "There are other parts of you I want to taste."

Just the thought made her body shiver beneath his, and she moaned as his erection slid lower, rubbing against her in the most provocative way.

He echoed her moan as he began to work his way down her wet body with kisses. When his head was between her breasts, she hugged him to her. As he sucked her nipple into his mouth, she arched her back and offered up everything to him. She whispered his name over and over as his tongue teased her breasts. When he slid farther down her body, she felt bereft and tried to pull him back. He laughed at her, white teeth gleaming in the firelight, pale blue eyes shining, as most of his body dropped off the tall bed and he braced himself against the floor. Only his chest was between her legs, and even that slid away from her.

When he started kissing her inner thighs, she shuddered with each touch. He lifted her knees, pressing them up toward her chest, exposing her in a way that should have felt embarrassing but wasn't, because she trusted him so completely. When he kissed her there, letting his tongue part her flesh and swirl across her swollen wetness, she cried out his name and gave herself up to the passion that overwhelmed her.

When she finally came back to herself, sprawled so languorously beneath him, she realized that he was watching her face intently. She pulled on his arms, wanting him to come back onto the bed, onto her body, but he resisted.

"Edmund?" she whispered uncertainly.

And then she knew that still he worried about her, that maybe some part of him thought he'd hurt Elizabeth with his lovemaking. She would disabuse him of that notion. She'd only experienced half of a wife's pleasure, and she wanted it all.

"We're not done yet," she said firmly, sitting up. Her legs dangled over the edge of the bed, and he straightened as he stood between them. She reached out and took his penis in her hand.

She heard his breath leave him in a gasp, felt his erection pulse against her. He was hot and hard, yet silky soft, and she wanted to give him the same pleasure that he'd given her. With her free hand, she grasped his hip and pulled him toward her. When she bent her head, he groaned and held back.

"Gwyn, nay—not now. I couldn't—last." His words sounded hoarse and forced out of him.

"Then let us do it together." She slid both of her hands up his hard stomach and rubbed his nipples between her fingers. He groaned, obviously liking the feeling as much as she did. He pushed her back on the bed, and she scrambled into the center. He came up beside her, then over her, settling between her thighs, his large palms on either side of her head. It wasn't enough, so she lifted her knees to feel even more of him.

His breathing was harsh, his face looked pained, as she felt him probing her moist, swollen flesh. He slid inside her by slow increments, then back out again. He repeated the motion again and again, stretching her. She was mildly uncomfortable, but that was nothing compared to her frantic need to feel him inside her.

Desperate, she lifted her feet right off the bed, pressing her hips up toward him. He sank all the way inside her, filling her, and she gave a little gasp as pain blossomed and faded away.

Edmund straightened his elbows, looking down into her face with worry. "Did I hurt you?"

A slow grin widened her mouth and she shook her head. He was heavy and full inside her, and she loved it. She raised her arms over her head, reveling in the way his wide eyes watched her breasts. She trailed her foot along his backside, and he shuddered.

She almost cried out her disappointment when he slid out of her, but then he surged back inside her hard, making her slide up the bed. That wonderful ache began again low in her stomach, stroked into outright need with every thrust of his body. Soon she was pressed against the headboard, gasping his name, feeling more alive and aware of herself as a woman than she'd ever felt before.

This time she cried out with her climax, then could only hold onto him as he shuddered and released his seed inside her stroke after stroke.

Feeling as weak as a newborn lamb, Edmund lifted his chest off Gwyneth. He felt a little tremor in her muscles where she held his cock inside her. He groaned and moved slowly, knowing it wouldn't take much at all to make him come again.

"Edmund?"

He opened his eyes and suddenly realized he had forced her so hard against the headboard that her head was tilted to the side. With his hands beneath her hips and shoulders, he sat back on his heel, bringing her with him to the edge of the bed. While she straddled his lap, he managed to stay inside her. Laughing, she clutched his shoulders to lean back, with her hair dangling down past her hips.

He bent her even farther backward and tasted the sweetness of her breasts again. Even as she sighed, she ran her hands through his hair, and he turned to kiss her palm.

"You were right, Edmund," she said.

He pulled her upright until they were face to face. He moved gently inside, watching her exquisite expressions. He had never imagined a woman could enjoy sex this much or how it would make him feel to know that they gave each other pleasure. And he'd thought being married to her would be a hardship. "And what was I right about?" he murmured, kissing the sweet, soft spot behind her ear, inhaling the seductive scent that was all hers.

"If we'd done this on our wedding night, it would not have been the same."

He lifted his head and looked at her, shuddering when she rose up, then took him back inside. "Why?"

"We were strangers, and I was very nervous. I do not think I would have felt so"—she tilted his head back so she could kiss the hollow between his collarbones—"so free and comfortable with you."

Her tongue darted out to lick him, and he shuddered again. He would have enjoyed having sex with her on that first afternoon. But women were different. Though she was brave, he knew she'd been frightened marrying a stranger. She wouldn't have squirmed so joyously in his lap, not that first day. And it would only have been a release for him.

Guilt swept through him, leading his thoughts away from this pleasant encounter with his astonishingly passionate wife. She never had to know what he'd meant to do with their marriage, with her trust. The plan had existed only in his mind after all and had affected no one. She was even grateful that he'd waited to consummate their vows.

She squirmed again, and his guilt slipped away for the night. He lay back in his bed and taught his wife how to ride him.

Chapter 18

The most difficult thing Edmund ever had to do was lie in bed in the morning and watch his wife bathe in the cool bath water and dress. He knew she would be sore, and he'd even felt uneasy when he'd seen the spots of blood on her thighs. But he wanted to be inside her again, where it was hot and tight.

When she walked over to him, Edmund sat up and swung his legs over the side, pulling her against him. He nipped between her breasts with his teeth.

"I wish you would wear the gown you wore when we were married. I could uncover your breasts whenever I wanted to."

She laughed and rested her hands on his shoulders. "Would we not have to be in our bedchamber first?"

"I can think of a dozen places where we could find enough privacy for a quick viewing. In fact, you covered yourself far too quickly."

Gwyneth giggled as her husband unbuttoned her bodice and peered inside her gaping clothing. She barely resisted the urge to hug him close and tell him how much she loved him.

But that would have been foolish, because she was starting to know him too well. Although they'd just spent hours doing the most intimate things together, he'd never spoken words of love—or even trust. There was a part of him he held away from her, a distance she wished he wouldn't keep. She was glad that he had finally shared his bed with her, yet she wanted him to share his soul.

But there was all the time in the world for him to fall in love with her, and she considered their night together a wonderful start.

"I must leave," she said breathlessly, when he'd pulled her bodice wide and her smock down to take her nipple into his mouth.

"Wait a moment," he murmured against her.

Only when she was shuddering, bent back over his arm, as his tongue licked and tormented her, did she blurt out, "This is not fair."

He pulled her upright. "Not fair? How?"

"I feel . . . I feel all . . . restless inside."

He released her, and she stumbled back as he stood up, rising so tall above her. "Ah, then we shall feel the same thing all day until we're alone again. Of course, we could meet for a private dinner instead."

When he raised his eyebrows playfully, she burst into laughter. "I cannot. What would I say to my family on their first full day here?"

"So you mean we should have done this much sooner, when no one would have cared if we had disappeared for an hour in the middle of the day?"

"I wanted to, if you'll remember," she said sternly.

"And you are not going to let me forget, are you, my lady?"

He caught her to him and kissed her hard, and she showed all her love for him with her tight embrace. But he only smiled down at her and let her go.

Edmund felt distracted as he watched the masons begin their daily work on the wall. He should have been joining them, but instead he found himself wandering into the lady's garden, which Gwyneth had worked so hard on throughout the autumn. The sounds of men working seemed distant, muted, and instead he heard the call of chirping birds as they chased one another from tree limb to tree limb. Though most of the flowers were now gone, a few late-blooming daisies still shivered in the wind. He stared down at them and thought of his wife, who'd fought him for a real marriage as hard as these flowers fought the coming winter. And she'd won. She'd practically tamed him, made him choose her and an uncertain future.

He picked a daisy and stared at its stubborn petals. His body was pleasantly sated, his mind overcrowded with memories of her passion. He didn't hear anyone approaching until the crunch of boots on dead leaves. He glanced over his shoulder to see Geoff leaning against the gate. His friend wore a smile, but his gaze was more probing.

"You're picking flowers," Geoff said.

"Without thinking, I assure you," he replied, tossing the daisy onto a bench.

"Don't throw it away. Your wife might want a remembrance. This is the first morning after she made a true husband out of you."

Edmund frowned at him.

"Don't bother to deny it. And I haven't been spying on you either. I've seen Gwyneth's smile, and now I've seen you picking flowers. You could have written it on a banner across the great hall, and it wouldn't have been any clearer."

"Geoff—"

"Worry not, your shouts of pleasure did not echo through the castle."

Edmund rolled his eyes. "I am not worried. I am merely asking you to refrain from discussing what goes on between my wife and myself. After all, it is none of your concern."

"Ah, but it is my concern, because I brought it all about."

"Only if your name is Earl Langston."

"Who do you think made you jealous enough to feel protective of your wife?"

"Jealous?" Edmund asked, his eyebrows raised. "There is nothing to be jealous about, because she is my wife."

Geoff sauntered forward. " 'My wife.' I can hear the possessiveness even now. You can thank me any time."

"I do not see why—"

"For a man well renowned for his ability to bluff an enemy, your face has been a study in openness. All I had to do was bring a cloak out to her when it was raining or take her on a private tour of the estate or dance with her on the village green. You were *steeped* in jealousy, though to be fair, I don't think you knew it."

Though Edmund wanted to issue a sharp denial, Geoff's words had the ring of truth. "I remember being annoyed with you, not jealous."

"Ah, an admission of guilt."

He reluctantly smiled. "I suggest you go about your business."

"I'll let you get back to the daisies. Give Gwyneth my best wishes for a happy marriage."

Gwyneth found her mother and sisters in the kitchen, getting to know Mrs. Haskell and the rest of the staff. It pleased her that the two older women conversed easily, as if they might become friends. Even Lucy joined in the fun, for once acting more like a friend than a servant.

When Lydia put her hands on her hips and stared hard at Gwyneth, Gwyneth was amazed to see that her littlest sister was now taller than she was.

"Gwyn, you never showed us your room yesterday."

She felt herself blush and glanced at Mrs. Haskell, who was suddenly polishing a pot with great determination. Surely the woman had known that their marriage had had a shaky start.

"Lydia," her mother began in a warning voice.

"Nay, Mama, 'tis all right. Lydia, I wasn't certain my husband would want you to see our room. The castle was much worse when he first came here, so he took a room in the servants' wing."

"Good of him," Lydia said, nodding. "I like him."

"You barely know him," Gwyneth said with a smile.

Athelina studied her. "Neither did you when you married him. You did not talk about your wedding much in your letters."

"I was more concerned with Papa and all of you, I guess. My wedding was very small, at a church in Richmond. There were only a few people there. See—not much to tell," she finished brightly. She looked at Lucy, who returned her smile.

Caroline put her arm around Gwyneth's shoulder. "Regardless, you were very brave. Now come sit and break your fast with me."

Her sister led her out of the kitchen. The great hall was mostly deserted, as the servants were already about their business. Gwyneth knew she too had to get to the orchard, but she could spare a moment for her sister.

Caroline pulled her down on a bench, then broke a loaf of bread and handed her half. "So, do you like all the people here?"

"They've been very nice, especially Mrs. Haskell." She lowered her voice. "You must understand that when I first arrived, none of the servants would even spend the night in the castle. They were very afraid of Edmund."

"Did that have something to do with those rumors that he murdered Elizabeth?"

"Rumors only, and you know that. But see how things have changed! It feels like a home to me now."

"Did the soldiers feel the same as the servants?"

"No, they'd been with him in France. They trusted him. It just took me a little longer to do the same."

"What about his friend, Geoffrey Drake?"

With new attentiveness, Gwyneth studied Caroline. "Geoffrey is Edmund's good friend, and he's a very kind man."

"Is he?" Caroline asked innocently.

"He's handsome too, is he not?"

Her sister's face reddened, and she immediately began to eat with gusto. Gwyneth could only laugh.

Later that morning, while the kitchen staff was preparing dinner, Lucy pulled Gwyneth aside.

"Lady Blackwell—Gwyn—I just wanted to tell ye how . . . happy ye look."

Surprised, she could only stare down at the girl who was brave enough to travel all the way north with her. "Why, Lucy, what a sweet thing to say."

Lucy brushed the compliment aside. "I guess I just wanted to know if ye were happy in truth. Are ye?"

Her eyes were direct, and Gwyneth was touched that the girl took their friendship so seriously. "More and more every day. Are you trying to find out if it's all right for you to return to London?"

Her eyes widened. "Oh, no, milady. I am content here."

"And Hugh Ludlow is here," Gwyneth added.

Lucy's face went fiery red. "Aye . . . he's here too."

"Then we're both content."

Two weeks passed, and they were the happiest of Gwyneth's life. At night she lay in her husband's arms, experiencing his gentleness and passion, falling more and more in love with him every day. She knew she should be grateful and fulfilled—but always there was a nagging sense of incompleteness, a feeling that he was holding something back. She was not fool enough to think that he had left his anger with the Langston family behind, not when he believed the earl was responsible for the rumors about Elizabeth's death.

She made it a point to talk often to Edmund, to tell him of her life before their marriage, hoping that he would reveal something that would make her understand him better. He told her about his time in London with his friend Alex Thornton. She listened, fascinated, to the stories of the court parties he'd attended and how the ladies dressed. But every time he made a personal comment and she thought she was getting closer to him, he would give her his seductive, wicked smile, and she'd be mindless with passion again.

Her family accepted Edmund and their new life quite easily. They loved living in the country again, even though a colder autumn foreshadowed a bitter winter. Caroline and Athelina made friends in the village, while Lydia contented herself following Edmund about and getting in the soldiers' way. Instead of being angry, Edmund only teased her, and Gwyneth knew he'd made a lasting friend in her youngest sister.

Gwyneth should have known her idyllic time couldn't last. A flock of sheep was stolen, and when she heard about it, she followed Geoffrey and Edmund to her bedchamber after supper.

Without knocking, she pushed open the door and found the two men sitting at the small table, conversing.

Her husband frowned at her. "Gwyneth?"

She shut the door behind her and climbed up the short set of stairs to sit on the edge of the bed. While her feet dangled, the two men stared at her.

"I'd like to hear about the stolen sheep too," she said. "Go ahead, Geoffrey."

Smiling faintly, Geoffrey looked from her to Edmund and shook his head. "She deserves to hear this too. 'Tis her home now."

She could tell Edmund wanted her to leave but was too polite to throw her out—at least not in front of Geoffrey. She wished he wouldn't try to protect her.

Edmund sighed. "Go ahead, Geoff."

"There's not much more to say," he said. "I heard from the shepherds an hour ago that a flock of sheep disappeared during the night."

"Why did they not tell us this morning?"

He shrugged. "They thought the sheep might have just wandered off. So they searched the high pastures before coming to me."

"Edmund," Gwyneth said, "these occurrences are not accidents or something so easy to explain away. They *must* be deliberate."

Edmund glanced at her. "I will not deny that it seems evident that someone enjoys making mischief for Castle Wintering."

" 'Tis not just mischief," Geoffrey said.

"But who could be doing it? And why?" Gwyneth asked.

Edmund got to his feet and began to pace, as if his outrage would no longer allow him to sit still. The anger and frustration rolled off him, and she could sense he wished his sword were the only answer he needed. Though she admired his commanding figure, she hoped he would find a solution other than violence, something he'd had to give up since his injury. He could be killed, she thought bleakly. She ached for him, wishing there was another way.

When no one answered her question, Gwyneth offered her own response. "Who is angry with you, Edmund?"

He smiled wryly. "Someone is not?"

"*We're* not angry with you, are we, Geoffrey?" she asked, trying to lighten the somber mood.

Geoffrey shook his head playfully. "Not I. But perhaps being married to Edmund isn't as easy as you make it appear."

She sent her husband a secret smile. "Now, Geoffrey, you must understand that Sir Edmund Blackwell is not an easy man to live with. I have suffered great personal sacrifice to remain his wife."

While Geoffrey chuckled, Edmund advanced on her, and with a laugh, she scrambled backward on the bed until she sat in the middle of it. With sly eyes, she sent him a daring look. His smile faded, and his eyes smoldered beneath his dark brows, but with a shrug he turned back to Geoffrey.

The knight slumped back in his chair and folded his arms across his chest as he watched them. "Tell her the truth, Edmund."

Gwyneth caught her breath as she looked at them both.

"Geoff—" Edmund began, but she interrupted.

"He is right, Edmund," she said. "I would have to be a fool not to know that something is going on. I can bear the truth."

When her husband remained silent, Geoff leaned forward, wearing a serious expression. "Not knowing could get her hurt."

With a sigh, Edmund leaned back against the bed at her side. He took her hand and looked into her eyes. "There is more between me and Earl Langston than you already know. He used this marriage as a challenge, a duel between us, knowing that I could not refuse the dowry money. He told me outright that he means to ruin me but that I'll have to discover how on my own."

With every word he spoke, she felt a sickening sensation clamp down tighter on her stomach. "But . . . you know not what he has planned, or . . . what he'll do?"

Edmund shook his head. "Nay, but I think he has begun."

"With sheep?" she demanded in astonishment.

"Before that. I think he has someone under his

control living either here or in the village. It started with the stolen linens and money, and now 'tis sheep."

When he said nothing else, she clutched his hand tighter and whispered, "You think it's going to get worse, do you not?"

He nodded and put his arm around her, but she shrugged him off and slid off the bed to face them both, hands on her hips.

"Why did you not tell me this from the beginning? I would have been more aware of anything suspicious. I might have seen something and not known what I was looking at!"

"And you could have put yourself in danger," Edmund said.

"We're all in danger," she answered angrily. "Why would you not tell me what the earl was up to?"

When neither of them responded, the answer swept over her like a cold bath on a hot summer day, chilling her. She hugged herself and said, "Because you thought I might be involved."

Geoff reddened and looked away.

Edmund continued to watch her, his face inscrutable, like a soldier dealing with a difficult subordinate. She wanted to stay angry; if only it weren't so easy to understand why he'd suspected her.

"Gwyn, Langston *gave* you to me, though he hates me. I had to think there was a sinister reason for offering me a woman as wonderful as you."

Instead of saying more, he closed his mouth and appeared chagrined at what he'd revealed.

Her anger began to fade away, replaced by weariness. "I do understand. And I'm thankful that you now trust me enough to reveal the truth. But we still don't know who could be the earl's accomplice. We should make a list of people that he could easily sway. Edmund, did you tell Geoff about the Widow Atwater?"

Her husband shot her a warning look.

"Prudence Atwater?" Geoffrey said, his eyebrows raised. "Will's mother?"

Gwyneth reached for the bedpost and leaned against it. "She tried to seduce Edmund when he was still married to Elizabeth. He refused her, which did not make her happy."

"So that is why she is angry with you," Geoffrey said slowly.

"She is but a woman," Edmund said.

Gwyneth tilted her chin. "I could do any of the things that have been done to us so far. Most women could."

Edmund smiled. "I do not think these are enough reasons for Prudence to risk her life."

"Gentlemen, I still think the widow should be a suspect. And what about Hugh Ludlow? Was he not angry that you replaced him, Geoffrey?"

"And Martin Fitzjames," Edmund said. "You are his replacement too."

"At this rate, why isn't someone trying to kill *me*?" Geoffrey said dryly.

"Martin was a loyal servant of the Langstons," Edmund continued. "I know he said he feared for his life because of the earl's threats, but he could have been lying."

Gwyneth hesitated. "You said he was the one who gave Elizabeth the castle profits, did you not? Well, I had a conversation with Mrs. Haskell about who she believed started the rumors about Elizabeth's death."

"Gwyneth," Edmund began.

"I know—I should not be discussing such things behind your back, but the Langstons are my kinsmen, and I am embarrassed by their behavior. I had to know, and I trusted Mrs. Haskell to tell me."

"And what did she say?" her husband asked guardedly.

"She says the guilty person wasn't fool enough to tell her his lies, but in her opinion, it could only have been Mr. Fitzjames."

Edmund shrugged. "He was always my first choice. Who else had been proven to be under Langston control? Yet I felt that I would rather keep an eye on him than banish him from the estate and wonder how desperate that might make him."

Geoffrey grimaced perceptibly. "And speaking of the Langstons—"

"Harold," he said with a nod. "Getting himself put in jail might have been deliberate, so I'd have to come for him."

"I don't think he is a bad sort," Gwyneth said. "The servants tell me his arrogance has quite receded. I've actually had a pleasant conversation with him once or twice."

Edmund scowled but said nothing.

She went to stand beside him and linked her arm through his. "You have many potential enemies, Edmund, and that's just right here. Could there be others from your soldiering days, men who'd want to see you fail?"

"None that I've seen lurking about Swaledale. And I would have heard if strangers had come here to live. Geoff was keeping watch on a man who came to our wedding, then appeared on our land the next day, but he has not been seen again. For now, we shall concentrate on the people we've mentioned. Geoff, keep an eye on Ludlow, while I take Langston. We shall both watch Fitzjames."

"I did see Prudence at the castle recently," Gwyneth said. "I'll watch for her."

Edmund glanced down at her. "You are not to put yourself in danger, Gwyn."

She smiled and leaned against his shoulder. "I promise."

As they stared into each other's eyes, her smile died at the passion that she could read in him. As if from far away, she heard Geoff clear his throat and bid them a good evening, but then her senses forgot everything but the heat in Edmund's eyes and in his touch. Roughly he lifted her and set her on the edge of the bed, spread her legs and pressed himself against her, regardless of the garments bunched between them.

There was no slow fondling, no gentleness, only a feeling of sinful excitement. Kissing him deeply, she pulled her own skirt back and felt him unbuttoning his breeches. She started to slide back on the bed, but he only pulled her closer to the edge and entered her swiftly.

Moaning, she linked her legs about his hips, felt his hands slide up her thighs to cup her backside. She was no longer even resting on the bed but held to Edmund's body by his incredible strength. He lifted and brought her down over and over. She felt the tension in his thighs splayed beneath her, the hardness of his arms where she gripped him. The hot fever of release called to her, and the rubbing of his hips against hers made her blind to everything but her aching need. Edmund gave a final groan and buried himself deep inside her. Feeling the flexing of his muscles as he climaxed, she realized that she wasn't ready to join him.

She found herself dropped back onto the bed, his perspiring head resting against her neck.

Should she tell him she had not experienced . . . everything? But then he lifted his head and trailed his cheek along her bodice. She tensed, squirming against his penis still buried inside her. He lifted his laughing eyes to her and then gently bit her nipple through her garments. When she gasped, he nibbled at the other one and tweaked the first with his fingers.

"I am wearing too many clothes," she said, trailing off into a groan as he sucked hard on her nipple.

"I can work around such hardship," he murmured, and then reached between their bodies to stroke her.

With his mouth teasing her breasts, his hand pleasuring her, and his erection thrusting hard inside her, she erupted in a quick climax and smiled through her satisfied stupor as he did too.

Feet still braced on the floor, Edmund put his hands on the bed and looked down at her. "This did not make me totally mindless, Gwyn. You are to let Geoff and I deal with whoever is targeting me."

She gave him a slow smile and reached beneath his shirt to feel the hard muscles of his abdomen. "I hear you—although *I* am quite mindless. I am so mindless that you could easily take advantage of me again."

With a groan, he left her body and crawled up on the bed to sprawl on his back. "You are an insatiable woman."

A woman in love, she thought to herself. She just snuggled against his side and said a little prayer that someday her husband would fall in love with her.

When Gwyneth awoke the next morning, the sun was already well above the horizon and Edmund's side of the bed was cold. She stretched and then hugged herself, remembering the pleasurable hours she'd spent in her husband's arms. But there was much work to do, and how would she explain to her family why she'd overslept?

She madly dashed out of bed and was dressed in her smock and stockings before she noticed that something was on the floor. Frowning, she walked to the door, where a sheaf of papers now lay, as if someone had slipped them beneath the door while she slept. It must have been done after Edmund had left, for surely he would have picked them up otherwise. She set them on the table and continued to dress.

When she heard footsteps in the corridor, she ducked her head out to find Mrs. Haskell passing by.

"A good morning, my lady," the housekeeper said with a smile.

"The same to you, Mrs. Haskell. Could you tell me—did you see someone slide papers beneath my door?"

"Papers, my lady? What are they?"

She pointed to the table. "I have not read them yet, so I know not what they are."

"I saw nothing," the housekeeper said with a frown. "I can ask the maidservants."

"Nay, do not bother. I'm sure 'tis nothing important."

But suddenly she knew it *was* important, or someone would not have been so devious as to hide his or her identity.

"I am sorry to keep you from your duties, Mrs. Haskell. I shall come to the kitchen as soon as I'm ready."

She ducked back into her room to finish dressing while staring at the papers, feeling a looming sense of dread that she couldn't explain.

She finally sat down at the table and began to read. Someone had written a copy of the marriage contract that Edmund had signed. Instead of her father, Earl Langston had acted as her guardian, offering an impressive dowry.

But why would someone want her to read it now?

Glancing through it again, she stumbled on a clause that she'd only skimmed the first time. It stated that should Edmund die without a son, the castle and its lands would revert to the Langston family instead of going to an heir designated by him.

Was someone trying to warn her that if Edmund died, she'd be penniless again? But nothing was mentioned about his own money and any newly purchased land. Surely he would provide for her.

Then why was she supposed to read the contract, and who had made sure she did?

Even more confusing, why would the Langstons insist that Edmund have a son and put it in writing?

Gwyneth spent the day puzzling over her little mystery. Though she was careful to watch out for

Prudence Atwater, the woman never appeared, and Gwyneth's mind lingered over the contract as she waited for the evening, when she could discuss it in private with her husband.

She spent the day in the kitchen, preserving fruit from the orchard, hard work that left her fingers and back sore. That night her mother and sisters gathered before the fire in the great hall to sew together and exchange stories of the day. But she felt distant and preoccupied as she stood watching them from the kitchen corridor.

Suddenly an image came to mind of a firelit hearth in London and a grander home she'd visited often as a child. She remembered being a little girl, listening to her mother's many sisters gossip and laugh as they, too, spent an evening together.

Just like her own mother, her grandmother had never borne boys. And now that Gwyneth thought on it, none of her aunts had sons either.

Was this a pattern she had never seen but the Langstons had? Had they written the marriage contract with this in mind, knowing that her side of the family never had sons? Was this the way the earl meant to ruin her husband?

Married to her and denied a son, Edmund would lose everything he'd worked so hard for.

Chapter 19

Pleading a headache—which wasn't a lie—Gwyneth escaped to the quiet of her bedchamber to pace with ever-growing frustration and despair.

Had Edmund read the contract? Even if he had, surely he wouldn't understand what that one terrible clause could mean. She hadn't understood either until this moment. She had never thought about children in so mercenary a way. To her, they were a blessing. But to the Langstons, a girl child was nothing but revenge. She felt overwhelmed by hatred for the first time in her life.

The anxiety and despair she'd felt when Edmund wouldn't treat her like a wife came back in double strength. He'd maybe begun to love her a little, and now he might lose his land because of her family. He would surely set her aside if he found out she couldn't bear him a son.

This land, this castle, was everything to him. He wasn't a soldier any more. How would he feel if every improvement he'd made at Castle Wintering went into Langston coffers?

His legacy and future were at stake—but so were hers. She'd finally begun to help her family and see them settled. Even if her sisters never had dowries, they would not starve. Yet if she told Edmund what she suspected, her family would lose everything. He'd try to annul the marriage and give back the dowry, for surely he wouldn't want to risk forfeiting his land.

Honesty and trust—things she valued above all else. But now she'd have to break them. She would lie to Edmund and pray she'd be the first in her family to bear a son. Then her falsehood wouldn't matter, would it? After all, every woman had to trust in God that she'd bear a healthy child.

Gwyneth slid her arm about the bedpost and pressed her face against the cold wood, telling herself that she was doing the right thing. But a hollow, sick feeling had invaded her stomach. She was betraying a man who gave his trust so cautiously, so carefully. And it hurt.

Arms around her middle, she sat down on a chair and bent forward, as if she could keep her sobs buried inside her. They emerged as hot tears on her cheeks and a faint moan of despair. Had she been lying to herself all along? Had she insisted that it was her family, her sisters, she wanted to save when it was only a desire to protect herself?

Never in her life had she felt secure. Marriage to Edmund had staved off the oppression of poverty, the looming threat of starvation. Deep inside, a selfish, desperate part of her had wanted security for herself. Perhaps she was no better than her cousin Elizabeth. Gwyneth wanted Edmund's money too—and she would remain silent to keep it.

She had never imagined how worthless she could feel.

When Edmund came to bed, Gwyneth lay still, pretending to be asleep. She felt the mattress dip when he slid under the coverlet, closed her eyes in despair when he pressed up against her from behind. Still she didn't move, even when his arm slid about her waist.

"You are not asleep," he whispered into her ear.

She forced a smile onto her face and looked over her shoulder to find him braced on his elbow over her. "As if you would ever be fooled."

"Your mother said you were not feeling well." He slid his big hand over her stomach. "Could there be a very motherly reason?"

Chilled to the bone, she shook her head. " 'Tis surely too soon, Edmund."

"Then it must be because you have been working so hard. You are the lady of the castle. There is no need for you to spend every day in the orchard or in the kitchen."

"I cannot sit about while others work."

"Then humor me just for tomorrow. You are not well. Everyone will understand."

She opened her mouth, and he covered it with his hand.

"No protests. Sleep." He grinned down at her, then gave her a kiss. "Though it pains me greatly, even I can leave you alone for one night."

Gwyneth blinked rapidly, trying to repress the tears that stung her eyes because of Edmund's thoughtfulness. She didn't deserve it. He lay back on his pillow and moved away from her, leaving her strangely cold, even with the blankets piled on her. She could not begin to comprehend the depth of her sorrow if he never came to her bed again.

Edmund lay still, waiting for Gwyneth's breathing to slow. Something was wrong. There was a tension about her he'd never felt before. Surely it was only this illness.

Just the touch of her soft lips had made him want to forget her comfort and satisfy his desires. Instead, he slid farther away from her, so she would not notice how easily she aroused him.

But whatever was bothering her did not go away in the coming days. Her usual vibrancy and joy seemed flat. In bed at night, she abandoned herself to him feverishly yet afterward seemed almost sad.

Was she worried about being pregnant? The thought of her swollen with his child both frightened and lured him. He needed the security of a male heir, but he did not want to harm her. When he thought about losing her to childbirth, he felt sick inside. He couldn't imagine his life without her any more. What would be the purpose?

But a pregnant Gwyneth worried him, so he found himself searching for privacy to speak to her mother. After he saw Sir Chester enter the great hall early one morning, Edmund went up to the tower room. Lady Hall was already dressed and gladly welcomed him inside.

No longer did the chamber hold Elizabeth's angry ghost. He could only remember the image of Gwyneth sleeping here and how at the time he wished he could have too. Now he had her in his bed, and the consequences worried him.

"Lady Hall," he began.

She put up a hand to stop him. "Please, Edmund, you are my son by marriage. Do call me Alyce."

"Very well, Alyce," he said. "I thank you."

"You have made my daughter happy, and my gratitude for that will never end."

"*Is* she happy, Alyce? Do you think . . . a baby would make her happy?" He grimaced at his lack of subtlety, but he had no other way to bring up the subject.

Her eyes widened. "Only God can know such

things, my son. Has she said she carries your child? It would bring us all great joy."

"She has said nothing to me. I just . . . worry." He took a deep breath and then blurted out the truth. "I was a large baby, and my mother died birthing me. I wouldn't want—that is, I worry that—" He broke off, feeling foolish.

But Alyce gave him a warm smile and put her hand on his arm. "Your worry for my daughter touches me, Edmund. But we cannot live wondering what will happen every day of our lives. We have to enjoy life for what it is and cherish the good times we spend together. Besides, it will likely take Gwyneth many births before she has a baby boy."

"What do you mean? Surely 'tis God's will what sex the child is," he said, feeling a growing sense of unease.

"It is not easy for my family to have sons." She frowned. "In fact, all of my sisters had girls, who have since birthed daughters."

He opened his mouth, but he could think of nothing to say. That foolish clause in his marriage contract seemed to emblazon itself on his brain.

"But surely you, my son, will easily put this silly family curse to rest."

Family curse?

Edmund knew he smiled at her, knew he somehow took his leave, but he remembered little of it. He found himself climbing higher up into the castle until he was out on the battlements, overlooking the whole valley. The brisk wind chilled him and blew the last of the colorful leaves from the trees. The encroaching winter matched the bleakness that hovered over his soul.

Gwyneth's family only had girls. No wonder they were the poor branch of the Langston family. All their money had been given away in dowries generations ago.

It explained why Earl Langston had been almost cheerful as he handed over another wife and dowry to a man he hated. In his arrogance, Edmund had thought they could do nothing to harm him except damage his estate, and even then he would catch the culprit eventually.

But when he wouldn't sell them Castle Wintering, they had made sure it would come back to them someday.

He refused to believe that Gwyneth had known of this, not his innocent wife. She would have told him. How *could* she have known—surely the earl hadn't shown her the contract.

But he found himself striding down through the levels of the castle until he reached his bedchamber. He didn't have to worry that Gwyneth would find him. She was in the weaving room, off her feet, as he'd requested, but unable to keep her fingers idle. Pushing away his guilt at pawing through her things, he made himself look through her trunk.

At the bottom, he found a copy of their marriage contract. Since she was not the kind of woman who'd ignore such a document once it was in her possession, she'd certainly read it and knew the clause about having a son. How could she not know that her family only birthed girls? And yet she'd said nothing to him.

He got to his feet, letting the papers drop to the table and staring blankly at them. Why had she withheld the truth?

Edmund had always known that Gwyneth was desperate to become a true wife to him and that she needed his help for her family. After all, hadn't he married her for the money and the land? Perhaps she was just afraid to tell him. But that would mean she didn't trust him, yet she'd promised that she did.

And now he knew how she had felt that night so many weeks ago when he'd told her he didn't know if he could trust her. He had taken Gwyneth's trust for granted, and now it broke his heart to know she felt she couldn't confide in him about something that could damage their future.

The door suddenly opened, and he saw Mrs. Haskell give a start and put her hand to her chest.

"Do forgive me, Sir Edmund," she said. "I came in to change the bedsheets."

He nodded distractedly and looked back at the table.

"Sir Edmund, did Lady Blackwell ever find out who gave her those papers?"

He glanced at her sharply. "*These* papers?"

"Aye. A few days ago she asked me if I knew who had slipped them beneath the door."

"Did she say what they were?" he asked, feeling tension crackle through him.

"She had not read them when we spoke. Is it something important, my lord?"

"No, 'tis nothing. But I have work to do here. Could you change the bed later?"

With a nod, she left the room.

Edmund stared down at the papers again. So Gwyneth had only seen them for the first time a few days ago. Though he was relieved that she hadn't known from the beginning, why hadn't she told him the truth about her family when she read the contract? He saw now that he'd been right, that he couldn't trust this closeness between them. It was better to reserve a part of himself than to give it all to her.

He couldn't confront her; he needed to know if she meant to tell him the truth. He decided to wait and judge her by her actions. But her sadness was one answer, and he didn't know how to make it better without revealing his own.

He would keep some distance between them. But that proved very difficult to do. He was drawn to her like a frozen man to a fire. She had brought his entire castle to life, filled it with people who no longer feared him. She joined in every task, whether it was herding pigs out of the woods or helping hang the meat for smoking. She made him realize that success with the land was not as rewarding as success with his people.

Yet even that was melting away. When he could not find his unseen enemy, the mill was targeted next. People were forced to grind grain by hand over the week it took to fix the problem. The worry in their eyes only made his frustration and rage grow. Everything—including his marriage—seemed to be falling apart, and he couldn't stop it.

But nights were the worst. He had not made love to his wife since he'd discovered the truth about her family. Always there was a reason: her sickness, his exhaustion from the harvest. Because when Gwyneth lay in his arms, the pain he tried not to feel became unbearable. Did it hurt so much because he was falling in love with her and had sworn not to?

Earl Langston was sitting at his elaborately carved desk in his withdrawing chamber when his wife swept in, holding a bedraggled, folded piece of paper between two fingers.

"This arrived for you, my lord. The man insisted that I see it into your hands personally, and then he fled."

Langston arched a brow and set aside his quill, inspecting his fingers meticulously for ink before he reached out a hand to his wife. She gave him the missive with reluctance and stood there watching impatiently.

And then he saw the discreet identifying mark carefully drawn on a corner of the paper, and his anticipation increased.

"This is from our agent at Castle Wintering."

"Our agent?" she repeated. "Surely you can tell me the identity now."

"I cannot take that risk, my lady wife. If even one soul finds out—and you would brag to your sister before the day is out—all of my carefully laid plans could fall into ruin. Surely you understand that." He gave her the smile that always pacified her, even as he wondered how much longer he could bear to have her in London. He would have to send her to their Lincolnshire country house soon.

He broke the wax on the stained letter and then held it to his chest when Letitia leaned over the desk to read it.

"My lord—"

"Be patient," he said in a low voice tinged with the menace he knew cowed her.

She stiffened, then began to pace while he read. When he was done, he folded the letter, set it before him, and stared at it for several moments until his wife was gripping her skirts with frustration. Then he slowly began to smile, looking up at Letitia in triumph.

"'Tis all coming together," he said. "My plan has succeeded beyond what I'd hoped. Blackwell's control of the estate is slipping away because he's been unable to find the person responsible for the crimes. The villagers are about to revolt. My agent asks if we would come take control before the lawlessness gets out of hand."

She shared his grin. "It has not been three months yet, and already we have almost vanquished Blackwell. We can be mining for lead ore by spring. Who will you trust to go to Wintering?"

"I shan't trust a soul but ourselves, my lady wife. I must be there to enjoy Blackwell's defeat. How do you feel about spending a Christmas holiday in the wilds of Yorkshire with our son?"

Chapter 20

Gwyneth had never lived with a lie before, and it weighed on her soul. A cheerful demeanor was a chore, and pretending everything was fine wasn't going to work much longer. She knew her mother was watching her closely, and Caroline was giving her puzzled looks. Even her husband made excuses to keep his distance from her. If any of them actually questioned her, she knew the dam behind which she held back her tears would burst. Then they'd all know what kind of person she was: a liar.

She couldn't blame Edmund for his distraction. He was worried about the person jeopardizing their winter stores. There was violence inside him now as he plotted with Geoffrey for ways to catch the villain. It seemed to shimmer beneath his skin—a burning anger that she feared would turn on her if she told him the truth. She was such a coward.

Yet for all her self-preoccupation, she was the one who noticed Prudence Atwater sneaking into the castle just after most of the men had left to spend the day slaughtering pigs for winter meat. Gwyneth was so grateful to be distracted from her morbid thoughts that she followed the widow without alerting anyone to what she was doing. Prudence hurried down a corridor into a wing of the castle that wasn't repaired yet. Both of them had to stumble over rubble littering the floor. Prudence at least held a torch, while Gwyneth didn't dare grab one for fear of being seen.

When she lost sight of Prudence, Gwyneth peered around a corner in time to see a door being opened from the inside. She held her breath as Martin Fitzjames, the old steward, leaned out, grinned at the widow, and then pulled her inside.

Gwyneth leaned back against the wall in amazement. Were Prudence and Martin conspiring together? Fearing that they'd leave before she could return, she ran back the way she'd come as fast as she could, tripping over objects that had previously been illuminated by Prudence's torch.

When she finally found Mrs. Haskell, the woman's eyes widened when Gwyneth leaned out of breath against the kitchen wall.

"My lady!" she cried, grabbing her arm.

Gwyneth shook her head. "Forgive me—I am well. I forgot to tell Sir Edmund something, and I was trying to catch him. Do you know where he went?"

"The last I saw him, my lady, he and Sir Geoffrey were heading for the stables. Allow me to send one of the servants with a message."

"Nay, I shall do it myself. Thank you!"

As she approached the stables, Will Atwater was leaving. His eyes were big with worry, and suddenly she tried to imagine what his life would be like if his mother was proven guilty.

"Milady, ye don't want to go in there. His lordship is talkin' real serious to Sir Geoff, and they want to be alone."

"Thank you, Will, but they'll see me."

She found the two men engaged in an intense discussion. She didn't even want to know what it was about, just simply barged between them and looked up at Edmund.

"Prudence is here," she said, glancing back to the courtyard to make sure Will couldn't hear her. "I followed her into an unused section of the castle."

Edmund grasped her upper arms. "Gwyneth, I told you to be careful."

"I was. I did not approach her. But I saw her meet Mr. Fitzjames."

She watched the two men exchange glances over her head.

"Tell me where they are," Edmund said.

" 'Tis easier to show you. Follow me." Before he could protest, she left the stables, not bothering to make sure they were behind her. She was beyond caring how they must look, all marching across the courtyard in a line. She just wanted this over with, so Edmund's anger would fade. But how could things be the way they were, since she was lying to him?

Shoving the bleak thought aside, she concentrated on quieting her steps as they neared the room where Prudence and Martin were. At the last corner, she pointed to the chamber, and Edmund and Geoffrey moved into the lead. The three of them paused at the door, listening. When they heard a giggle, Gwyneth looked up at the men with wide eyes. Shrugging, Geoffrey slammed the door open.

As the two men moved in before her, she could see nothing but their broad shoulders. They came to a sudden stop, and she was able to squeeze between them in time to see Martin and Prudence in bed together, a single blanket clutched up to their chins. The room was bare of all else save cobwebs. In dead silence, they all gaped at one another.

At the same moment as Prudence began, "How dare ye—" Martin yelled, "'Tis not what you think!"

Biting her lip to keep from laughing, Gwyneth touched Edmund's arm and already felt some of his tension fading.

He raised a hand, and Martin and Prudence stuttered into silence. "Dress yourselves quickly, or in my impatience, I will toss you out into the courtyard however you're dressed. We will be waiting in the corridor."

The three of them trooped back out of the room. Gwyneth tried not to smile hearing frantic whispers and scrambling feet. Edmund and Geoffrey said nothing as they exchanged glances.

When the door flew open, Martin was standing there, the collar of his doublet half bent, his feet bare. Prudence sat on the edge of the bed fully dressed, her hands clutched together in her lap.

Edmund shouldered his way into the room, followed by Gwyneth and Geoffrey, and Martin hastily backed away to stand at Prudence's side.

"There was great secrecy to this meeting, Fitzjames."

Prudence's chin came up. "There be nothin' wrong with what we're doin'."

Martin shot her a pleading look. "Allow me to speak, Pru."

"Aye, please, do," Edmund said. "Many other things have been done in secret at Castle Wintering. Are the two of you conspiring against me?"

Martin's bewhiskered jaw sagged open. "Conspiring—surely you—" His voice trailed off as he looked between Prudence and Edmund. "My lord, we just want to be together and could find no privacy to do so. If you're talking about the crimes that have been committed lately against the castle, I can assure you that neither of us was involved in such things."

"And why should I believe you? You have made your feelings against me known."

"But my feelings were because of Pru!" he cried.

When the woman in question stared suspiciously at him, he addressed his words to her.

"Pru, I knew how you used to feel about him. I thought after his wife died, he'd stay away, and you would be mine. But then he returned. Naturally I was angry! I didn't want to lose you."

Prudence sighed. "Ye haven't lost me, Marty. All I want is a man to love me and take care of me. And that'll never be him."

Martin reached for her hand, and she smiled at him and rose to stand at his side.

Gwyneth stepped forward and looked at the widow. "Then why did I see you ask my husband to dance only weeks ago?"

Prudence blushed. "Just tryin' to make Marty jealous."

Martin leaned toward her, devotion shining from his eyes. "That wasn't necessary, my dove."

"That is enough," Edmund said, shaking his head. "Fitzjames, you were angry that I replaced you as steward."

The man shrugged. "I knew I'd miss the money, but that paled in comparison to the relief of not being hated any more."

"Hated?" Edmund echoed.

"How do you think it felt having to carry out the earl's dreadful orders? I had no wife, no friends. I was glad to give it up. And glad, too, to see you make this place come alive again, my lord."

"Even though I was a murderer?" Edmund asked impassively.

Martin's face paled. "It was me that said those things, my lord, you know that, don't you?"

"Aye."

"I couldn't . . . they wouldn't let me stop."

"Who?"

"Lord Langston. It was a horrible thing he made me do, and afterward I wrote and told him I was finished and that if he tried to harm me, I would make sure people found out what he'd been up to."

" 'Twas my idea," Prudence said with a proud lift of her chin. "The old earl never answered back, so we thought Marty was safe."

"I ask your forgiveness, Sir Edmund," Martin said, going down on one knee. "You have my allegiance, and you hold my fate in your hands."

Catching her breath, Gwyneth stared up at Edmund, whose face betrayed nothing. She had a good feeling about the lovers and believed they had both put their pasts behind them. But mayhap her husband needed more proof.

Edmund sighed. "I accept your apology. I suggest the two of you formalize this union or else find a safer place to meet. This section of the castle is dangerous. And do not speak of our discussion to anyone else. Do you understand?"

"Of course, my lord. Thank you!" Martin grinned at Prudence. "Do you want to get married, my dove?"

Prudence glanced at the three of them. "Perhaps ye could ask me at a more . . . romantic time?"

Geoffrey and Gwyneth filed into the corridor, and then Edmund pulled the door shut behind them. Gwyneth walked before the men, feeling relieved.

Edmund raised his torch higher. "You seem light in your step, wife."

Picking her way through the rubble, she glanced over her shoulder and smiled at him. "I am merely waiting for your congratulations."

"Congratulations?" He didn't smile back; rather, he stared at her intently.

"I did remove two suspects from your list, did I not?"

"That you did," Geoffrey agreed. "We thank you heartily, my lady."

"Oh, no thanks are necessary."

She heard Edmund grumble something.

"What was that, my lord?"

When they reached the great hall, she turned to face them.

"You performed admirably," he admitted.

Just looking up at him, remembering that things were no longer the same made her heart

give a painful shudder. She wanted that closeness back. She desperately wanted to have his
son. How to bridge this awkwardness she'd
caused?

She glanced from one man to the other. "What
were you two discussing so intently when I found
you in the stables?"

Edmund kept his face impassive, not wanting
to show how much he admired Gwyneth's pur-
suit of Prudence Atwater. "Nothing you need to
concern yourself with."

She put her fists on her hips and frowned up at
him, lovely as a brave kitten. He wanted to hold
her close, to ask why she would keep secrets
from him. He must love her, for his heart was
breaking.

Traitorous Geoff smiled at Gwyneth. "I've had
men high up in the dale, looking for lead ore. It's
been mined in these parts for centuries, so why
should Edmund's land be any different?"

"Did they find some?" she asked, her lovely
brown eyes alive with excitement.

"That they did. 'Tis Castle Wintering's future.
I've told Edmund where it is. Why don't the two
of you go look?"

Edmund opened his mouth to protest, but it
was too late. In their excitement, Gwyneth and
Geoff crossed the great hall. His wife picked up a
cloak from the chair by the door and wrapped
herself in it before stepping out into the courtyard.
He followed them.

The wind was cold, and the sky was muddy with clouds that hinted of snow.

"The weather might change, Gwyneth," Edmund said. "You should remain here."

Geoff entered the stables, but before she followed him, she turned back to face Edmund. "I want to be there with you for this. Mining could save our people, save our home, regardless of what this villain does."

Our home. He wanted to share it with her, but all he could think of was the Langstons taking back all his hard work someday. When he died, all of his daughters and Gwyneth would be left with nowhere to live. Why did she not say something, so they could make plans together?

But her eyes called to him, her body drew him, and he could only watch as Geoff brought out Star for her to ride.

Two hours later, Edmund led his wife into a small cave, from which a stream of water flowed down the hillside to join the River Swale. He could barely stand upright, and when Gwyneth joined him inside, they were pressed close together. He could feel her warmth, smell the flowery scent of her. It had been a week since he'd been inside her, a week without her passion.

She touched his arm. "Edmund, where is the ore?"

He pointed to the stream. "Buried here. We have to dam the water to see the veins. Then we keep digging into the hillside."

"This will help the castle, will it not?"

In the murky light, her eyes glittered. She pushed her cloak back from her shoulders, and he saw the curves of her breasts.

"Not this winter," he said hoarsely, fighting the worry that simmered inside him. "We'll have to ship it to the smelting mills in Richmond come spring."

"But if it's a good thing, why are you so upset?" When he said nothing, she nodded. "I know you're thinking of the crimes against the estate. Surely we're closer to discovering who is behind it."

"It has to be Harold Langston," he answered, transferring his anger to where it would do more good. "I want to shake the truth from him, to punish him with my fists before I send him back to jail."

"Edmund, nay," she said with dismay, grabbing the sleeves of his doublet as she leaned closer. "You mustn't. No one has seen who the villain is. And Harold is a trained knight, is he not? And you're—"

When she broke off, he laughed harshly. "And I am lame. Think you I cannot take that puppy, even like this?"

"I did not mean—I only wanted—" She pressed herself against him, reaching up to cup his face in her hands. "Edmund, please, this is torture for me. I only want to help."

"There is only one way you can help."

The words sounded angry, even to him, but it was anger with himself, for he could not keep from kissing her. She moaned beneath his mouth, and her hands slid from his waist up his back. He could feel her grip his garments with a desperation he knew too well.

"Aye," she whispered.

Her tongue tracing his lips induced a madness he no longer tried to control. She was his wife—he wanted her—she wanted him. He let passion thrust everything else aside. As his hands unlaced her gown at her back, he tasted her neck, sucked on her skin until she shuddered and moaned.

In a dazed voice, she asked, "Could someone see us?"

"Do you care?" He stared down into her eyes.

"No—just touch me, please."

But he didn't, not until he'd stripped every article of clothing from her body. She was fearless, and he admired that. He yanked at his own shirt, felt buttons at his neck pop free, and then let her hands push his aside. He couldn't wait, but she worked just as feverishly as he would have. And the feel of her hands pulling on him raised his desire to uncontrollable heights.

When they were both naked, he pulled her down onto the pile of their garments and spread her out for his viewing. She lay on her back, trembling, reaching for him, but he pressed her arms above her head with one hand and looked his fill. With his fingers, he skimmed her breasts and belly, and she moaned and writhed for him. He cupped the heat between her thighs, and though she was already wet for him, he stroked her anyway, needing to see in her eyes what he could make her feel, this thing between them that she couldn't deny.

He bent over her and suckled her breasts, still not allowing her to touch him. When she was so close that she couldn't stop shuddering, he came down between her legs and entered her in one hot thrust. They gasped against each other's mouth, and he felt her bare arms hugging his ribcage. As he braced himself on his arms to move inside her, her fingers teased his nipples. Her beautiful face was flushed; her breasts trembled with each movement of his body.

She was his, his body said, claiming her over and over. Nothing would separate them; he would find a way. He kissed her hard, and when he felt her woman's pleasure shudder about his cock, he poured his seed—their future—into her.

Gwyneth held back her cries, holding Edmund's body close against her. She took his frustration, his violent need for her inside her, made it a part of her. She wanted him focused on her, not on his quest to destroy Earl Langston.

"You don't have to prove anything to me,"

she whispered against the damp hair behind his ear.

He slowly lifted his head. "What?"

"I am worried for you." She pressed kisses to his chin, his cheek, and his lips. "I'm frightened where this villain is leading you."

"You think I am proving something to you?" he demanded with disbelief.

"Are you not? We can call the constable to deal with the earl and his son."

"They are trying to destroy what is mine." Edmund pulled out of her and got up on one knee. "I shall not stand back like a coward."

A chill of despair and anxiety deepened as she watched him floundering in his anger.

"Do you not understand?" He grabbed up his braies and breeches and pulled them on. "I have to do this alone, I have to prove—"

"To prove what—that you can kill again? That you are still a soldier?"

He froze, his shirt hanging from one hand, his eyes pale blue flame. "I care nothing about that. I have to protect what's mine. I have to protect *you!*"

Stunned, she fell back on her elbows to stare up at him.

"I will not let him destroy everything I've worked for, everything I want to leave to my children."

Her despair deepened into nausea. "Edmund, please—"

He pulled his shirt over his head. "What, Gwyneth? Please what?"

Her tears spilled over. She needed to tell him everything, but how could she say the words that would damn her in his eyes?

Chapter 21

⁓⟡⟡⁓

Gwyneth watched Edmund pull his doublet on and stride to the mouth of the cave, keeping his back to her as he looked out at the valley. She dressed herself, unable to stop crying. She couldn't lie to her husband for another minute. His anger had to be better than this horrible deception that hovered between them like a vulture.

"Edmund!"

He turned to face her as she approached him, holding her gown up at her shoulders, her cloak over her arm. Showing no emotion, he turned her about and laced up the back.

"Edmund." This time his name was but a whisper. When she looked into his beloved face, it was even harder to admit what she knew she must. "I have to tell you something."

His narrowed eyes studied her, but he said

nothing; instead he drew her out into the sunlight, took the cloak from her hands and wrapped it about her. The valley—their valley—spread out before them. Far in the distance was Castle Wintering, only a speck beside the sparkling river.

Taking a deep breath, she forced herself to gaze into his eyes. "Ten days ago, someone slid a copy of our marriage contract beneath our chamber door when I was in there alone. I cannot imagine who might have had a copy. I read it, but I still did not understand why someone wanted me to. It wasn't until I puzzled over the clause about everything reverting to the Langstons should we not have a son that I began to think. It never occurred to me before I read that contract, that—that there might be something wrong with my family."

His eyes remained impassive, even as she silently begged him to believe her.

"Only then did it dawn on me that my grandmother never had sons, my mother's sisters never had sons, and my parents never had a son. I realized that the earl must have figured this out long ago and decided to use it against you. And I felt . . . terrible." She rubbed her wet eyes, wishing desperately that he would say something.

"But even though you supposedly trust me, you did not confide in me."

"I was afraid you would set me aside! You are the most wonderful, gentle man, and I could not bear being parted from you. And I also could not help fearing for my family's welfare."

Edmund turned to look out over the valley. "When you discovered the purpose of the clause in our marriage contract, you could have told me immediately and given us both a chance to come up with a solution. Instead, you kept it hidden."

"But I'm telling you now!" she cried, pulling on his arm until he looked down at her. "I admit it was a mistake, but I was frightened of your reaction. I was worried you would annul our marriage if I couldn't bear a son. I couldn't do that to my family or to us. We had discovered something wonderful between us. I was praying every night that I would eventually give you the heir we need."

"I didn't want to trust you. I have never trusted many people, because when a hidden truth comes out, it always feels like betrayal."

"Edmund—"

"Allow me to finish. There's one more truth unsaid between us, and I see now that holding it back will only cause more harm. I've told you almost everything about this plot by Langston to ruin me except my own response to it. My plan was to earn enough money to pay back the dowry and annul our marriage. And then I was going to find another wife, one not connected to the Langstons."

His words were like a physical blow. Shocked and sick at heart, Gwyneth said, "Was that why you never came to my bed?"

Something flickered in his eyes, but he only nodded.

"It wasn't because we needed to know each other better or because you cared that I wasn't hurt?"

"I did not want to hurt you," Edmund said, his voice hoarse. "I thought you would be better off with your family, able to find a husband of your own choosing. I would have given you a settlement to see to your comfort."

"But I forced you to take me, didn't I," she said sadly. "That changed all of your plans."

"*I* changed my own plans. I could have resisted you. But I had thought we could make this marriage work, that we would have a son and then the contract wouldn't matter. But you didn't tell me the truth."

"It was just one lie," she whispered, "and only a few days old. But you've lied from the beginning, planning a temporary marriage when I wanted a real one."

Stunned by the truth of her words, Edmund knew in his heart that it was only hurt that made him speak, hurt he thought he'd never feel again. "I thought you were being forced to wed, that you would be better off without me."

Lifting her chin, she gave him a sad look. "You had your reasons to lie, and I had mine. Are you saying we can never trust each other? Isn't there a way past this?"

"Maybe there is, Gwyn, but I don't know how to do it. As you know from my first marriage, I didn't succeed before."

"Can we not begin again, to find love now that there are no secrets between us?"

"I will not put you aside, if that is what you're asking. I can become content again with this marriage, as I was before. But love?" How could he give her that power over him, when he didn't know if there was any trust left between them?

Her eyes filled with tears. "I love *you*."

She turned and fled from the mouth of the cave. She mounted Star and rode back to the castle, leaving him to follow on The General.

Could she honestly love him? If he let himself love her in return, she could hurt him worse than Elizabeth ever had.

Gwyneth had managed to compose her face before guiding Star into the courtyard. She gave a tired smile to the groom who took her horse, then entered the great hall, only to find everyone gathering for dinner. She wanted to run sobbing to her mother, but no one but herself could make this marriage work. She couldn't even regret what she'd told Edmund, because she'd finally spoken the truth. She loved him, and it was time he knew it.

Now that she understood him, she saw where his plan to defeat Earl Langston had come from.

He was a man who'd been rejected at every turn and saw only one way to make things better—all on his own. He had built his life on the ashes of his childhood poverty and then rebuilt it again after the Langstons had stolen his hard work. Why should he have trusted her when no one else had ever proven trustworthy? How could she make him see that he was an honorable man and that all she wanted to do was love him?

And how could she stop him from risking his life in a desperate plan of revenge against the Langstons?

Gwyneth went to sleep that night thinking that Edmund hadn't returned to the castle. But in the middle of the night, when someone pounded on their door, he was there beside her, a warmth she'd unconsciously burrowed into. He threw back the blankets and vaulted from the bed, and as she blearily sat up, she noticed he wore his breeches. He flung back the door to see Geoffrey, who was still tucking in his shirt.

"What is it?" her husband demanded.

"Edmund, one of the small sheds is afire, though 'tis not near the main barn. The alarm has already gone out to the workers here at the castle."

"I'm coming," he said grimly, shutting the door and picking up a shirt.

His face looked cold and empty—deadly. Feeling panic at the rage that must be building up inside him, Gwyneth slid out of bed and pulled on her dressing gown. "Edmund, please do not just assume this is another attack against us. This could be an accident."

"An accident?" he said with weary disbelief. "This *is* an attack, and I will not be made to look like the fool."

"But if you send for the constable instead of trying to deal with it yourself—"

"This is what I have been trained for, Gwyneth." He buttoned up his jerkin and bent to open up a coffer near the door.

She had never been so afraid in her life. He could never be the soldier he once was—but would he kill himself trying? Especially when he seemed so resigned. "Please, Edmund, you must listen to me. I'm so afraid for you."

He lifted his sword and the scabbard that covered it from the coffer. As he strapped it about his waist, the metal glittered in the firelight. Words failed her as she stared in horrified fascination.

"I thought I wanted more out of life than soldiering," he said in a low, husky voice. "But 'tis what I am good at."

"But not all," she cried, grabbing for his arm.

Edmund gently released her, even as he surrendered to the bloodlust of battle, which honed his senses and banished emotions from his thoughts. It made things easier.

He spent several hours fighting a fire in the bitter cold of December. If he could have found Harold Langston, he would have insisted he work at his side before putting him in jail.

At dawn, he returned to Castle Wintering to find Gwyneth and her family still in their night-clothes, waiting for him. The servants rushed to feed the other men who'd worked at his side, while his wife stared at him, wide-eyed, before taking his arm.

"Edmund, you're hurt," she said, reaching up to turn his head so that she could see his face.

" 'Tis nothing. I don't feel it."

"You will if that burn on your cheek worsens. Sit down and let me see what else is damaged."

He did as she requested, then watched her determination as she cleaned the wound on his face and one on the back of his hand.

In a low voice, he said, "Is Langston here? I was a fool to remove his guards."

She spared him only a quick glance, then returned to her work. "Mrs. Haskell said he was seen at the tavern last night, drinking."

"And who saw him?"

"Apparently one of the maidservants has begun a friendship with him."

"Do not tell me 'tis Nell, the girl I stopped him from attacking."

She shrugged as Mrs. Haskell set a tray of medicines at her side. "He always said he wasn't trying to hurt her. Apparently he was quite convincing in expressing his remorse." She looked into his eyes. "You know what I think about this whole matter."

" 'Send for the constable'—I know," he said heavily.

But before he could say anything more, the doors to the great hall were thrown back, and a tall stranger dressed for the cold entered.

"I need to speak with Sir Edmund Blackwell," he said to the first serving maid he saw.

Edmund stood up. "I am Sir Edmund. What is your errand?"

The man produced a sealed letter from inside his cloak. "For you, sir."

Edmund studied the elaborate script that his name was written in before glancing back up at the messenger. "Do you await a reply?" When the man shook his head, Edmund ordered a hot meal served to him and then walked over to sit before the fire and break the letter's seal.

Gwyneth followed him. "Who is it from?"

He spread the paper wide and frowned at the elaborate signature. "Your cousin the earl."

He glanced up to see her face whiten, but she said nothing until he'd read the letter.

"What does he want?"

"He says they are coming to spend the Christmas holidays with us—and their son, of course. Good timing, is it not?"

"Why would you say that? You despise them."

"Perhaps we can end this duel between him and me. Do you not you wish for that, Gwyneth?"

She nodded solemnly. "More than anything. But Edmund, what about Harold? Are you going to send for the constable?"

He sighed. "I shall look into the matter of where he was last night. If I find no definite proof that he was involved, I will wait until his parents arrive, when I can confront them all together. Christmas is only a few days away."

Gwyneth looked worried, but he knew no words would reassure her.

Chapter 22

❦

On Christmas morning, Gwyneth awoke alone, as usual. Edmund always left before dawn. She knew a holiday could not make everything right, especially not with Earl Langston due to arrive at any moment. But she had dreamed of her family warm and safe by Christmas, and since they were, she was determined to pretend everything was all right rather than worry them.

She had thrown herself into preparations for the season, decking every room in the castle with holly and ivy. Wonderful smells wafted from the kitchen for days as the feast was prepared. Last night, the Yule log, still dripping with snow, had been dragged into the great hall, and one of the woodsmen had been Harold Langston himself. Gwyneth had watched her husband most carefully, but all he'd done was smile as all the castle residents had gathered around the hearth to sing.

Though she'd gone to bed alone and awakened in the same state, he had been at her side through the night, which offered her comfort—and hope. She lifted his pillow to her face and breathed deeply of his scent and prayed that somehow on this glorious day she could magically make him love and trust her.

Hearing a soft knock at the door, Gwyneth drew on her dressing gown and opened it. When she saw Lucy's tentative smile, she drew the girl inside.

"So how is it being the consort of the Lord of Misrule?" Gwyneth asked, smiling. Hugh Ludlow had been elected by the villagers as the head of the Christmas festivities. Both Hugh and Lucy had become so much a part of Swintongate that Gwyneth assumed they'd soon be living there as husband and wife.

Lucy smiled tremulously, then dissolved into tears, throwing her arm over her eyes.

"What is it?" Gwyneth cried, ushering her friend to a chair before the fire. She pressed a handkerchief into Lucy's trembling hands and watched her mop her face. "Have you and Hugh had a quarrel?"

"Oh, 'tis not that, Gwyn. I fear I've done somethin' awful and ye'll never forgive me."

"You couldn't have done something as drastic as that," she said, pulling up the other chair to sit across from her friend. "Do tell me, so I can make you feel better."

"Nothin' can do that," Lucy wailed, burying her face in the handkerchief.

Gwyneth waited for her sobs to lessen. The girl finally composed herself and stared with anguish into Gwyneth's eyes.

"'Tis all me fault," she whispered, then hiccuped on a sob. "The earl is comin' because of me."

The first hint of worry settled in Gwyneth's stomach. "I do not understand."

"We sent him a letter, Hugh and me. We didn't know what else to do. We thought that surely Sir Edmund could deal with him!"

"Why did you send him a letter?"

"Because 'tis me who's at fault, me who persuaded Hugh to do these horrible deeds."

Gwyneth sat back in her chair and stared aghast at Lucy, whose tears dripped onto her bodice. "What are you saying?"

"I only came with ye to Yorkshire because the earl forced me to. He said he'd hurt me family if I didn't do what he wanted. He paid me so they wouldn't starve."

"You're behind all the problems we have had?" Gwyneth said in a faint voice.

"Me and Hugh," she whispered mournfully. "I hated every moment of it, but Gwyn, I had no choice! He threatened me parents! He told me he has someone nearby watchin' me, ready to kill me. I didn't know what to do! I . . . I persuaded

Hugh to help me when I saw how angry he was at Sir Edmund. We did only little things, though, didn't we? I tried not to hurt anyone. Say ye can forgive me, Gwyn."

"A fire is not a little thing," she said, feeling the sad heaviness of betrayal.

Lucy's tears started again. "Hugh set it where he thought no one would be, away from anythin' important, but we never thought about people comin' to put it out. Someone could have"—her sobs shook her chest—"d-died. I couldn't live with it any longer, even if the earl decides to kill me."

Gwyneth sighed and rubbed her eyes. "Edmund takes great pride in what he's accomplished at Castle Wintering, and you've tried to ruin it."

Lucy's face went sickly white, and she put her trembling hand to her mouth. "Do ye think he'll have us killed?"

Gwyneth frowned. "Have you learned nothing about him in all these months?"

"But I seen him angry over this, Gwyn, and I'm afraid."

"I will speak to him with you." She would calm Edmund's temper and make everything right. She *had* to.

"Could ye? We'd be so grateful, milady. I know things have not been . . . right between you and Sir Edmund, and 'tis my fault, too. Lord Langston told me to put those papers under your door just when ye seemed happiest. I don't know why, but it worked to make ye sad." More tears slid down her cheeks as she whispered, "I felt like I killed somethin' inside ye when I saw your face."

"You almost did," Gwyneth said gravely.

Lucy pulled another handkerchief from her sleeve and noisily blew her nose. "I know I don't deserve your help, but Hugh and me, we love each other and want to be married, but we don't know how to escape the earl. I know he's goin' to kill us!"

"How did you make him come all the way to Yorkshire?"

"We told him a lie, that the village was ready to revolt against Sir Edmund's rule, and that they needed to come take control. But 'tis not true, milady. If Hugh and me weren't makin' mischief, everyone would be happy with Sir Edmund. Do ye think he'll ever forgive us? Will you?" Her voice broke.

"I can't answer that now. Let me get dressed, and we'll both pay a visit to Mr. Ludlow."

Lucy brought Hugh to meet Gwyneth in the cold, bare lady's garden, where the burly young man twisted his hat in shame. He couldn't meet Gwyneth's eyes as she berated them both for not coming to her earlier.

Hugh cleared his throat. "Milady, can ye not keep our identities secret from Captain Blackwell? Surely he'll rest easy knowing it's all over now."

"I will not lie to my husband," she said sternly. *Not ever again.* "And it's not over, is it? I shall expect both of you to help me when the Langstons arrive. If only you'd told me this sooner. Did you think Sir Edmund could confront the earl without complete knowledge of what's happened?"

And she must have said that forcefully, because neither of them dared respond.

Gwyneth went back into the kitchen to help with the preparations for the feast, but all she could hope was that with this information, Edmund would be able to plan his confrontation with the Langstons. At the first opportunity, she would speak to him privately.

But the earl and his countess arrived at midmorning, before Gwyneth even saw her husband in passing.

With his arms across his chest, Edmund stood in the courtyard as a soft snow fell and watched his enemies arrive. They came in an elaborately decorated coach followed by a train of carts and wagons that stretched out through the gates. Shivering footmen climbed down stiffly from their perch at the back of the coach to open the door and help the occupants out.

The earl emerged first, dressed in a shimmering golden cloak, as if the queen would be in attendance at a Yorkshire Christmas. His wife came next, her face fixed in a dour frown and her arms clasped about herself, shivering. When they both saw him and barely masked their hatred, Edmund was even more determined to show them that their son's villainy had not succeeded, that Castle Wintering was full of happy people—especially the lord and lady. He was determined to win this challenge, but it was a hollow feeling.

He nodded instead of bowing. "A merry Christmas to you, Lord Langston."

"Hardly merry in such a harsh climate," the earl grumbled, sweeping past Edmund with his wife on his arm.

"Then 'tis a good thing I own this estate now."

The barb hit its mark when the earl stiffened but didn't look back.

Edmund followed them inside and watched Gwyneth lead her relatives away. Then he saw Alyce Hall standing inconspicuously to one side, as if she was avoiding her cousin.

"Alyce?" he said. "Is there something you need?"

"I have been waiting for you, Edmund." She smiled fondly and took his arm. "My three younger daughters and I have a gift for you, but I didn't want to wait until the New Year's celebration to give it to you."

"That is very generous," he answered, not seeing a package in her hands.

She laughed. "You have to come with me to receive it."

Arm in arm, they walked through the castle to the weaving room, which was empty because of the holiday. Alyce approached a cloth that was hanging on one wall and tugged it down to reveal a small tapestry. It had been woven and then embroidered, and he inhaled quickly as he realized it pictured Castle Wintering, the River Swale at its side, sparkling beneath the sun. There were shepherds guarding flocks on the hillside and people in the orchards. And at the gate, small but central, were two people—Gwyneth and himself, he realized. They were holding hands.

Amazed, Edmund reached out to touch the little figures.

At his side, Alyce said softly, "I've left room to add your children someday. We made this so you could see what you've done here."

He stared down at her, not knowing what to say.

"I give it to you now," she continued, "because I can sense that things are difficult between you and my daughter. She has not confided in me, so I can say little to help, except that no marriage is perfect. There will always be the occasional arguments, the disappointments. But as long as you love each other and talk about your differences and forgive each other—that is all that matters."

"You are a good woman, Alyce," Edmund said hoarsely.

"I would be honored if you would let me call you my son."

She put her small arms about him, and he felt

embraced by the mother's love he'd never thought to have.

An hour later, Gwyneth saw the earl and countess settled in the tower room her parents had graciously vacated. She left the Langstons to her parents' company, then escaped down to the kitchen, to the servants bustling with their preparations. She had just thought of an idea for how to deal with the Langstons.

"Mrs. Haskell," she called, "please do me a favor. Send people to every part of the castle. I need to speak with all the servants immediately."

In half an hour, the kitchen was full to bursting with serving maids, scullery boys, grooms, footmen, shepherds, and farm workers. More waited in the courtyard for the message to be passed back to them. Gwyneth stood upon a chair, and their merry conversations died into silence.

"I've called you all here because I have a favor to ask. I know things have been uneasy, since we have someone among us trying to make life difficult." She noticed that Lucy dropped her gaze. "But you must trust me when I say we have almost put it all behind us. The earl is here because he wants this land back, and he's done all he can to make sure my husband fails. Do you want him to be your lord again?"

There were immediate cries of "Nay!" and looks of worry and fear.

"Then help me—help us. Go out to Swinton-gate and invite everyone you know here for Christmas dinner. We need your support, but we only have three hours to fill the great hall. I promise all your doubts will be answered this day."

She watched in relief as people rushed out of the room in twos and threes, talking excitedly.

Edmund stood at the doors and watched with amazement as the whole village arrived at Castle Wintering for Christmas dinner. The hospitality of his household enveloped even the Langstons. Everywhere people toasted each other and the season. Beggars were brought in to eat with the residents of Wintering and Swintongate. Servants in red livery danced attendance. Tray upon tray of beef, lamb, and goose were laid across elegant tables covered in damask cloths. White breads and cheeses overflowed baskets. A peacock, roasted then sewn back up, complete with feathers and beak adorned the head table.

He realized how much Castle Wintering had changed in the few months of his marriage. It truly was the tapestry come to life. What had once been a decrepit, cavernous abode for one lonely man had become a healthy home for many. Amazed and relieved, he suddenly knew that he'd succeeded in his quest to become a landowner, lord of this castle. He'd allowed his frustration with what was really a small series of crimes to overshadow everything that had been accomplished at Castle Wintering. He could honestly say he'd helped better the lives of many people.

In the center of it all was his wife. Gwyneth moved among beggar and servant and guest with good-natured ease. Her authority was unquestioned, her kindness a certainty. Everything he enjoyed now was due to her. Even his dogs waited obediently in the corner for her attention.

He watched with pride as she greeted the earl and his wife with a polite curtsy. He hadn't had time to warn her of his plan to behave normally and see what the Langstons did. But without prompting, she played the joyous, loving wife so successfully that it made his chest tight with remorse. She slid her arm about his waist, and he rested his about her shoulders. He listened as she answered the countess's questions about the changes in the castle. She graciously introduced her sisters to the Langstons as if the girls had never been slighted by their wealthy relations.

He couldn't take his eyes off her, this fearless woman who'd braved a cold husband and a broken-down castle. He was staring in a besotted fashion into her lovely face when she stood on tiptoe and leaned toward him, her hand resting on his chest. His heart started pounding.

Staring with imploring eyes, she whispered, "Trust me—just this once. I have a plan. Pretend that you love me."

He could only nod, but his love wouldn't be

pretend. He could no longer lie to himself. Gwyneth had pierced his armor and found the heart he thought he lacked. He loved her, her warmth and compassion, her bravery in taking a man like him in marriage. His worries faded, and he let himself trust her completely, knowing that this was his only chance for the happiness he'd thought he didn't deserve. He'd been using his doubt and her small faults almost as a last barrier between himself and his wife, but no more. There would be mistakes aplenty between them in the coming years, but none they couldn't talk through.

Before they could all sit down for Christmas dinner, there was another commotion out in the courtyard. When the doors were again thrown back, in strode Alexander Thornton, the man whose family had saved Edmund from poverty. Through a wager, Alex had led Edmund to Elizabeth—and through her to Gwyneth. Alex's wife, Emmeline, carried their year-old son, Nicholas.

"Edmund!" Alex called, stepping forward to shake his hand. "We made it in time."

Edmund returned his grip and stared uncomprehending at Gwyneth.

She shrugged and smiled ruefully. "He's one of my presents to you."

He grinned at her, and she blushed.

Alex turned to give her his usual scoundrel's look. "So this is your wife, Edmund. How did someone like you become so lucky? And when are you going to introduce us?"

Edmund laughed, even as he hugged Gwyneth to him. "This is my bride, Gwyneth, who has made our first Christmas together very memorable indeed." He gave her a quick kiss, and her smile grew even more brilliant than he'd imagined. The light from hundreds of candles was reflected in the sheen of her eyes.

"Lady Emmeline," Gwyneth said, "could I hold the baby for you while you remove your cloak?"

Smiling at each other, the two women talked quietly, and Edmund stared at Gwyneth as she looked wistfully at the child she bounced on her hip.

"Edmund," Alex said, "I've never seen you look quite so contented. And it must all be due to your bride here."

Gwyneth glanced at Edmund with hope in her eyes.

"It is a good life we've made for ourselves," he said.

"Then I say we keep this good will going through another generation. I shall make you a wager that we can persuade two of our offspring to marry."

Edmund and both the women stared at Alex in amazement. Before he could say anything else, Gwyneth laughed.

"Sir Alexander, my husband tells me I am not to wager with you."

"That is not a wise decision," Alex said. "After all, the result of a wager of mine brought the four of us here."

They were all still smiling and shaking their heads when the clear tones of a handbell called everyone to crowd about the tables. Geoffrey, as steward, brought silence to the room for the chaplain from Swintongate to say grace. Then the noise rose and the food was served.

Though Edmund enjoyed renewing his friendship with Alex and Emmeline, he found himself watching the bemused faces of the earl and countess. To Edmund's astonishment, Harold barely acknowledged his parents and spent his meal below the salt, keeping Nell and the masons company.

Gwyneth watched too, waiting for the Langstons to make their move. She'd deliberately placed Lucy nearby, where they could see her. As the last plum pudding was consumed, the Lord of Misrule himself, Hugh Ludlow, came marching into the hall, leading a parade of mummers and hobbyhorses. Dozens of people cleared tables in preparation for dancing. Gwyneth watched with satisfaction as the earl and his wife drew Lucy through the crowd and out the hall doors to the courtyard.

Gwyneth gripped Edmund's arm and pulled him away from Alex. "You have to come with me."

"What is it?" he asked, hugging her close as he looked about protectively.

"Nay, I'm fine. You must come with me after the Langstons."

This time he didn't protest as she led him out of the hall. A soft snow was falling, but it was still easy to see the Langstons and Lucy disappearing into the lady's garden. Edmund gave her a quizzical look, but she covered his mouth until he nodded and pulled her hand away. Silently she led him into the cold shadows beside the garden wall.

They could clearly hear the earl's voice.

"So where are these villagers in revolt?"

"I know not, milord," said Lucy in a subdued voice. "I did everythin' ye wanted me to."

Gwyneth saw Edmund's eyes widen, but she put up a hand and shook her head. Whispering into his ear, she said, "She confessed all this to me this morn. I shall explain later."

With a nod, he took her hand and held it.

Shrilly the countess said, "They all seem *happy*!"

"I did me best! Some of the villagers left, and I thought people were afraid of Sir Edmund again, but I guess not." She burst into noisy tears. "Please don't hurt me parents!"

"What about the marriage contract?" the earl demanded. "Are you certain she saw it?"

When Edmund gripped her hand harder, Gwyneth nodded.

"They had angry words, I know they did," Lucy said miserably. "But—"

Releasing Gwyneth's hand, Edmund stepped out of the shadows and into the lady's garden, and no one said a word.

Chapter 23

When Gwyneth followed Edmund into the garden, she saw the countess's white face, heard the woman's swiftly inhaled breath. Earl Langston had smoothed his expression into an emotionless mask. They stood on either side of a cowering Lucy, who hugged herself and cried.

The earl opened his mouth, but Edmund took a threatening step forward.

"Do not insult me with any more lies. I heard everything."

"I do not understand what you're talking about," the earl said stiffly.

With a sob, Lucy came running to Gwyneth, who wrapped her arms around her.

"Of course you do. It wasn't enough that you tried to ruin me through your daughter and then through Gwyneth. You needed to complete the task by forcing an innocent girl to commit your crimes. But 'tis over now."

The earl said nothing, but his eyes glittered.

Gwyneth looked over her shoulder to find that Geoffrey and Alex Thornton were standing just outside the garden and Mrs. Haskell was making her way across the courtyard. Other curious people were beginning to emerge from the castle. Hugh Ludlow, wearing an elaborate hat in the shape of a dragon, came into the garden and took Lucy into his embrace. As she cried against his chest, he spoke softly into her ear.

"Your plan failed," Edmund said. "And I surmise it had to do with lead ore rather than the sentimentality of owning your family land again. You underestimated the people here, especially Gwyneth. I cannot even be that angry, because your manipulations gave her to me."

He smiled down at her, and she leaned against his side, finally beginning to feel that everything might work out in the end.

The earl found his voice. "If you think to threaten me with the law, remember that no court will believe you over me."

"Then I shall have to go right to the queen. Did you know that I saved the life of the Earl of Leicester, her favorite courtier, while I was stationed in the Low Countries? 'Tis why I was knighted. I am certain I shall have some sway with her."

The earl's mouth worked, but nothing emerged. His wife slumped onto a bench.

"And if Queen Elizabeth won't listen to Edmund," said Alex, stepping forward, "then she'll listen to me. I'm not sure we have met, my lord. I am Sir Alexander Thornton, and I *am* the queen's favorite dance partner, you know. And there is the matter of my brother and I saving all of England from the Spanish. Did you hear that story?"

Gwyneth watched as the earl looked about him and saw all the tenants and villagers who now gathered in the courtyard staring angrily at him. But when she saw a cold light suddenly gleam in the old man's eyes, she felt a renewed sense of fear.

"You'll not spill your lies to the queen, Blackwell," he said. "There are family matters between you and me where Her Majesty can do nothing. Gwyneth, if you let him slander us, you will have doomed your sisters to lives of spinsterhood. No one will marry them after we spread certain . . . rumors."

Though Gwyneth's stomach was in knots, she lifted her chin and spoke strongly. "You mean like the rumors you spread about your own daughter being murdered? You cannot hurt me or my family any more. I trust my husband to do what is best for us."

She could tell that her cousin was desperate now.

"There is still the marriage contract, which is legally binding. The land will be ours again when you cannot produce an heir."

Gwyneth's mother stepped forward. "What nonsense is this?"

Gwyneth smiled. "I can handle this, Mama." Putting her fists on her hips, she turned her anger on the Langstons. "I have already begun work on your contract. I carry Edmund's child, and I can assure you that no matter how many times we have to try, we will have a boy."

When she felt an arm come about her shoulders, she looked up into the smiling blue eyes of her husband, who watched her with tenderness.

"It will be a difficult duty," he said seriously, "but I shall manage."

Gwyneth knew that the people in the courtyard had erupted into cheers, but she only had eyes for her husband, whose expression had sobered as he cupped her face in his hands.

"It will be easy because I love her," he said softly, using his thumbs to wipe the tears that fell from her eyes. "Even this land is not as important to me as you are, Gwyn. I would gladly lose it all if you'll stay with me."

"Oh, Edmund," she whispered, overwhelmed that her every dream of happiness had come true.

"A foolish sentiment," the earl said scornfully, "because now I'll—"

"Enough!" Harold Langston pushed his way through the crowd. He stopped before his parents and gave them a scornful look. "I am ashamed to be a part of this family. All of this was because you could not deal with the truth about what kind of a woman your daughter— my sister—was. She made Edmund miserable with her selfish ways, and you helped her do it. She will not rest in peace until the truth is known."

"Harold!" his father said sharply.

But Harold only put up a hand. "She killed herself out of vanity, Father, trying to be a different person than she was. What does that say to you about what you've done to your children? I never knew that good people existed until I came here."

The countess started to sob, but he ignored her. "Now there are no more secrets unspoken and no reason to torment people who have done nothing to harm you. As for this land, you already have more than you will ever need. Why don't you just go home and leave us in peace?"

"Harold," his mother said weakly, "come home with us. Let me tell you what really happened."

Her son only shook his head. "Save your speeches for your other son, although I am not sure he'll believe you either. You'll have to arrive home before my letter reaches him."

The earl gripped his wife's arm and hauled her

off the bench. Gwyneth was worried that the crowd might do them harm, but the villagers stepped aside and let them return to the court-yard, where Lord Langston shouted for his coach.

When everyone had left the lady's garden, Gwyneth and Edmund remained still, staring at each other. They both began to smile.

"So what will you do if the Langstons develop a new scheme against us?" she asked.

He gripped her waist and drew her against him. "I honestly have no proof of their crimes except Lucy's word."

"And Hugh's."

"Hugh?" he echoed, puzzled.

"Lucy seduced him into doing her bidding, then they fell in love. When they realized they wanted to get out from under the earl's control, they came to me first."

He frowned and opened his mouth, which she quickly covered. "I told you that I only found out this morn. I was looking for a moment to explain everything, but the Langstons arrived. Then this plan occurred to me." She let her fingers slide down his cheek. "You will not punish Lucy and Hugh, will you? Lucy only acted out of fear for her family and her life."

"And what is Hugh's excuse?"

"Love—and immature anger, perhaps. He re-grets what they did."

"I am certain that I can find a very difficult way for him to make it up to me."

"As long as you allow them to marry."

"Hmm."

She smiled brightly. "I do have more proof against the Langstons." From beneath the girdle at her waist, she drew out a folded paper and handed it to him. " 'Tis a letter they sent to Lucy. She saved it. They were foolish enough to say an incriminating thing or two."

He stared down at the paper, then shook his head and grinned.

"Edmund, 'tis time to let all this go," she said softly, pressing herself against him. "You have nothing to prove to anyone. You are more worthy of love and respect than any man I've ever known."

"I have made so many mistakes, Gwyn. I know not how to make our marriage work, but I want to try."

He touched her stomach, and she held his hand there.

"I do not know if this will be a son," she whispered. "Will you love our daughters just as much?"

He cupped her face between his large, warm hands. His eyes, once so fierce and cold, were a warm, pure blue. "Such an easy thing to do, when they're sure to take after their mother. 'Tis the start of a new year, the start of our life together. Will you let me show you how much I love you?"

"Yes, please do."

Their kiss was warm and loving and full of a lifetime of promises.

"Merry Christmas, my love," he whispered.

Epilogue

When Mrs. Haskell announced a visit from Geoffrey Drake, Edmund rose from the table in the winter parlor and shook his friend's hand. It had been many months since he'd last seen Geoff in London.

"Edmund, congratulations on the birth of your son."

Edmund smiled and nodded. "My thanks. Come sit down. I am sure Mrs. Haskell went to inform Gwyn of your arrival."

Geoff took a seat across from him and accepted a tankard of ale. "You must finally be at peace in regard to the troublesome Lord Langston."

"I was never worried about it. The estate and the lead mine have succeeded so well that I could have offered him a price to leave us alone."

"Especially with the persuasion of that letter

they'd sent to Lucy. You've taken good care of it, I presume."

Edmund grinned. "Naturally."

The door opened, and Gwyneth walked in, carrying their new baby at her shoulder, followed by their four daughters. The girls raced each other to climb into his lap and onto his shoulders, arguing over whose turn it was to hold the baby. He exchanged smiles with his wife, deeply grateful for the love they shared and the life she'd given him.

Chestnuts are roasting by the fire this holiday season, so curl up with the best in romance from Avon Books

THE IRRESISTIBLE MACRAE by Karen Ranney
An Avon Romantic Treasure

Riona McKinsey is captivated by dashing stranger James MacRae, whose kisses ignite a burning passion deep within her heart. But the dutiful daughter is promised in marriage to another man—and responsibility comes before love. Or does it?

RISKY BUSINESS by Suzanne MacPherson
An Avon Contemporary Romance

When beautiful but klutzy model Marla Meyers takes one spill too many, it becomes Tom Riley's job to keep an eye on her. Yet as passion flares between them, who is going to protect Marla from a sexy heartbreaker like Tom?

THE MACKENZIES: COLE by Ana Leigh
An Avon Romance

The last time Cole MacKenzie saw Maggie O'Shea, she was a scruffy kid with dirt on her cheeks. Now the tomboy is all grown up, but she hasn't outgrown her teenage crush. And she's about to prove to this cowboy how much of a woman she's become.

HER SCANDALOUS INTENTIONS by Sari Robins
An Avon Romance

The dashing Duke of Girard believes Charlotte Hastings holds the key to ensnaring a traitorous villain . . . so he kidnaps the spirited miss and claims her as his betrothed! Charlotte is willing to maintain this ruse, but succumbing to her "fiancé's" sinful charms is another matter.

REL 1102

Avon Romantic Treasures

Unforgettable, enthralling love stories,
sparkling with passion and adventure
from Romance's bestselling authors